WHAT WE ALL WANT

MICHELLE BERRY

Vintage Canada

A Division of Random House of Canada Limited

VINTAGE CANADA EDITION, 2002

Copyright © 2001 by Michelle Berry

Published in Canada by Vintage Canada, a division of Random House of Canada Limited, in 2002. First published in hardcover in Canada by Random House Canada, Toronto, in 2001. Distributed by Random House of Canada Limited, Toronto.

Vintage Canada and colophon are registered trademarks of Random House of Canada Limited.

National Library of Canada Cataloguing in Publication Data

Berry, Michelle, 1968–
    What we all want

ISBN 0-679-31128-9

I. Title.

PS8553.E7723W42 2002   C813'.54   C2001-902596-3
PR9199.3.B4164W42 2002

Cover design: CS Richardson

www.randomhouse.ca

Printed and bound in the United States of America

10 9 8 7 6 5 4 3 2 1

Praise for WHAT WE ALL WANT

"Oddly spellbinding.... Berry has one of the drollest, most cunning sensibilities in Canadian fiction. A spiritual child of novelist Barbara Gowdy, she creates characters who are so profoundly isolated they seem to live in separate universes." *Maclean's*

"Berry's fine writing shows that she understands that the space between the words can be important and that what is implied speaks volumes." *National Post*

"This book has all the makings of a Peter Sellers movie with a little angst thrown in for good measure. A good read that delivers more than unremittingly grim social commentary.... Its cynicism is infused with hope; social realism butts up against the grotesque, making the fiction vital and playful." *Calgary Straight*

"Berry is a writer of disciplined restraint, one who always seems as though she's about to speak the unspeakable before she rears back, keeping things on this side of the credible, the recognizable. In the end, against all odds, she achieves a fine balance." *Quill & Quire*

"[A] crafty piece of writing.... Berry uses a spare and direct style to convey her characters' dilemmas.... And she has a way of letting the situation speak for itself, without cluttering things up with intricate or adjective-heavy wordplay.... This is a really good first novel." *NOW*

"Berry seems to recognize, as her strange story unfolds, that sometimes happiness is a more interesting and complicated outcome than despair." *The Gazette* (Montreal)

"Berry's attention to average people is what makes her novel...so good.... *What We All Want* is an endearing and amusing novel that is bizarre while remaining credible." *FFWD*

For S.B.

Acknowledgements

Sincere thanks to Rick E. Downey, Director Funeral Planning Services, Sherrin Funeral Home, and Brandi Battle and Aaron Battle, Licensed Funeral Directors, for taking the time to teach me a little about their profession. Thanks also to Dr. Cheryl Wagner for giving medical advice on parts of the novel. And Janice Zawerbny, thanks for hooking me up with your cast of interesting friends.

Jennifer Barclay, I couldn't have done this without your editing abilities, your patience, your encouragement, and the occasional pint of Guinness. Also, Hilary Stanley and Bruce Westwood, thanks for becoming my new agents during that wild, and appropriately symbolic, thunderstorm.

I am indebted to Eliza Clark for reading and editing the manuscript. And to Patrick Crean who got this book almost all the way there. Also to Sarah Davies, who took it the rest of the way, and Anne Collins for all you said the first time I met you.

Barb Tyler — thanks for trying to keep me sane as I learned all about motherhood. Rowan and Maya Cress and Jessica Tyler —

thank you for being such good friends to Abby and Zoe. Shawna Destin, thank you for teaching me, by example, about patience and kindness. I am grateful to Jonathan Bennett for commiserating with me, and Wendy Morgan for your constant optimism and for shamelessly promoting my writing. For their support and encouragement thank you to Beverly and David Baird, Susan Swan, Natalee Caple, Allison Sekuler, Ande Hecht Endewardt and Stacia Sekuler Miehe at Trailopolis, Lisa and Richard Ziegler, Ken Wright, and the staff and board of PEN Canada, especially Charlotte Gray, Clayton Ruby and Ann Ireland.

And, of course, big thanks to all the friends I don't have room to mention.

I'm grateful to the Ontario Arts Council and the Canada Council for financial support.

Thanks to The Pogues for the inspiration from their song, "Tuesday Morning," on the *Waiting for Herb* CD.

Most especially, most importantly, I am indebted to my beautiful, loving, honest, talented family: Mom, Dad, Dave, Stu, Abby, and Zoe.

Prologue

The grey van arrives on the quiet suburban street, rolling over a stray Coke can, crunching it flat. The windows of the van are tinted black. The van pulls up in front of the two-storey brick house and the driver throws his cigarette out of the window and wipes the crumbs from a chocolate donut off his shirt.

"This is the house," the man in the passenger seat says. He sighs and finishes off his donut in one bite. The dough sticks in his throat and he coughs to clear it.

The house is on a cul-de-sac and the neighbourhood is varied. Some houses look clean and peaceful, they have short front driveways and basketball nets propped on large plastic poles. Some have empty flower boxes stacked neatly beside driveways and rose bushes wrapped in burlap for the winter. The front walks of these houses have been swept clean of leaves and dirt. Other houses have lawns grown over with weeds. Two bent bicycle tires are propped against a tree and candy wrappers litter the grass. The front screen door of one house hangs off its hinges and squeaks in the wind and an old soup can used as an ashtray sits beside a rusted-out car used for parts. The van stops in front of a house with a small front porch and a lawn spotted yellow and brown. Spatterings of green paint are all that is left on the stairs, chipped and worn from years of neglect. There is a broken wicker chair lying in a heap at the bottom of the stairs next to a snow shovel, a rusty broom and rake, and an old baby stroller missing a wheel. A dog barks.

Hilary is standing out front on the sidewalk. With one hand she is clutching an oversized cardigan around her thin body. With the other hand she is rubbing her face, as if trying to wipe something off. She is staring up into the sky.

"I thought I saw a hawk," she says to the men when they get out of the van. "Are there hawks around here?"

"I don't know." The men look up into the sky.

"Seems like it would be the wrong season for hawks."

"Is there a season for hawks?"

All three stand for a minute staring up at the sky. It is a chilly, blue fall day. Everything glows. The wind has picked up and the litter from the lawn beside them blows towards them.

"Hawks, I think, migrate," one of the men says. "Surely they'd be gone by now."

"No, they don't. They aren't geese," the other man says.

"Yes they do."

"Where do they go? Florida?"

"Why not?"

"Hang out in the parks with those pink birds?"

"Flamingos," Hilary says. "I've never seen a flamingo."

"That's all right," one of the men says. "He doesn't know what he's talking about."

Hilary pulls her cardigan closer. Her eyes are large and soft. Her brown hair falls to her waist and is thick and tangled.

"You should come in," Hilary says. "She's inside."

The flat Coke can clatters across the street loudly in a gush of cool wind. The men nod. Hilary points towards the front door of her house and the men busy themselves in the van. One man carries a folded stretcher up the creaking stairs and the other carries a body bag.

"Are you interested in birds, then?"

"Not really," Hilary says. "I just thought I saw a hawk. I wasn't sure."

The men enter the house. The front hallway is cluttered with yellowing newspaper piled high, all sizes of coats and boots, broken umbrellas. Several rolls of pink-patterned wallpaper, mildewed, lean up against the staircase. In the living room the curtains are drawn and the lights are off. An overstuffed old couch, a large boxed television set, and a glass coffee table crouch in the dim shadows. The table is covered with dirty glasses and several bowls of popcorn kernels. Around the room are bookshelves full of dolls. Hundreds of them. Some porcelain, some plastic, eyes open wide and closed shut, hair in ribbons and bows, held down with hats, dresses of every colour. So many dolls in one place. It looks like a museum.

"So you collect dolls?" one of the men asks.

"Yes," Hilary says. She turns the light on in the living room. "My mother collected them first. And then she stopped going out. Now I collect them."

"That's a lot of dolls."

Hilary nods.

"There's that store in the mall," one man says. "The one with all the dolls in the window. You have more dolls in here than they do in that store." He steps into the room to take a closer look at the dolls. His ankle gives way a bit and he stumbles.

"I used to stand before that store and stare in the window when I was a child," Hilary says. "I used to just stand there and stare."

The man looks down at the floor. The entire floor of the living room is covered with pebbles. Stones. Rocks. Gravel-size pieces, smooth and worn. Like a driveway. "I thought this was carpet," the man says. He tries to laugh. "It looked like grey carpet."

"No," Hilary says. "Not carpet."

The men look at each other. They move carefully back out into the hall.

The dolls stare out at the men from above the pebbled floor. A dump-truck worth of stones, stopping up against the furniture. Glass eyes glowing. Soft hair, pink lips, delicate hands, and feet in leather shoes. The men are careful where they step.

Hilary watches them. "Don't you think it's like a beach?" she says. "I think it's like walking beside a lake."

"Yeah, that's all right," one man says. "That's fine with us. You don't have to tell us. We've seen lots of things."

"I never get to travel. I've never been anywhere really." Every evening Hilary pads lightly over the rocks and settles on the couch to watch TV. She likes to feel their smoothness on her bare feet. They remind her of her childhood, of summertime, of the fact that the earth is solid and hard.

"I'm cooped up inside this house," she says.

One man clears his throat.

"Upstairs," Hilary says. "She's up there. The door at the end of the hall."

The man with the stretcher walks up the stairs. The man carrying the body bag follows. They walk behind the woman who steps lightly down a dirty, worn trail in the carpet. The small bit of sun coming through the bathroom window patterns the air with dust particles. The hallway is dark and narrow. There are more dolls resting on the floor here and there, but no more stones. One of the men hums nervously under his breath. Hilary flicks on the lights as they move closer to the final door.

"These are antiques," she says, pointing to the dolls on the floor. "They are porcelain. Their hair is real human hair." Hilary stops and touches her long hair. Pulls it before her and stares at it. "Imagine," she says. "Where do you think they get real human hair from?"

"Which room again?" one man asks.

"Down here. At the end of the hall." Hilary points but doesn't move. "My mother started her doll collection when she was eight. She would get a different doll for Christmas every year and one for her birthday. Sometimes an extra one for Easter or Valentine's Day. When she was fourteen years old she had over twenty dolls. I had thirty-eight dolls when I was fourteen." Hilary starts walking again. The men follow. "I've named them all," she says. "They each have their own names. They have their own personalities. My mother gave me my first doll the day I was born."

"I feel like they're looking at me," one of the men says and Hilary stops again and stares down at the dolls on the hallway floor.

She says, "Sometimes it's as if their eyes follow you."

The men walk quickly around Hilary towards the room at the end of the hall. "This room?"

Hilary nods.

The air feels muted and thick. The furnace blows stifling heat around the house.

"Collections," Hilary suddenly says. "I suppose I collect preserves too. I have so many of them. Remind me to give you some on your way out. I have a wonderful pepper jelly. You can never have enough preserves. Mother and I made them. Pickles, relishes, jams, jellies, chutneys. I like to be prepared."

The air in the hallway smells like sweat and mildew. One of the men coughs. "We'll just go in now," he says.

"I also stock up on things that are on sale." Hilary begins again. She clears her throat. They are standing in front of the door at the end of the hall. The men look down at their feet. "Toilet paper. Paper towels. Kleenexes. You never know when you'll need something and the stores will be out of stock."

"My mother does that," one of the men says. "There's nothing wrong with buying a couple of extra things each time you shop."

"Mother always says that we don't want to be caught without." Hilary moves to the men, reaches around them, and puts her hand on the doorknob. "Here we are. This is her room."

Hilary slowly opens the door. Her breathing quickens. Bright sunlight dazzles them as they enter. The room is spotless and dust-free. In the air there is the pleasant scent of lime or lemon or lilac. On the bed, tucked tightly under white sheets, is what they have come for. The dead woman is bald and if it weren't for the high lace nightgown collar, she could be a man. For a brief instant the men think the dead woman could be another doll. She's so still.

"Liver cancer?"

Hilary nods. She turns from the image on the bed.

"Sorry," the men say.

The dead woman is bright yellow. Her mouth and eyes are closed tight. Her face is turned up to the ceiling and her neck is bent back slightly.

Beside the bed an old desk is laden with bottles of medicine, jars of pills, hypodermic needles, Kleenex boxes.

"God," one of the men says as he moves to lift the old woman. "She's all bones."

Hilary leans in the doorway, twisting her hair around her fingers. She tries not to look at her mother. There is a dull, thudding pain in her head, just over the bridge of her nose, that won't go away. She can't help herself. She watches the two men carefully lift her mother onto the stretcher, stick-like arms and legs, head thrown back. They place her on top of the body bag and then tuck her limbs into the bag and carefully zip it shut. The noise from the zipper travels down Hilary's spine. The men roll the full stretcher through the hallway and lift it down the carpeted stairs and out the front doorway to the waiting van. They roll it quickly away from the dolls and the rocks on the living room floor. Away from the claustrophobic feeling, away from Hilary. The cold air outside is fresh and alive.

"We're taking her to Mortimer's Funeral Home on Oakwood and Landley," one of the men says. He is panting from the exertion, from the race to get out of the house. "Sometime today you should go down there. Bring some of her clothes and a picture of her when she wasn't . . . you know, yellow." He wipes the sweat collecting above his eyebrows.

"Mortimer's," Hilary says. "You're from Mortimer's?" Her hands flutter up to her neck. The wind whips her hair around her face. "She can't go to Mortimer's."

"Mortimer's. That's right. You called us."

"Mortimer's," she says again. "The doctor called. Not me. I didn't know. She can't go there." Her hair hides her face from the men. "I haven't seen Dick in years."

"Oh, you know him?"

"Yes. We knew each other once." Hilary looks up at the sky. "When we were younger." She watches the clouds float slowly past. She is still and silent. "Does she have to go there?"

"Yes, we're from there. You'll have to talk to the director if you want her to be moved later."

Hilary nods. She stands silently for a while. "Do you think the hawks will come back?" she asks finally.

"You should get some rest," one man says. "You've had a trying experience."

"Yes," Hilary says. "You are probably right. Thank you."

The men climb into the front of the van and shut their doors. Hilary taps on the window.

"Excuse me," she says.

The man rolls down his window. "Yes?"

"You'll take care of her, won't you?"

"Of course."

"Because she's all I have left. I have nothing any more."

The men watch Hilary walk back up her stairs, onto her porch, and then shut the front door behind her. There is a sudden silence in the van.

"Hey, back there." One of the men turns to the body in the back of the van. "You wouldn't mind if we stopped for coffee, would you? We're just a bit cold."

"You know," the man driving the car says, "I see those kids standing in front of that store window in the mall, with all the dolls staring out at them, and I think that's cute. I think, they want a doll for Christmas. Just one doll. Maybe two. I think it's cute. Do you know what I mean?"

He speeds the van around the corner.

In the house Hilary stands on her pebbles in the living room and watches the grey van drive quickly down the quiet street. She takes a deep breath. Her eyes tear up. She swallows loudly. She looks around at the still neighbourhood, over at the deserted park at the end of the street, at the houses around her full of people she doesn't know. Over the houses she sees the city lit up in the afternoon sunshine, the high-rise office towers glowing gold and silver. She searches the air for birds. More hawks.

"Mother," she whispers.

It is a Thursday afternoon in late November.

She turns from the window and walks into her kitchen where the dishes are piled high in the sink. There are dolls on the counters, on the windowsill. The table is caked with spilt food: blood-red spaghetti sauce, toast crumbs, mayonnaise. Hilary moves some of the dishes from the sink, piles them on the counter, and begins to wash her face. Then she dries her face, puts the dishes back in the sink, and looks around the room, unsure of what to do first, what to do next. She walks back into the living room, tiptoes across the rocks, and sits on the couch. She looks at the dolls settled beside her, the dolls all around her.

"Everything will be just fine," she tells a doll in an emerald green dress. She pulls the doll onto her lap and holds it facing her. "Everything is fine."

Her eyes light upon the telephone beside her and she picks it up softly, as if afraid to make a noise. She dials. As she waits for the person on the other end to answer, Hilary tidies the doll's hair and places it back on the couch, plastic hands clasped in front, resting on its green velvet dress. The doll smiles brightly, red lips and dimpled cheeks. Then one eye closes. The hinge that holds the eye open when the doll is sitting and closed when the doll is lying down is broken. Hilary leans over and pries open the eyelid. She pushes hard and the lid stays open. Its eyes shine.

"Hello?" she whispers into the phone. "Hello? It's Hilary. Mother died . . . this morning. . . . We have to bury her soon. . . . You'll have to come home now."

Rebecca Mount lies naked under a sheet in the preparation room at Mortimer's Funeral Home. Scalpels, scissors, forceps, clamps, needles, pumps, tubes, bowls, basins. A surgical room. Her body is yellow, chalky, cold. The jaundice from her faulty liver has not faded. Her hands have been crossed in front of her. Her body is splotched with darker patches of colour: green, white, grey. Her left big toe has been tagged for identification purposes. The tag reads: "Rebecca Hilary Mount. Age sixty years. Liver cancer. Death: Thursday, 10 a.m. — burial unspecified." The nails on her toes are long and yellow, crooked, ingrown. There is a bit of black lint from her socks in the corners of her big toes.

Rebecca Mount's stretched skin hangs off of her like baggy clothing. Her scalp is bald and smooth. Her face is wrinkled. Eyes closed. Her nose seems hooked now, seems bent a little towards her cheek as if it has fallen. Her neck is bruised. Her breasts sag to the sides, resting lightly on her upper arms, the nipples pale and flat. Her hips poke, the bones so sharp they look as if they might cut out through the paper-like skin. Her pelvic region collapses upon itself, hollows out, a valley centred by a belly button. The once-expanded, cancerous liver has flattened in death. Slightly bloated legs stretch out, skin loose, gradually dehydrating, knees bony and thick, ankles swollen and veiny.

Soon there will be a cut on the right side of her clavicle where the mortician will pull up her vein to drain her blood and then pull up her artery to fill with embalming solution. There will be another cut above the belly button where the mortician will insert a long, hollow needle attached to a tube. He will poke around the entrails and chest cavity. He will pump out the contents and replace it with cavity fluid. Both cuts will be sewn with skill. Then the mortician will sew Rebecca Mount's mouth shut with a needle directed upward between her lip and gum and brought out through her left nostril. He will raise the corners slightly for a more pleasant expression. Her eyes will be sealed shut with flesh-tinted eye caps and eye cement.

It is quiet in the embalming room.

Rebecca Mount is on table 2.

Mr. Grant, heart attack, is on table 6.

Rita Paisley, car accident, is on table 10.

The room is cold and dry, the air stale and stinky. The tables are shining silver. The occupants are still.

Silent.

Speechless.

Bodies lying in a state of rest. Waiting for someone to carry on.

Waiting.

I

Fear of Flying

Luggage is being loaded onto an airplane on the tarmac. Thomas stares at it. He swallows and reaches up to his brow as if trying to wipe off sweat.

"Don't worry," Jonathan says. "It's one of the newer ones. That's not your plane out there. That's an old one."

"I can't fly. God, you know I can't fly."

"We could get another drink."

"I'll be sick."

"You'll be fine."

"I can't do this." Thomas walks away from the window. He sits on a plastic bench beside a flowerpot. He watches the children play in the huge rocket-ship shaped structure in the centre of the lounge. Sliding down the tube slide. Screeching. In the lounge they can see everything inside and out.

"Thomas, you have to go."

"I know. I don't want to go."

Jonathan sits beside Thomas.

Thomas looks at his watch. "It's almost time to board the plane."

"I could come with you."

"No, you can't."

"Why not? I could see if they have any standby tickets."

"We talked about this." Thomas takes Jonathan's hand.

"I'd like to meet them, Thomas. It's been fifteen years."

A small voice sounds through the airport: *Now boarding flight 742A. All passengers please report to gate 8B.*

"That's me." Thomas squeezes Jonathan's hand. "Remember," he says. "When the plane goes down, you can have the oil paintings and the granite sculpture in the garden but you can't have my clothes. You look awful in my clothes. Give them to Geoffrey."

Jonathan laughs. He stands and Thomas stands. The men hug. "Are you sure I can't come?"

"Positive."

The men take the escalator to the departures level. Thomas walks towards the metal detector. He stops and empties his pockets into the plastic bucket. He places his raincoat and carry-on baggage on the belt. He walks through the metal detector and picks up his things, fills his pockets back up, and turns to look at Jonathan but Jonathan is gone. He is leaving the airport, holding his coat around him, battling the fierce November wind.

Thomas settles into his seat and clutches his paperback book close to his heart. He remembers watching a movie once where a terrorist shot at a passenger but the passenger lived because her paperback romance novel stopped the bullet from entering her body.

Terrorists. That's all Thomas needs to think about right now. *Jesus.*

A young woman sits beside him. "Hi," she says.

Thomas nods. He turns to the window. He wasn't sure if the window seat was the safest. Now that he looks at the thick glass he thinks that he could never break it to escape and that the aisle seat seems safer. At least he could run. But run where? He shakes his head. *Jesus, Jesus, Jesus.*

"You okay?"

"Yes, fine."

"You're sweating a lot." The woman points to his forehead. He is an attractive man, well dressed, tall, muscular. She smiles at him.

"I'm just hot." He wipes his forehead on a ironed handkerchief that he pulls from his breast pocket. He moves his book to do so and the woman sees the title.

"Oh," she says. "Look."

Thomas looks. She holds up her book. "We're reading the same book."

A best-seller. On the best-seller lists for ten months.

"That's fate, don't you think?" The woman leans into him. "Do you like it?"

"Like what?" The plane starts to taxi down the runway. *Jesus, Jesus, Jesus.* Thomas feels his heart is about to explode. He can feel the intense beats in his arms, his stomach, his neck.

"The book."

"What?"

"Do you like the book?"

"Oh God," Thomas says as the plane begins to soar. He reaches instinctively for the woman's hand and he clutches at it, grasps it hard, pulls it towards his chest, on top of his book.

"What?" she says.

"Oh my God," Thomas says. "We're going to die."

"We're just flying in a plane," the woman says, taking her hand back, prying her fingers from his. "We're not going to die."

"We're going to crash," Thomas pants. "Almost all crashes occur during takeoff and landing."

The woman looks past Thomas, out his window. "Well, we're up now. We're in the air. So we made it through takeoff, in about five hours we'll just see if we make it through landing." She shakes her hand out. Her rings were pushed into her fingers when Thomas clutched her hand so hard. They have dented the flesh.

"I'm sorry," Thomas says, peeking out his window. "I'm sorry about your hand."

"How can you not like flying?" the woman says. "I do it about three times a month for business."

"I've always been afraid to fly."

"Why are you flying then? Why didn't you drive?"

"I have to get home," he says. "For a funeral. It would take too long to drive."

"Oh, I'm sorry. Whose funeral?"

"My mother's."

"God, I'm so sorry." The woman puts her hand on Thomas's. He pulls away.

"It's all right. She was quite sick. She's been dying for a long time. Cancer."

The woman makes sympathetic noises. Clucking sounds. She sniffs. "And when did you see her last?"

Thomas looks again out his window. They are high in the clouds. He can't see anything but whiteness below him and blue sky above. He wonders if this is heaven. Walking on clouds. Whiteness and blueness. But he doesn't believe in heaven and hell. He believes in nothing, really. He wonders if he should start believing in something. Because if human beings can fly in a machine this heavy, hurtling through the air, then maybe there is something more to death, something other than just ceasing to exist. Anything seems possible when you are thirty-five thousand feet up.

"I haven't been home in a long time," Thomas says. "Years."

The woman shakes her head. "That's too bad. My mother is my best friend. I don't know what I'd do without her."

Thomas opens his paperback novel. He starts reading. His hands are still shaking. But his heart has slowed down. He wishes that Jonathan were here beside him instead of this woman, going on about her mother. But it would have been impossible for Jonathan to come to the funeral.

Thomas turns the pages without focusing on what he is reading. In less than five hours he will be home again. He will see his younger sister and brother again. He will bury his dead mother, get her affairs in order, sell the house, settle his sister into an apartment somewhere, and then, one week later, turn around and fly back to Jonathan. Christ, Thomas thinks, he has to do this flying thing again. He has to fly home somehow, without dying, without plummeting to the earth and exploding in a burst of flames. Thomas's heart speeds up as he tries to steady his breathing. He wishes he were in the gym riding the bicycle or playing squash or drinking a non-fat cappuccino or watching a movie, even watching a game show on TV, anything other than riding in this beast.

Jesus, Jesus, Jesus.

Billy picks his sister up at the house. He doesn't go inside. He waits on the front porch and looks around the neighbourhood. He thinks about nothing in particular. Instead he looks at his car parked up on the sidewalk, the blinkers flashing. Hilary comes out of the house wearing a fur coat.

"What the hell is that?"

"Mother's coat."

"It's not winter yet."

"But I'm cold." Hilary puts her hands in the pockets. She takes out a dirty Kleenex and some loose change — a penny, two dimes. She stuffs the Kleenex in the old baby carriage on the porch, puts the coins back in her pocket, and follows Billy down the stairs and across the front walk to the car. She doesn't want to get in the car.

"This doesn't look safe," she says. "It's not a safe car, Billy. The consumer reports say that it is not a safe car."

"You read consumer reports?"

"Sometimes."

"Get in, Hilary. I drive this car every day. It's safe."

Hilary walks around the car, staring at it.

"Just get in."

"It's not safe. There are no side air bags. The panels will collapse in a side collision."

"How else are you going to get there?"

Hilary stares at Billy. "I could walk," she says.

"That would take you hours." Billy guides Hilary around to the passenger side. "I'll clip you in with a seat belt."

"Do you have front air bags?"

"Yeah," Billy lies. "I had them installed a week ago."

Hilary lowers herself into the bucket seat. "I don't believe you and I don't like this one bit," she says. "I don't like it at all."

"How the hell do you get around?" Billy asks.

"I walk everywhere."

"Explains your thinness," Billy says under his breath. "You and Thomas. You're both chickenshit."

Billy buckles Hilary into the seat and then slams the door. Hilary jumps. Billy climbs in the driver's side and starts the engine.

"So, how've you been?" Billy asks.

"What's that thumping noise?"

"What thumping noise?"

"Listen."

Billy listens. He doesn't hear anything. "That's just the way a car sounds. How the hell did you take Becka to a doctor if you didn't drive a car or take a taxi?"

"Oh," Hilary brightens. "Taxis are fine. Mother and I love taxis."

"What?" Billy shakes his head. "You love taxis?"

"Taxis are safe."

"Safe?"

"We could take a taxi now," Hilary says. She starts to undo her seat belt.

"Hilary. I'm driving to the funeral home. Jesus. Stay in the car."

Hilary buckles herself up again.

"Taxis don't even have seat belts," Billy says. "And the drivers are crazy. How the hell can you say they are safe?"

"No," Hilary says. "That's not true. They are safe."

Billy wishes he had more to drink before he picked his sister up. He could have used two beers instead of one. He sighs loudly.

"Well," Hilary says, "you still look tall." Billy has always been gangly, tall, awkward. His arms hang down at his sides like a gorilla.

"I haven't gotten any taller." Billy turns the corner and heads west.

"Are there hawks around here?"

"Hawks?"

"You know, the birds."

Billy shrugs. "I don't know. Why?"

"Just wondering. Watch out for that car."

"I'm watching." Billy drives quickly through a stale-yellow light. "I imagine there probably are hawks. I think they even live in the tops of the office towers downtown."

"Really?"

"Or maybe that's falcons."

They drive towards Mortimer's Funeral Home. Hilary keeps her hands on the seat belt, clutches it around her.

"How are the kids?" Hilary asks.

"Kid, Hilary. I only have one daughter."

"That's right," Hilary takes one hand off the seat belt when Billy stops at a light. She twirls her hair around her finger. She rubs her cheeks. She sucks on a strand.

"Sue's fine. She's about three months now."

"Three months what?"

"Pregnant."

"That little girl is pregnant?" Hilary sits up in her seat and stares at her brother.

"Sue's not that little. She's seventeen."

"Oh, I forgot."

"That's still too young, though," Billy says. "The whole thing pisses me off. She won't tell us who the father is. Or she doesn't know. I'm not sure which."

"You haven't been to see us in a long time, have you, Billy?"

"About five months," Billy says. "That's all." Billy drives and Hilary holds on to the door.

"When was the last time I saw Sue?"

"About two years ago."

"I can't remember. Time seems to stand still and pass quickly all at once." The fur coat Hilary is wearing is hot and smells of mothballs. Her skirt is too small. Her tights have been stretched too long and have runs in them.

Billy's breath smells like beer, like rotten socks. He scratches his thigh and turns on the radio.

"So," he says. "How was it?"

"What?"

"You know."

"What?" Hilary stares out the car window. She marvels at the change in seasons. The trees are bare and the grass and plants are brown. "You're going too fast."

"How was she at the end?"

"Oh." Hilary looks down at her shoes. "You should have come to visit," she says. "You should have said goodbye. She asked about you all the time. She wondered where you were."

"I know that. Don't you think I know that?"

"But, why — Billy, that man is turning left. Slow down."

"Jesus. I'm a busy man, Hilary." Billy closes his eyes for a second, tight, and then opens them again and watches the road. "I have two jobs. I'm working nights and days." Had two jobs, Billy thinks. He lost both of them recently.

"What about weekends?" Hilary says.

"I'm not good with sick people," Billy says. "I didn't want to have to say goodbye."

They drive through the suburban streets, Billy's headlights shining through the dimming evening. Hilary watches people walking their dogs on the bare sidewalks, restaurant signs lit up with neon tubes, a couple arguing in front of a Pet Valu store, the woman's head turned away from the man, the man holding a bag of cat food and looking out at the road, looking into Hilary's eyes.

"She didn't suffer much, I guess," Hilary says. "It was pretty quick when it happened."

Billy breathes out loudly. "Did Thomas ever come to say goodbye?"

"No," Hilary says. "Of course not. You know how he is on airplanes." She clutches her seat belt tighter around her body, holds on to it.

"Yeah, like you are in cars."

"That's not the same. Cars are much more dangerous."

"Not even once? He didn't come home once?"

"He hasn't been home in years, Billy. I would have called you. Thomas would have seen you."

"Did he call Becka?"

"Not often."

"I don't know why," Billy says. "I wanted to come see her."

"You don't live that far away."

"I know."

"I could have used the help," Hilary whispers.

"Shit. I'm sorry. I have my family— we got so busy, I guess."

"Mother would have liked to see you."

In the funeral home parking lot Billy gets out of the car and stands tall and watches the sun setting orange. The evening air is chilly. Hilary gets out of the car on shaky legs and steadies herself before walking up to the front door. She is clutching a grocery bag of her mother's clothes, a wig, and a picture. She straightens her fur coat and pats down her hair.

"Come on," Billy says. "Let's get this over with. What happened to your face? Looks like your skin is chapped."

Hilary puts her hands up to her cheeks. "Chapped? You can't see the stain? I can't get it off."

"What stain?"

Hilary stares at her brother. "What stain? This black stain." Hilary points.

Billy shrugs. He says, "It must be the dry heat in the house. It'll get you every time. Makes my back itch." He scratches his back to illustrate his point. "Hey, isn't this Dick Mortimer's father's place? The fat kid. You used to hang out with him, didn't you?"

Hilary nods. "We used to come here," she says. "After school."

"To the funeral home? That's creepy."

"It wasn't really. They lived up there." Hilary points to the fire escape stairs that lead to an apartment above the building. "His mother made it very bright. Cheery almost. I think I used to be in love with him."

"With Dick's father?"

"No." Hilary looks shocked. "Not his father. With Dick. He was my only friend."

Billy can't remember one specific friend in high school. His teammates on the basketball team or on the volleyball court, but no one specific. No particularly close person. He wasn't even close to his brother. He mostly hung out with Tess and then he married her.

"Tess wanted me home for supper. She wants to have fried

chicken tonight," Billy says. "I tell her my mother is dead and she says we'll have fried chicken and gravy." Billy shakes his head. "The woman does nothing but eat."

As they walk into the funeral home the odour hits them immediately. Chemicals. Formaldehyde. Billy would recognize it anywhere. He remembers the pickled fetal pigs in biology class at high school. He remembers flunking the class, putting the pigs' eyeballs in his pockets and using them to scare the girls in homeroom.

"Can I help you?" A receptionist peers out from behind a glass enclosure. Billy walks up to her.

"We're here to talk about what to do with our mother," he says. "Becka Mount, Rebecca Mount. She came in this afternoon." He pauses. "She died."

"Yes, of course. Mr. Mortimer is waiting for you in the conference room. Let me just page him."

Billy and Hilary stand together awkwardly. They look at the heavy oak furniture, intricately carved, at the thick pile carpet overlain with Persian carpets, at the mottled glass windows. There are floor-length burgundy velvet drapes over all the windows. Hilary feels as if she's in a womb, the place is throbbing, soft and warm. A soothing luxury.

"Hilary Mount." Dick Mortimer stands suddenly before them. His shoes make no sound on the thick carpet. "It's great to see you."

"Hello," Hilary says. She holds out her hand and Dick takes it and a spark of static leaps between them.

"Sorry about that."

Hilary rubs her hand.

"Hey," Billy says. "Hi there, Dick." They shake hands. "We're waiting for your father. Our mother died."

"I think we want to take her somewhere else," Hilary says.

"Why?" Billy asks.

"If you are waiting for my father," Dick says, "you'll have a long wait. My father died about ten years ago."

"Oh, I'm sorry," Hilary says.

"Why would we want to take her anywhere else?" Billy asks.

"I run the business now."

"You do?" Hilary says. "Then we won't need to move her. She can stay right here."

Billy scratches his head.

"I went to school," Dick says. "I'm a funeral director now."

"Business good?" Billy asks.

"Fine. Thanks for asking. How are you two doing?"

"A funeral director," Hilary says.

"I should get into that," Billy says. "Funerals are a sure thing. They're all about fear. Put that together with making money and you've got it made."

Hilary pulls her fur coat tight around her body.

"Come with me," Dick says. "It's good to see you two again. I'm sorry about your mother. Let me take that." Dick takes the bag from Hilary and gives it to the receptionist. She places it behind the counter, out of sight. Dick is a large man. He holds his hands before his belly, clutches them together. He looks down at Hilary. "It's been a long time, Hilary."

Hilary nods but Dick doesn't see her head bob. He is walking ahead of her.

Dick was in Billy's class in school but they weren't friends. He was Hilary's friend. She remembers the smell of him, the chemical smell of the funeral home. It lingered in his clothes, his hair. He was always sweating and he breathed heavily when he walked. Dick was smart in school. Especially in biology. He would help her with her homework, sitting together at the kitchen table in his parents' apartment above the funeral home.

"Things have changed here, Hilary. I should show you around. I've renovated a bit since my Dad died," Dick says. "I've added a few new things. A new wing. A new office. But you probably don't remember this place anyway. Do you?" Dick talks fast. Several drops of spit fly out of his mouth. He wipes his hand on his lips. He points out the rooms they are passing. Then he stops and turns towards Hilary. "Your mother arrived a couple of hours ago. Again, I'm really sorry about your loss."

Silence. The two men stare at Hilary. She looks down at the fur coat wrapped around her and then farther down at her shoes.

Once Dick's mother asked them to find Dick's father. She wanted him to open a jar or fix something. Dick and Hilary wandered the funeral home. Dick lay down in a casket, squeezed his large body in, and said, "Look at me, look at me." The wood creaked around him. He was sure-footed in the funeral home, moving quickly around in the darkness of the basement, in a world he was comfortable with. And they came upon his father in the embalming room. They entered the room without knocking. There was a body, a young woman, hooked up to a machine, a tube draining blood from near her neck. Hilary gasped. The woman was naked. Her breasts lay flat against her ribs, the nipples erect. Her pubic hair black and dark against her white skin. Her hands draped over her belly. Richard Mortimer turned away from his work towards the children. His face was tired and sad. His eyes were anxious. He stopped the machine and his arms moved up and down as he waved them out of the room. "Get out. Get out."

"Well, we need to plan her funeral," Billy says.

"Yes, of course. We're heading in that direction." Dick starts walking again and leads them down a corridor and into a small room with a large oak table surrounded by covered red-velvet chairs pushed tightly together.

"Have a seat. I'll get coffee." Dick leaves the room. As he idles by the coffee machine, watching the brown liquid pour out, he thinks about Hilary, about how much she has changed since they were kids. Her hair is tangled, she's so thin, and she has raw marks on her cheeks. He wonders what he ever saw in her but then he thinks about his life now, how lonely he is, and he wishes they had never stopped being friends.

Things didn't work out for Dick quite the way he planned. He wanted to be a forensic scientist. But Dick's father, the first Richard Mortimer, left him the funeral home, a small business, ten years ago when he choked on a hot dog at a family picnic. It surprised Dick (and surprised his mother even more) that the home was willed to him. But after finishing an embalming course at the local community college, Dick sat down and thought it all out. Something entrepreneurial clicked when his father died, something about the trust his father had in him to run the home, and to everyone's surprise, in the short span of ten years, Dick has made a killing. Dick found that he had a knack for running a business. Slowly the money came in. He doesn't know what to do with it half of the time. He renovated extensively. He bought himself a new car and a new Cadillac for the home. He gave his mother the burial of a Queen. But still the money keeps coming.

Dick Mortimer advertises. He persuades folks to buy their plots early, to prepay for caskets, vaults, urns, to come tour Mortimer's, to register their wishes in a Family Preference Guide. "Prepare early" is his motto. Preplan. You never know when death will come knocking. You never know when it'll strike. Like a tornado or a flood. At Christmas Dick sends turkeys to all the doctors who work at the geriatric hospital in the city. A little card stuffed inside the bird with his name and phone number. And cut flowers to all the nursing homes.

There isn't a person in a forty-mile radius who would go anywhere else to buy a casket or have a service. And Dick, a shy man, with his new wealth, has become expansive, loud, and even mildly generous. Once every six months he takes a dozen cans of beans with pork to the food bank in the back of the fire hall. At New Year's Dick sends each of his employees home with a ham and a cheque for fifty dollars.

But Dick has no family any more. His mother died shortly after his father, and his brother, Steve, moved to New York and disappeared somewhere into his high-powered-business job. Dick hasn't talked to him in years. And he doesn't have many friends. Really, he doesn't have any friends. And now that his mother is gone he doesn't have anyone to love. Dick thinks about getting a dog or a cat or a hamster. Something that would move a little when he walked in the front door after work every night. But he usually works so late he would forget to walk it or feed it and then he would come home at night, after a hard day, and there would be another damn thing he'd have to bury.

The coffee stops and the smell is lovely. Dick pours several large mugs and makes up a tray with cream and sugar and spoons.

"He'll probably put formaldehyde in the coffee," Billy whispers to Hilary in the conference room. "Preserve us now so he won't have to work so hard when we're dead."

"I can't believe he's a mortician. I can't believe how tall he is."

"He was always pretty short, wasn't he? Looks like he sprung up after high school."

Hilary touches the soft chair below her.

"What I really want is a cold beer," Billy calls out to Dick. "Forget about the coffee."

"I can't believe Mother is dead," Hilary says.

Billy looks closely at Hilary. The whites of her eyes are red. "She was really sick, Hilary."

"In pain," Hilary says. "The pain needed to stop."

"In pain," Billy echoes. He shakes his head.

Hilary rests her head in her hands on the table. Her long hair hangs around her like a curtain. She is tired.

"You must feel a bit relieved? I mean, it's over. She's dead. At least she's not in pain any more. You've spent your whole life taking care of her. Now you can move on."

Hilary presses against the table until there is an ache on her forehead and in her nose. She thought her mother's death would make her feel better, she thought she would feel relieved, but all she feels now is a big empty chasm in her stomach and a pain in her head that won't go away. She feels abandoned and scared.

Dick comes into the room carrying a tray of mugs. "Here you go." Dick hands out the mugs, giving Hilary one of his favourites, a blue mug with a picture of a cow standing on its hind legs putting several farmers out into a field to graze. The caption reads, "I'm the boss around here." Dick was given the mug by one of his employees in the Christmas gift exchange several years ago. Dick still smiles every time he sees that mug.

"A beer would have been nice," Billy says. "Something cold."

"We have water," Dick says. "Or juice, or coffee. That's it. Let's get to work, shall we?" He clears his throat and sits at the table across from the Mounts.

Hilary is sitting on the edge of her seat. Billy is picking at his cuticles. He sits with his long legs wide open. Dick can see a rip in Billy's jeans. He pulls a list out of a filing cabinet behind him. "You'll be needing a casket, a coach, a burial site, a vault, and everything else, I take it. That includes embalming, dressing, and an open-casket service for the memory picture, right?"

"Memory picture?"

"The last glimpse of your loved one."

"What?" Billy's mouth is open.

"A viewing. It's sometimes called a viewing."

"Why do you need a vault?" Hilary asks.

"Oh, it prevents the ground from caving in," Dick says. "It protects your loved one's remains for all eternity."

Billy snorts. "She's still going to rot, isn't she? Isn't she going to rot, Hilary?"

Hilary's face pales.

Dick ignores Billy. He rattles off his list and then passes out a photocopied piece of paper with "Eighty-seven Things That Must Be Done by the Survivor" typed at the top. It starts with securing vital statistics and ends with notification of family members, attorney, and newspapers.

"You'll have to notify these people yourself," Dick says. "I can help, I can advise, but I can't call them for you. I'm sorry but that's not part of the service."

"Did she have an attorney?" Billy asks.

Hilary sits still in her chair, staring at the coffee before her.

"First we have to fill out a vital statistics sheet. Name, occupation, age, et cetera."

Dick takes out a pen and reaches for a form from the filing cabinet. He sits and begins to write down the information Hilary and Billy supply.

"Okay, any suggestions? Any ideas on the service?" Dick asks. "Where shall we start?"

"We have to discuss money," Billy says. "I haven't got much right now."

"Mother had nothing," Hilary whispers. "I have nothing."

Dick says, "Don't worry about the money. Just decide what you would like, later we can pare it down, simplify it, shall we say, to fit your financial position."

"Don't worry about money?" Hilary says. "I always worry about money."

"Hilary," Billy says. "Thomas is loaded. He'll pay."

Hilary looks at Billy. She suddenly wants to get back home. "I'm tired," she says. "I'm really very tired. I need to go home."

Dick clears his throat. "I'm sure you'd like to discuss your finances in private," he says.

"Did Becka say anything about what she wanted?" Billy asks.

"We didn't talk about it," Hilary says. She rubs her eyes. "It's not something you talk about. You don't just talk about death to a dying woman. You talk about when she gets better, what the two of you will do." Hilary covers her eyes. "Besides, there were too many other things to do. Change diapers and bedpans, feed her, give her sponge baths, give her medicine, do the laundry."

Billy can't fault Hilary for that. He would never have asked Becka what she wanted either. The odd time Billy visited he just peeked in Becka's room and spent the rest of his time there in front of the TV with the dolls, resting his feet on Hilary's rock collection, feeling as if he was in an orphanage close to the water. Silent, small bodies watching TV with him. It was comforting really. He doesn't know why he didn't go more often.

"Okay," Dick says, leaning back. He clears his throat. "Why don't we just check out the selection room? That way you'll get some ideas as to what you are looking for. You can always come back later, tomorrow maybe, and settle on a definite plan." Dick stands. He hates this part of his job. He prefers embalming and makeup, dealing with the corpse, not the living, angry, grieving, unhappy family. Dick, in general, prefers the dead to the living. Less complications. They seem, somehow, more grateful.

Hilary and Billy follow Dick out of the room and down the hall-way. Hilary feels like a mouse behind an elephant. Dick is so large and round. She notices that he is balding in patches on the back of his head. Patterned baldness, Hilary wonders if the spray-on hair she sees on late-night TV might be useful to Dick.

"Have you thought of where you want to bury her?" Dick asks.

Hilary shakes her head. "I just can't believe she's finally dead."

"Because all the cemeteries have different charges."

Hilary nods.

"I'm sure you're suffering now," Dick says. "We have a grief ther-apist who comes in twice a week. If you're interested, I could make an appointment for you."

This is the first time someone has acknowledged Hilary's own pain and her heart speeds up slightly and she suddenly feels warm. She looks up at Dick and, even though she doesn't want to talk to a grief therapist about her mother, she feels an overwhelming sense of gratitude. A weight has lifted from her shoulders.

Dick can't imagine not planning in advance for a funeral. It happens all the time but it still knocks him out. Clients coming in unprepared. He's had his funeral planned from the day he turned four. He remembers his father sitting him down on his lap at the kitchen table and working out the details — casket, service, coach, plot. He still has the piece of paper his father wrote on.

Behind Dick and then Hilary, Billy walks. He runs his fingers over the wainscotting and is amazed that there is no dust. A place this big, Billy figures, must take hours to clean. Billy wonders who Dick gets to clean the funeral home and then he wonders if, perhaps, he should start a cleaning business. It couldn't be all that hard — a few mops, dusters, a vacuum. Hell, he could use Tess's vacuum. It's not as if he sees her lugging it around the house that often.

In the selection room, Billy stands beside Dick and sizes him up. They were classmates, Billy reminds Dick, but Dick shakes his head and says, "Can't matter much on the price, Billy. A casket is a casket. I can't up or down the cost for anyone. You have to pick the one that suits your feelings for your mother, that makes you feel good about laying her to rest."

Hilary puts her hand over her mouth and swallows. The whole thing is ludicrous. She can't move. The caskets are large before her. Her fingers ache around her lips, they feel tight, arthritic. Mother was in so much pain this morning and now she's dead. Just like that. Everything happens so slowly and then so quickly. Hilary can't keep track of time.

Billy walks around the room checking out prices on the open-lidded boxes, adding sums up in his mind, tapping each casket, looking for defects, for solid structure, for a good buy. Dick follows him around, giving him the sales speech. He doesn't push too hard. He knows Billy isn't the one with the chequebook. He'll wait for Thomas before he hard-sells. Hilary stands like an awed child, one hand up to her mouth, eyes wide open.

"You can get an eternal casket," Dick says. He taps a bronze one. "It will protect your loved one forever."

"I bet they aren't as solid as they look," Billy says. He knocks on the casket.

Hilary thinks the caskets are beautiful. She remembers feeling this way about them when she would come here years ago, as if they were merely large beds, a pretty place to sleep. A place where you could shut the door and get some peace and quiet. Be alone with your thoughts. They look comfy and peaceful, with large pillows and shiny wood. And there are the eternal caskets too, copper and brass and bronze and a particularly pretty one called Blue Diamond that shines in the dim lights of the viewing room like a summer night sky, the gold-coloured handles like stars.

Billy heads towards the pine box, the three-hundred-dollar special, but Dick says this box is only used for cremation. In his best salesman-like voice, Dick says that no one buys the pine box for a service. And Billy touches the tiny, cotton pillow once, runs his hand along the unfinished wood, and turns towards the Oak Memory casket, lined in white satin, dotted with roses. The average-price casket. Fifteen hundred dollars. Billy imagines what he could do with that kind of money.

The room is large and quiet. Their footsteps are muffled in the thick rug, the walls are solid and seem to cushion any noise.

"Is it true that you guys break the dead person's legs if they don't fit into the coffin?" Billy asks. "Or saw them off?"

Dick clears his throat.

Hilary looks startled.

"I'm tall," Billy says. "You'd have to break my legs, I guess."

"This is a fine model," Dick says. "The Oak Memory casket. It's a popular selection."

Hilary wants to curl up in a casket. They look so soft and warm. She wants to shut the lid and sleep for years and years, sleep backwards in time, if possible. Wake up on the day her daddy walked out of their lives, but do everything differently. Stop him at the front door. Stand in front of him. Hold him down. Pin him with her little-girl arms. Hilary moves up close to the Blue Diamond casket and touches the surface and then the inside. She shivers.

"What do you think?" Dick asks. He is close behind her. He can smell a musty odour, mothballs, coming off of her coat. He is amazed because he thought his sense of smell had left him years ago. He figured the formaldehyde had stripped his nose of all its nerve endings.

"This one is beautiful." Hilary points to the Blue Diamond.

"Ah, a favourite."

"Too expensive," Billy says. "Even for Thomas. Look at the price."

"Why don't we talk about all this with Thomas later," Hilary says. She is starting to get nervous. The room feels stuffy and close. "We'll talk it over and get back to Dick."

"That's fine with me," Dick says. "Consult among your family and then make an appointment to see me. Hilary brought me some clothes, a wig, and a picture. You go home. You call me tomorrow. In the meantime, I'll begin to preserve your mother."

Dick watches Hilary and Billy Mount leave the funeral home. He watches Hilary stand beside the car, he watches Billy help her in and then move around and open the trunk. Dick feels strange suddenly, as if he has the flu. His stomach rumbles and his bowels churn. Stress sometimes makes him feel this way but Dick doesn't think he's stressed. He doesn't know why he would be stressed. Although part of his childhood did just walk through the funeral home. Part of something he often tries to forget. He's spent so long trying to boost himself up, turn himself inside out, that seeing his past creeping in, remembering what he once was, may possibly be the cause of his stomach worries. What was he once, Dick thinks: fat, shy, pimply, short, ugly, friendless, the son of a funeral director. He shuffles his weight from one foot to the other. And what is he now: fat, shy, friendless, and a funeral director.

He's moved up on the ladder, he supposes.

At least he's taller now. No pimples. He's grown into his ugliness. It almost suits him.

He looks again at Hilary in the car. She looks angry. She is shouting something at Billy who has just started the engine. She is waving one hand in the air, the other is clutching at her seat belt.

Hilary has to get back in that car again. "Really, Billy, we should just take a taxi."

"To the airport? Do you know how much that would cost?"

"Maybe Thomas could just take a taxi to my house."

"You told him we'd pick him up."

"I could take a taxi home and then you could both come back after you pick him up."

"Hilary, just get in the car. We're halfway to the airport now."

"Oh God, oh God," Hilary says as she sits back down in the passenger seat.

Billy moves around the car to the trunk. He opens it and pulls out a bottle of Scotch in a paper bag. He unscrews the cap and gulps. The liquid burns his throat. He gulps again. Hilary is rattling her door, trying to get out. Billy put the child safety locks on the doors. He wipes his lips with the back of his hand and then takes another gulp.

"What are you doing?" Hilary screams at him as he gets into the car. "You left me in the car. You locked me in. I could have suffocated."

"Calm down." Billy starts the engine.

"You idiot," Hilary shouts.

"I'm not an idiot." Billy drives towards the airport. "Don't ever call me that. If I didn't lock you in you would have —"

Hilary is breathing heavily. "I can't stand cars, I can't stand cars, I can't stand cars."

Billy turns on the radio. He thinks it's as if Becka didn't really die. She's right here beside him, only thirty-nine years old instead of however old she was. Billy doesn't know. Who the hell knows how old their mother is? Hilary and Becka lived together for too long. They fed off each other's fears and paranoia. It's almost all right for an older woman to be afraid of everything, but Hilary is still young. And Thomas is afraid to fly. Billy sighs. He wonders how his brother is coping up there in the sky. Of course, Billy thinks, that could just be an excuse that Thomas has dreamed up in order not to visit. Who knows? Thomas wasn't afraid of much when they were kids. He was always the first to jump off the high dive at the public pool, or the first to try the rope swing in the garden. Matter of fact, Thomas taught Billy everything he knows about taking risks. He taught Billy not to pay attention to kids when they laughed at him, taunted him because he had no father and his mother stayed locked in the house, because his mother didn't sew his clothes or buy new ones, because he had to do the grocery shopping with his red wagon dragging behind him, or because his sister talked to herself as she walked to school. He taught Billy how to fight, where to punch the hardest, where his knuckles should connect to break a nose. Thomas himself never got in fights. He managed to skirt around trouble, leaving it behind. But Billy came home bloody almost every day. He would wipe off the blood with the kitchen sponge and eat whatever crap Hilary had made for dinner.

And she wonders why he rarely visited. Who wants to remember?

"There's something behind the furnace," Becka would whisper to them at the table. "I think it's a rat."

"We don't have rats," Thomas would say.

"Then I don't know what it is. It was staring at me. It had red eyes." She would hold herself together with her thin arms, clutch at the sweater wrapped tight around her. "I want you to get rid of it. I want it out of here or I won't be able to sleep all night."

"Are we there yet?" Hilary says. "Are we almost there? I'm going to take a taxi back."

"We're almost there. It's just up ahead."

Hilary sees the lights of the airport ahead of the car. "Do you wonder what he'll look like?" she asks. "I've been wondering."

"Like Thomas," Billy says. "Only older."

"Like Daddy?"

Billy looks at Hilary. "Do you remember what he looked like?"

"Not really," she says. "But Mother has those pictures. To me they are just black-and-white pictures of a man who looks familiar."

"I was too young, I guess," Billy says.

They pull into the parking garage and Billy steers Hilary through the airport to wait at the gate for Thomas. She looks awkward in her fur coat and ripped tights, her hair all messy, her face red and chapped. She is biting her fingernails. Billy feels ashamed to be standing there with her. He roams over to the computer terminals to see if Thomas's plane is on time.

Hilary starts talking to the man standing beside her. He is at the airport, he says, to pick up his girlfriend. He is carrying a bouquet of roses which he will give to her to make up for the fight they had before she left.

"She left to visit her mother," he says. "She was mad at me and so she went home."

"Why was she mad at you?"

The man shrugs.

"My mother just died," Hilary says. "I'm here to pick up my brother."

"I'm sorry."

"Thank you."

"I think she left because I'm always working," the man says. "I'm always at the office. I'm really busy."

The man's cellphone rings.

"I'm not going to get it," he says, obviously agitated. "I've promised myself that I'm not going to answer it all the time. Only half the time. Every second call."

"He's my older brother," Hilary says, ignoring the ringing. "He hasn't been home in years. I don't know what he looks like any more."

The man's hands keep moving down to the phone in his coat pocket. He fingers it. The ringing continues. The man's eyes are searching the airport.

"I could answer it quickly," he whispers. "Before she comes."

"Thomas might have a cellphone," Hilary says. "I never thought of that. He's rich. He sends wonderful Christmas presents. He has everything."

"Yeah, what?" the man answers his cellphone and his manner instantly changes. He is loud and confident, holding his finger in the air to stop Hilary from talking. "What do you want? Quit your nattering and get to the point."

Just then the doors open and a woman comes out carrying her suitcase. She is lovely, dark-haired, tall. Hilary watches her. Her eyes light upon the man. He waves at her but doesn't stop talking on the phone. She walks up to him and takes the flowers out of his hand. She walks past him and out the front doors of the airport. Hilary saw the look in her eyes. The woman hails the first taxi, hops in, and disappears. The man stands there, holding his phone away from his ear. Hilary can hear a small voice buzzing from the phone. He stands there with the phone out, his shoulders slumped, his eyes weary. Then he closes it up, puts it in his pocket, and walks alone slowly out of the airport into the cold evening air. As he walks out his phone begins to ring again. Hilary can hear the tiny, muffled sound coming from his coat pocket.

"My mother just died," Hilary whispers to herself. "And I'm all alone."

Billy moves over to stand again beside Hilary. "You really shouldn't wear that fur coat," he says. "You look like a prostitute."

"A prostitute?" Hilary looks around at the people mulling at the airport, waiting for their families and friends to come out from behind the mottled glass doors, and she touches the fur on her chest. People are looking at her. They are always looking at her. She touches her hair, her lips. She catches her reflection in the glass doors. Her reflection disappears as the doors open and Thomas, on unsteady legs, walks towards them. His face is pale and drawn, his eyes are sunken. He is talking to a young woman. He nods at her and says goodbye and then he looks up and sees Billy and Hilary and he straightens up tall and walks, suddenly confident, towards them. His face flushes, his eyes brighten. It is the same Thomas who left them years ago, only older.

"How was your flight?" Billy asks, shaking Thomas's hand and taking his luggage.

"You look tired," Hilary says.

"I'm fine, I'm fine." Thomas gives Hilary a hug. He smells mothballs and feels the old fur warm and soft and slightly holed, under his grasp. He can't believe he is alive. The world looks fresh and vibrant, the browns and golds and oranges of the airport explode before his eyes. "It's good to be here. How are you both?"

Billy starts walking towards the exit doors. He has swung Thomas's small suitcase over his back. He turns to watch his brother and sister come towards him. Thomas walks with his arm around

Hilary's shoulders. He leans into her, listening carefully to what she is saying. Billy looks around the airport and notices people turning to watch them — the beautiful man and the strange-looking woman, her hair hanging ratty around her face. Hilary is so thin she is walking on stilts.

"Mother's dead, Thomas," Hilary says and it's only then that she begins to cry.

2

The House

It is late. They are in the kitchen.

"Jesus, Hilary. Where did you get all these dolls?" Thomas says. "I know you've always had dolls, but this is ridiculous. It's like a museum in here. They stare at me." Thomas picks one up and then quickly puts it down. It's like hundreds of little children looking straight into his soul. Silent watchers. And the house is dirty. There is a smell in the kitchen, something rotting somewhere, dishes piled high on the counters. He has the urge to breathe into his handkerchief, tie it around his face like a cowboy. The table has food crumbs and sauces caked on it. Thomas picks at this with a dirty knife that is sitting on the table. Chunks come up. He wipes his chair before he sits down but he still feels as if he's sitting on something hardened and aged with time. And he thought that flying in that airplane might be the worst of his experiences.

Hilary looks around. "They are mine and Mother's. We've always had dolls. You know that."

"So many? I remember only forty or so. And most of them were in the living room or your bedroom. Not all over the house."

"You've been gone a long time, Thomas. We buy them whenever we have extra money."

"And when did the house get so messy?"

Billy sits at the kitchen table. He looks around him. "Remember that man who lived in that brick house painted yellow?" Billy says. "Remember how we'd throw rocks at his windows just so we could watch him come outside in his pyjamas, a pot in each hand, waving them in the air? God, that old man smelled. And his house smelled. It smelled like shit and rotting meat and alcohol. I remember when he died the police found a bunch of dead cats in the basement and there were rats all over the place."

"It's not that messy," Hilary says. "I just haven't done dishes in a while. I haven't cleaned the counters or mopped the floors. I just haven't wiped the table. I don't even own a cat."

"I never threw rocks at his windows," Thomas says. "You threw rocks at his windows?"

"Yeah." Billy laughs. "Everyone did."

"We've never had rats here," Hilary says thoughtfully. "Although Mother sometimes thought she saw them. Maybe mice, but no rats. And we had ants all over the kitchen floor once. Remember that?"

"I can't believe Becka tolerated this mess," Thomas says. "You used to be so clean."

"Mother's been in bed, Thomas."

"Surely she must have come downstairs —"

"She lay in bed for a long, long time. Until she died. You don't know how sick she was." Hilary turns to look in the fridge for something to offer her brothers.

"Those ants," Billy says. "We couldn't get rid of them. I remember my socks were black on the bottom from stepping on them all the time."

Hilary's hands are shaking. She has been cold ever since she took off that fur coat and threw it on the hall floor by her shoes. She feels as if she has shed her skin, as if she were an animal who has moulted for the summer. Hilary pulls out an old can of frozen orange juice. "Yes," she says. "She was sick, sick, sick." She looks around for a container. "There's juice and water. Nothing else." Hilary finds a container in the cupboard over the sink. It's dirty. "There's preserves and pickles in the basement," she says. "Things like that."

Thomas says. "We'll have to clean this place."

"And then they were gone suddenly," Billy says. "They just picked up and left. All those ants."

"I could put out a pickle plate."

"We'll have to throw things away," Billy says. "Shit, we'll need a dumpster." He is holding a doll in his hand. Blonde hair and pink dress. Billy takes a peek under her dress. She is wearing lace underwear. Little-girl underwear, with frills and bows. "I have a friend who runs a construction business. He could probably get us a dumpster. If he put it in the driveway, we could throw things off the front porch."

Hilary looks away from the container. "Throw what away?" She looks at her brothers. She takes the doll away from Billy and cuddles it in her arms like a child.

"Everything." Billy circles his hands in the air.

"How do you go in there?" Thomas asks, indicating the living room. "How do you watch TV?"

"How do I go in there?"

"The rocks."

"What about them? What do you mean throw everything away?" Hilary turns from Thomas to Billy and then back to Thomas.

"How do you walk on them? Why the hell did you put rocks all over the floor."

"What was there before?" Billy asks. "I can't remember?"

"It's like walking on a stony beach. Why does everyone find that so hard to understand? Why is everyone giving me such a hard time about it? You just have to watch you don't twist your ankle. You have to tread lightly."

"Everyone?" Billy asks. "Who's everyone?"

"The two men who took Mother away thought it was strange."

"It is strange, Hilary," Thomas says. "Who else has rocks on their living room floor?"

Hilary shrugs. "It took me a long time to put them there," she says. "I'm not about to get rid of them easily. Now do you want a pickle plate or not?"

"I think it was carpet, wasn't it? A pinkish colour?"

"Hardwood floor," Hilary says. "It is hardwood. You can see it still if you just look between the rocks."

"Jesus, Hilary, do you know what kind of damage rocks will do to a hardwood floor?"

Billy is looking over Hilary's shoulder into the fridge. Hilary has given up on the orange juice. She puts it back in the freezer and puts the container in the sink with all the other dirty dishes. She puts the doll she is holding on the counter.

Thomas walks to the doorway of the living room and looks in. He puts one Italian leather shoe down on the floor and then the other. He inches forward, slipping slightly, catching his balance. It does feel like walking on the beach. There is a dent in the couch cushion from where Hilary must sit to watch TV. He looks at the dolls every-where, large dolls in various poses propped up against every available surface. He remembers how his mother would touch the dolls when she passed, run her fingers over them. They'll have to throw them all out, Thomas thinks, and picking up all these rocks will be a pain. Not to mention the sanding and refinishing of the floor.

"Do the dolls cost a lot?" Thomas asks, coming back into the kitchen.

"A little," Hilary says. She doesn't tell him that she spends the money he sends her on the dolls. She doesn't tell him that she hasn't eaten a proper meal in months. She pays cable bills, phone bills, hydro and water bills. And she buys dolls. There is a store close by that sells these dolls — not the one at the mall that the two men who took Mother away mentioned, another store, walking distance — and she visits it once a month, buys clothes and material to make new dresses and beads and pearls and ribbons for their hair. She has boy dolls and girl dolls and mother dolls and father dolls. There is even a grandfather doll up in her bedroom that she likes because she can comb his beard.

Billy goes out to his car and brings in some beer.

"This was in the trunk," he says. "Lucky us." He hands one to Thomas as he passes him leaving the living room. He hands one to Hilary in the kitchen. She looks at it. It is cold and heavy.

Billy twists off the cap and gulps the beer quickly. His throat feels parched and dry. Hilary sips at her beer with a bemused expression on her face. She stifles a burp.

"Well," Thomas says, "I guess we should figure out what to do with her."

"Mother never went anywhere," Hilary says, dreamily, sipping her beer. "I put the rocks there so she could feel as if she had travelled great distances. I put the rocks there so she could walk barefoot over them."

"Surely she went out, Hilary," Thomas says.

"No. Only to the doctor at the end. And to the hospital for chemotherapy."

"How long?"

"How long, what?"

"When did she last go out, go shopping or something?"

"A couple of years. Maybe five years."

"Five years," Thomas echoes. He imagines sitting in this house, being stared at by these dolls, for five whole years. Never going out for dinner or to the symphony or the opera.

"Everything we wanted was right here," Hilary says. "We didn't need to go out much."

"She just got worse and worse, didn't she?" Thomas says, looking at Billy.

Billy shrugs and sips his beer. His mother and sister were always crazy, this doesn't surprise him at all.

"Well, we have to bury her," Billy says. He lets out a large belch. "Hey, didn't Dad give you a doll once?"

Hilary goes rigid. Her bottle of beer is poised at her mouth.

"Did he?" Thomas asks. "That would explain a lot."

Hilary says nothing.

Billy says, "We have to bury her, have a small funeral, and then get on with our lives. I've got a teenage daughter who's having a baby. I've got a wife to feed."

"Hilary," Thomas says. He ignores Billy. "What do you think? Do you have any ideas about where to bury her? What did the funeral home say to do?"

"Daddy gave me the doll with the emerald green dress," Hilary says. "Her eye is broken. It keeps shutting. It's like she's winking at me. But Mother started my collection. She gave me my first doll the day I was born."

"I didn't get anything," Billy says. "I never got anything."

"You got married, Billy," Hilary says quietly to the kitchen sink. "You have a child."

"Lucky me," Billy says. He snorts. "Dick Mortimer said that we have to think of a good place to bury her and he'll arrange the details. He said each cemetery has a different fee. I think Sage Hill's nice. Or maybe Cresswood. Then we have to decide how much we want to spend on the funeral. I'm broke, Thomas. So is Hilary."

"That's not a problem," Thomas says. "I'll pay for it."

Billy smiles. "Told you he would, Hilary."

"Cresswood then?"

"No," Thomas says. "I never liked Cresswood. It looks too cheap. Plastic flowers, that kind of thing. We want something with character, with age."

Billy swirls the beer around his mouth and swallows loudly. "I'm lucky to be saddled with a pregnant teenager?" He shakes his head. "You don't know what you're saying."

"What about Inglehaus?" Thomas says with one hand cupped over his mouth, the other wrapped across his chest, his head down. "Or what about that other one — what was it called — Valeside?"

"Where," Hilary asks, her voice a whisper, "would Daddy have buried her?"

Thomas and Billy look at Hilary.

"That's beside the point," Thomas says.

"I think she would like Sage Hill," Hilary says. "All the pretty bushes. The bushes line the side of the road there. They keep the car exhaust off the headstones."

Thomas looks up at Hilary's face. She looks old and tired. Her eyes are unfocused. Thomas sits back in his chair, tilts it a bit, wraps both his arms around his chest and breathes deeply.

"Careful," Billy says. "Those legs aren't strong enough."

"That's my problem."

"You'll break the chair."

"I'll buy a new one."

"Big man," Billy laughs. "I suppose you have credit cards with huge limits. Do you drive a BMW?"

"Do you have a problem with that, Billy?"

"Jesus, a BMW?"

Hilary feels teary all of a sudden. The beer is going to her head. She knows her mother wouldn't like Sage Hill.

"I should go now," Thomas says, looking at his watch. "I'll call a taxi to take me to the motel. We'll decide everything in the morning."

"I don't like that chair anyway," Hilary says, rubbing her eyes. "You can break it if you want, Thomas."

"I don't want to break the chair."

"No, Thomas, you should stay here," Billy says. "Why don't you stay here?" He looks at his older brother. He opens another beer from the pack on the kitchen table. "Don't waste your hard-earned money on a motel."

"Here? I can't stay here."

"Yes you can. I'll help you clean up our bedroom. Just like old times."

"It's just . . . I can't stay here." He thinks of facing the kitchen in the morning, the dirty dishes, the smell. He thinks of all the dolls staring at him.

"We'll have to clean the house before we sell it anyway."

Thomas itches his thighs through his pants.

"Sell?" Hilary's beer is raised to her mouth. The air from her word makes the bottle whistle.

"What did you think we were going to do with it, Hilary? Open a bed and breakfast? Becka is dead. This house is too big for just you."

"You can't sell my house. This is my house, Billy. You can't sell my house."

"This was Becka's house," Thomas says. "Now it's our house and we have to make some sort of sensible decision. She had a will that told us to sell and divide. I think that's sensible, don't you?"

"A will?" Hilary says.

"Yes, it's at my office. I'll send you copies."

"It's my house. You can't sell my house. What will I do? Have you thought of that? Where will I go? What about my dolls? I have far too many dolls to move."

Silence.

Billy says, "What will she do?" He imagines her moving into his house. He shudders. All those dolls lining his garage shelves. Sharing a room with his daughter and her baby.

"Hilary, this house is falling apart. It needs too much work to stay here. The roof needs replacing, the eavestroughs look like they are falling off, it needs painting. We'll use part of the money to set you up somewhere nice. A condominium or apartment. Something close to the stores. We'll give you some sort of allowance, we'll figure it out."

Billy sits up in his chair and opens another beer. "I could use some money too."

He imagines what he could do with the money. He wonders what the house will sell for. Thomas is right. It will need a good coat of paint, some fixing up. Get rid of all the old furniture. "You can throw out the old dolls, keep the newer ones. We'll get you fancy cases for them. Glass with fluorescent lights. We have to sell the house, Hilary. I need the money."

"One thing at a time, Billy," Thomas says.

Hilary clutches her hands around her small chest. She starts to shake. At first the tremors are not noticeable, but they get stronger.

"You won't sell this house. You can't sell this house. It's my home. Everything I have is here. Right here. My dolls. . . ."

Billy rubs his chin. "Christ, Hilary. Don't be so selfish."

"I'm going to a motel," Thomas says. "We'll talk about this all after we've had a good night's sleep. And, Billy, don't count on anything. Hilary is the one who is going to need a place to live and money to live on. You've got a job."

"Jesus, Thomas. I think I deserve some of the money."

"We'll see."

"What are you? A lawyer? It's in the will."

Thomas shrugs. "I'm tired. I'm going to a motel."

"You really should stay here," Billy says. "Hilary needs you."

Hilary turns her head quickly, looking back and forth between brothers. "It's my house. You can't just sell my house."

"I could stay at your house, Billy."

"We don't have enough room. Besides, Hilary needs you."

Thomas leans back in his chair again, his toes barely touching the floor, and the legs suddenly crack right in half with a noise like a shotgun.

After Billy leaves, Hilary shows Thomas where she keeps the extra towels. She hasn't used them in at least ten years. She assumes they will be in good condition.

"In the attic?"

"Where else? Where else would you keep them?"

"In the linen closet."

"There's no room in there," she says.

"Why?"

"Why?" Hilary echoes, looking around. She looks at the boxes stacked four high in the crawl space of the attic. "Our old school textbooks are up here," she says. "And Christmas decorations. Mother kept everything. There's a box with your name on it. And another with Billy's."

Hilary is standing on the ladder that leans up against the trap door, peering into that space. Thomas steadies her below. "I can't keep the towels in the linen closet because the linen closet is full of preserves. So is the basement. We've got preserves everywhere. You won't believe how many things we've preserved."

"What for?" Thomas says. He looks at his manicured fingernails turning white from holding tightly to the ladder. Thomas shivers. The house is cold and damp. "Do you eat them all?"

"If we ate them all," Hilary says as she climbs down the ladder with a box of towels and takes Thomas by the arm and guides him to his old room, the one he shared with Billy when they were boys, "then we wouldn't have so many around the house, would we?" She puts the stale-smelling towels on one of the twin beds and folds the covers back. Thomas notices an old water glass on the night-stand, water now missing, evaporated years ago, but lip marks, probably his waxy teenage Chapstick marks, still stuck to the glass. Thomas has an urge to put his lips up to the glass now to see if they'll fit.

"We haven't had a guest for quite a while," Hilary says. "I'm so glad you are here."

"I'm not a guest, Hilary. I'm your brother."

"After she died, I was all alone. That was the first time I've ever been all alone. Mother has always been here."

"There are advantages to being alone," Thomas says. "You'll get used to it."

Thomas wishes he had stayed in a motel. The one out on Barclay Street, across from the old Chevron station. Alma's Hotel. He wishes he had a nice clean double bed, sweet-smelling towels in his own private bathroom, and a mini-bar. He wishes he were alone. Maybe he should just pack up and go back home. But that means he would have to fly again and he's not ready for that. It will take a couple of days at least to build his courage up again.

He sighs. He sits down on the bed he spent his childhood nights in and it squeaks. Loudly. If he were home, in the house they are renovating, Thomas would be lying in bed next to Jonathan. Sleeping peacefully. A nice thought, but he would probably be feeling guilty that he hadn't done more to help Becka when she was alive, feeling guilty that he wasn't at her funeral. He would probably be tossing and turning, thinking that he should have at least visited her once before she died.

"I was thinking," Hilary says. "I was thinking that maybe we should put something in the paper, in the obituaries, something about Mother's death."

"Why? She didn't have any friends, did she? And we have no living relatives."

"Daddy. Maybe Daddy would come to the funeral."

Thomas looks at Hilary. "Do you think he's still alive?"

"He wouldn't be that old."

"True." Thomas stares at the old posters on the walls. "I like to believe he's dead. I like to believe that there was a damn good reason he never came back to us." Sometimes he feels that he understands why his father left. The same reasons he did, he guesses. He just needed to get away in order to be himself again. "I don't know if I want him to come home. I don't know if I want to see him. He isn't really part of our lives any more, is he?"

Hilary sits beside Thomas. "That's from 'The Dukes of Hazzard,' isn't it?" She points to a poster beside Billy's bed. "I came in here last week and I spent about an hour trying to remember the name of that show."

"Yes," Thomas laughs.

"You and Billy."

"I think Billy liked the car better than the adventures the brothers had."

"He's still like that," Hilary says. "He'd still prefer the car."

"I don't know," Thomas says.

"I don't come in this room very much. I keep the door shut. It reminds me of you and Billy. It reminds me of all I miss . . . of all I've missed."

"I'm sorry I moved away, Hilary," Thomas says. He takes Hilary's hand. "I don't know what else to say. I went to university. I started my own life. I got away."

"Men are always leaving." Hilary pulls her hand away from Thomas and stands up and starts to walk out of the room. She pauses at the doorway. "Thomas?"

"Yes."

"Do you remember Dick Mortimer?"

"Who?"

"Dick? The boy who lived above the funeral home on Duncan Street?"

"Yes, I think so. Fat kid? Smelled funny?"

"He didn't smell funny."

"Yes, he did. Like formaldehyde. A chemical smell from the funeral home."

"He's a mortician now. He's burying Mother."

"That's not surprising. What else would he do for a living? Careers like that are usually passed down the line. There probably aren't that many people who just become funeral directors because they want to."

"It's just," Hilary says, "I haven't seen him in years." She stands awkwardly in the doorway to Thomas's room. "And I saw him today. It made me think about things."

"What things?"

Hilary shrugs. "About me. It made me think about me."

"It's always good, I guess, to think about who you are, where you're going, that kind of thing." Thomas yawns.

"It made me remember that I'm . . ." Hilary pauses.

Thomas yawns again.

"That you're what?"

"I don't know. I don't know what I'm trying to say." Hilary turns to leave the room. She turns back. "So you don't think we should put a death notice in the paper?"

"No, I don't. It's not necessary."

"Well, good night, Thomas."

"Good night."

Thomas sinks back onto the bed. He stares at his old desk, still littered with paper scraps. It amazes him that nothing has been tidied up, thrown out, put away. It's like a museum of his childhood.

When Thomas finally moved away from this house he never

wanted to go back. He couldn't go back. He formed a shell around himself, closed in his family and his past, and he continued on, remade himself, until he forgot he was wearing a hard, shiny exterior. Now it's as if, because he's home again, that shell is cracking. He feels nervous and responsible, he feels overwhelmed. He feels like a father, a husband, a brother again. Everything to everyone. He had so much to take care of when he lived at home.

Thomas lies down on the small bed in his clothes, drapes a stinky towel over his torso, and closes his eyes tight. He knows he'll be haunted by that airplane ride for years to come. Christ, Thomas thinks, once he gets back home he'll never, ever fly again. He'll take buses and trains. He'll drive his car.

Hilary stands in the hallway listening to the small sounds coming from Thomas's room, to the sigh and then the creak of the box spring. And then she listens carefully for the moan of her mother but realizes, suddenly, that the sound of her pain is gone for good.

What will she do now?

She has nothing to do.

She could do the dishes, dust, even vacuum. But she doesn't want to.

Seeing Dick again made her feel like a girl, like a woman, really. That's what she was trying to tell Thomas. But it makes no sense because she knows she's female. She's always known that. Seeing him just made her feel different somehow.

She wanders the hallway. She can smell Thomas's scent, his cologne, lingering in the air, and she remembers the strange smell of her brothers when they were young, the odour of their difference lingering behind their closed door. Sweat socks and body odour. They never let her in. They would shut the door, lock it. She would sit with her mother and their dolls in front of the TV. Her mother smelled of waxy lipstick and cigarettes and stale perfume. Later she smelled of medicine and urine and shit and vomit. Hilary sniffs her armpits, smells the cardigan she put on after she took off the fur coat to keep her warm. What does she smell like?

Hilary paces the hall one last time and then walks quietly to her mother's room and turns on the light. Her bed is a mass of pillows and sheets, all crumpled. Hilary can almost feel her mother's pain moving about her. She can see her mother's shape pushed into the mattress, a dent stained from urine and vomit, scrubbed hard every week and aired to dry. She moved her mother from one half of the double bed to the other. Back and forth. Cleaning each side carefully. She sees the medicine on the table — Valium, Lorazepam, Gravol, morphine, even Tylenol, melt-in-your-mouth pills and liquid, sharp-edged needles — anything to stop the pain. There's an empty water glass lying broken on the floor just under the bedskirt. Hilary sees her mother's slippers, white and bleached, looking for all the world as if she will step into them and shuffle around the house and down the stairs and out into the garden. That was where her mother was most comfortable. Before she stopped going outside altogether. Among her flowers and plants. Her knees caked in dirt, hair up in a bandana, a package of cigarettes close by. When Hilary was younger, her mother would spend hours in the garden, smoking, weeding, planting. It was the only time she ever seemed comfortable in her skin. Not afraid of who she was, of what was around her.

Day after day after day of sitting by the window, watching her garden grow over. Hilary trying to keep the weeds back, trying to trim the bushes, but to no avail. They were living that fairy tale where the castle gets covered over with vines. But there was never a prince to come home and chop at those vines and rescue her mother, rescue her. Hilary did it all on her own. First it was only shopping, cleaning, cooking, laundry, then medicine, doctors, bathing, nursing. From mature older woman to thin, caved-in child, her mother ate only applesauce and mushed vegetables. Their preserves. And Hilary bought baby food. Wax beans, summer vegetables, peaches, pears, apricots. The apricots were the best. Hilary took to eating them herself. Standing by the kitchen counter, licking the little jar clean. The sticky, sweet baby smell near her nose.

Hilary turns off the light and closes the door to her mother's bedroom. She catches her reflection in the hall mirror. It startles her because, for a brief instant, a flash, in her nose, her eyes, her lips, the way she holds her shoulders, she sees her mother standing there. Her mother before she fell over the edge of the world.

Billy lies beside his wife, Tess. He listens to her snore and watches the lights of the cars outside roam like rainbows over his bedroom ceiling. He has to pee but he doesn't want to wake Tess. He thinks of his sister in that big old house, his brother, sleeping in dirty sheets, his daughter, Sue, in her room, seventeen years old and pregnant, and he thinks of his mother dead and lying all undone at Dick Mortimer's funeral home. He wonders what clothes Hilary gave Dick to dress Becka up in. He wonders if it was Becka's violet- and red-flowered dress, the one she wore when she used to go out, the one she wore to his wedding. He wonders if Hilary included Becka's underwear, bra, nylon stockings. What about shoes? Do you put shoes on a corpse? Billy feels his mother is in a nowhere zone somewhere. Hovering. He misses her now but he doesn't know why. He's lived only an hour away for at least twenty years yet he still only visited her once in a while.

His daughter is pregnant and probably doesn't know who the father is and Billy can't think of that because it pains him in the chest and he often worries about his heart. His little girl pregnant. Jesus. Sue's baby will be born in May. And to top things off, to make life even more miserable, he lost his job at the photo shop several weeks ago and his job as a night security guard several days ago and he hasn't had the nerve to tell anyone about either. Christ, life is unfair. Money is lean. Tess is fat. Hilary is going to fight them over the sale of the house. Thomas is going to give all the money to Hilary. His mother is dead, dead, dead. Everything sucks, Billy thinks, and this thought makes him want a drink.

Tess pushes her beefy body up against his thin one.

He hasn't even told Tess he lost his jobs and he's not intending to tell her. Why should he? She hasn't done much for him lately.

Becka, Billy thinks. Dead. A mercy. After all, she suffered enough. But his mother's death makes losing his jobs even worse. Although she's been sick for such a long time it seems sometimes to Billy that everything is happening at once.

Billy really has to pee. "Move over, Tess," Billy whispers. "Jesus, just move a bit."

Billy slides out of his warm bed. He puts on his slippers and robe and leaves his room to go to the washroom. But on the way he gets distracted and he heads downstairs to the kitchen where he finds several bottles of beer and moves with them to the TV set in the living room. He sits on the couch with the remote control in his hand, twists off a beer cap, and tips the bottle into his mouth.

Billy has a list in his head of what he wants out of his life and money is the highest on that list. Thomas can't do anything about their mother's will. If it's written that the money is to be divided, then it will be divided. Three ways. Thomas can give his share to their sister but Billy is going to take his share and pay off some debts. He's going to try and get ahead, he's going to push himself like he did years ago when he was just married and Sue was a tiny baby. When Sue was sweet and small and innocent. When Billy was king of his house, when he could do nothing wrong.

3

Mould

"Have you made any decisions about your mother?" Dick Mortimer says on the phone to Hilary the next morning. Dick twirls the phone cord around his fingers. He thinks of Hilary's face as he talks, the way her nose seems to have shifted, her eyebrows are thicker. He sits back in his big easy chair in his dark office. The windows are leaded, old-fashioned, and the glass is thick. Dick can't see out and no one can see in.

Dick spent three hours last night embalming Hilary's mother. He is tired. Liver cancer is not a pretty sight. She was bright yellow. And then he almost used formaldehyde, which would have reacted with the jaundice and turned her green. Horrid green. Dark olive green, almost black. After seeing Hilary and Billy, he was a bit off, he wasn't thinking. His childhood coming back to him so quickly, so unexpectedly, thoughts of his own mother's death, memories of sneaking around the funeral home with Hilary. Last night Dick left Rebecca Mount in the embalming room when he was finished with her. He set her features, sealed her eyes, embalmed her, covered her with a sheet, and left her on a table.

"Not really." Hilary looks around the kitchen nervously. "We tried to figure out where to bury her but we can't come up with anything. We haven't been together in so long. We don't know each other any more." She suddenly doesn't want to put her mother in the ground. She likes this flurry of activity, the action and bodies around her. She wants to get to know her brothers again. She likes talking on the phone to Dick Mortimer, something she didn't even do when they were young. She knows that if she buries her mother, everyone will leave and she will be all alone. Alone with her dolls and preserves.

"I don't know my brother either," Dick says. "I haven't seen him in years."

"Steve? What's he doing?"

"He's some big lawyer in New York."

"I'd sort of like to keep my brothers here," Hilary says. "Go back to a time where we all lived together. Thomas is actually staying at the house. He's sleeping in his old room. I can hear him snore across the hall. I usually sit by my mother's bed and talk to her. I tell her about the weather or how I'm feeling or I read to her. I read her the *TV Guide*."

"But she's gone now, Hilary."

"I know that." Hilary twirls the cord around her fingers until her hair gets caught up in it and then she pulls at it, trying to release herself.

"When my mother died," Dick says, "it took me a long time to start talking about her in the past tense. I would say, Mom does this and that, instead of Mom did this and that."

"What did she do?"

"What do you mean?"

"This and that. What was this and that?"

"Oh, I don't know. Things." Dick looks at the notepad on his desk.Yesterday, before the doctor phoned from Hilary's house, Dick was adding up his monthly incomes from the previous year, tallying up how much he had made and deciding if he could give himself a raise. He sees the line of numbers and then he sees a doodle, just lines and circles. But the doodle looks like something to him now. It looks like the figure of a man with the head of a chicken. Dick turns the doodle upside down. Now it's a mountain with snow on top.

"See," Hilary says. "You've already forgotten her. I'm not going to forget my mother."

"She baked cookies," Dick says. "And watched TV a lot."

Hilary is silent on the other end of the phone.

"Are you still there?" Dick asks.

"Yes."

"Well," Dick sighs. "I know it's difficult but you'll have to make some decisions. She didn't mention where she'd like to be buried? Usually people talk about such things when they have cancer. It can be such a slow disease."

"No."

"Not a thing?"

"Nothing. She said nothing. She wasn't really dying."

"What do you mean by that?"

"I mean, we never believed she was dying."

"She had liver cancer. The odds of survival —"

"We thought the doctors could be wrong. Doctors are often wrong. I saw a show once where a doctor did prostate surgery on a man who only needed his gallstones removed." Hilary scuffs her slippers along the kitchen linoleum. She chews her fingernails. She wishes Dick were here with her in her kitchen. The phone is hot against her ear and her neck hurts from the position she is standing in. Hilary is not used to talking on the phone. She wonders if people develop phone muscles from stretching their necks to keep the phone under their chins. Maybe she doesn't have the right phone muscles.

When they were young Dick and Hilary spent hours in the library together doing homework. They rarely talked about anything more than school work but when they sometimes touched on a subject that was personal Hilary remembers that she would feel her heart speed up. Her brothers rarely talked to her. She had no friends. Her mother was her only friend but sometimes her mother would lock herself in her room, afraid to come out and talk to anyone, over-whelmed by her fears. Dick's constant presence was reassuring; his bulky figure, the whiff of formaldehyde, his loud laugh, comforted her. Then Thomas left home for university and Hilary dropped out of school to help her mother. Billy was never around, always at Tess's house. And Hilary lost touch with Dick. Gradually. Hilary was too busy doing laundry, dishes, shopping, cooking, and comforting her mother as her fears grew.

"I know this is hard, Hilary," Dick says. "Thomas will help you. Why doesn't one of you come in to talk to me soon and we'll sort things out. Or I could come over there and we could talk about it."

"I just want her to get up out of bed," Hilary says. "I want her to stop saying that she hurts."

"It's over now, Hilary. You need to move on."

"I know that."

"I'll be in touch, all right? I'll give you some time to get organized."

When Hilary hangs up the phone she feels her cheeks. They are flushed hot and dry. She runs cold water from the kitchen sink over her face. She watches the water fall into the rusty old soup cans, the crusty forks and knives, the banana peels, that are piled up in the sink. She feels like gagging.

Thomas is suddenly standing in the kitchen. He is wearing the same suit he had on last night but his shirt is hanging out and his tie is in his pocket. He looks wrinkled.

"Coffee?" he asks, rubbing his eyes.

"Coffee gives you cancer," Hilary says into the sink, her face dripping wet.

"Jesus, Hilary," Thomas says. "I just need a cup to wake up. I'm not going to bathe in the stuff."

"I think Daddy probably got cancer and died," Hilary says. "That's what I think. It seems to run in the family. Remember Uncle Hugh? And Grandma? Remember Grandma?"

"What time is it?"

"Ten o'clock."

"Isn't it too early in the morning to be talking about our family?" Thomas sits at the table. He rubs his hands over the stubble on his face.

"Why did you sleep in your suit?" Hilary dries her face on a dirty towel that is hanging on the handle of the stove.

"I was tired, I guess. I forgot to change."

"Billy would say something about that, wouldn't he?" Hilary says. "About you being so rich you can sleep in one-hundred-dollar suits."

"One hundred dollars?" Thomas laughs. "I'd like to see a suit that only costs one hundred dollars."

Hilary sits with Thomas at the table. "I could make you coffee, but we don't have any coffee. I could make you toast, but there is no bread. I could make you eggs, but there are no eggs, I could make you —"

"I get the picture. Looks like we should go shopping this morning."

Hilary says, "We can take a taxi."

"Whatever," Thomas shrugs. "Hilary," he says. "I had a dream last night about Becka. About her death."

Hilary stiffens.

"Did she suffer a lot at the end? I dreamed that she was suffering, that she was crying."

"She was in pain," Hilary whispers. "Why?"

"I should have come home," Thomas says. "Why didn't I come home?"

"I don't know, Thomas. That's all she wanted you to do."

"I'm so sorry, Hilary."

"It's over now. There's nothing you can do."

Thomas sits quietly at the table with his sister. They both look at the cupboards in front of them. Thomas sees the stains from sauces and food. Hilary sees whiteness before her. Thomas feels a need to get away from this house right now. He feels itchy here, not really himself, like he's covered in some sort of talcum powder and he can't see straight and can't breathe well and can't move without leaving imprints all around. Hilary feels at peace here, she doesn't really want to go out shopping. She wants to stay in this house, here with her brother, forever. She gets up from the table and stretches.

"Can you help me carry some things up from the basement?"

"Sure." Thomas gets up. "What things?"

Down in the basement, Hilary rummages. She thinks she should spend more time down here. Organizing, rearranging. Thomas looks around at the dolls everywhere, sitting high on shelves, at the water on the floor beside the furnace. The walls seem to be growing some sort of mould. Hilary is standing beside a stack of boxes.

"I'm looking for the red pepper jelly," she says. "I don't think it's in the upstairs closet. And I want to bring up some canned fruit and pickles. Then we would have something to eat. Then we wouldn't have to go shopping."

"Canned fruit and pickles for breakfast? No thanks." Thomas tries not to touch anything. He feels damp and cold. "We'll have to get the basement fixed before we sell."

Hilary ignores him.

"Where is the water coming from?" Thomas moves over to the window where he sees a large crack. Every time it rains, water must just pour through. "Jesus, Hilary, look at that crack."

"It's been there for years." Hilary picks up a box and moves it. She opens the one underneath and looks inside. "Here we go. Baby dills.

I've got chutney somewhere but we don't have any bread to dip."

"Years? Do you know how much money you're losing through there?"

Hilary stops searching through boxes and looks curiously at the window. "How can money go out the window?"

"The heating bills. All the heat seeps out through here."

"Oh," Hilary laughs. "I thought you meant that I was being robbed or something. I pictured money flying out the window."

"You are being robbed, almost," Thomas says. "And this mould on the walls. It can't be healthy living with that."

Hilary looks at the mould. "It's never bothered me. In fact, I never realized it was mould until last year."

"For someone worried that coffee will give me cancer —" Thomas begins.

"That's different." But Hilary stands back from the wall. "Isn't it?" Then she walks quickly up the stairs. "Bring up the baby dills," she shouts down. "And a jar or two of red pepper jelly in the box beside the pickles."

When Thomas comes up the stairs carrying the preserves he finds Hilary sitting in the living room, her slippered feet on the rocks. She is holding one of her dolls, a redhead with long braids and freckles.

"I'll have to get the mould removed," she says. "Do you know how much that will cost?"

"Hilary, we'll just get someone to paint over it," Thomas says. "Before we sell."

"Sell," Hilary says. "I told you I'm not selling this house."

Thomas sighs. He walks across the rocks, careful not to twist his ankles. "Tell me about Becka," he says. "What was your life like after I left? What was she like?"

Hilary doesn't even pause to think. She says, "Mother was afraid."

"She was always a bit paranoid."

"No, she was afraid of losing people. Afraid that if she got to know anyone, then that person would leave her, they would get hurt or killed or just leave. And it got worse. She never went outside except to garden because she thought she might meet someone outside. There were days when, talking to me, she would start crying. She would touch my hair — like this — touch my cheek. She loved me but was afraid to love me. Do you know what I mean?"

Thomas stands, steadies himself on the rocks, and walks over to the window. He stares out at the cold day, the leaves blowing on the street. He can see a man walking, hunched over in the wind.

"It's funny, though," Hilary says.

"What?"

"Mother was never afraid of getting sick and dying herself. She didn't believe the doctors when they told her she was dying. Even at the end, she thought she would live forever. She was saying, 'Don't you leave me now, Hilary, don't ever go away,' as if I would be the first to go."

"But you're afraid of that, aren't you? Of getting sick?"

"Isn't everyone afraid to die?" Hilary asks. "You are. You're afraid to fly and that's because when you fly you take a chance that could lead to your death."

"Thanks for reminding me."

Thomas watches the man walk away from them, down the street. He crosses over to the opposite sidewalk where he stops to light a cigarette. He cups his hands together over the cigarette and his hair rushes up in the wind.

Hilary has moved to Thomas's side and is watching the man too. "And liver cancer? She didn't even drink. She smoked. But she never drank. Why did she get liver cancer? Why not lung cancer?" She signals to the man outside.

"It tells you that you can never be sure about anything, doesn't it?"

"I have to get rid of that mould," Hilary says. "What if it was the mould that made her sick."

"I don't think so."

"But you don't know, right?"

"Maybe we should just clean the whole house. Do the dishes. Start from there."

"I just haven't had the energy lately," Hilary sighs. She gets up from the couch and walks carefully out into the kitchen. She starts to run the water in the sink. "I'll need dish soap if I'm going to do the dishes," she says. "You'll have to go shopping."

"Aren't you coming?"

"No. I'll make you a list."

"I should buy you some cream for your face. Your face is chapped from the weather outside or from the heat off the furnace. There's nothing there that can't be cured with some cream."

While Thomas showers and shaves Hilary thinks about what Thomas said, that everyone has their fears. Somehow that lifts her spirits a little, makes her feel lighter. Everyone is afraid of something, aren't they? She imagines that even purely evil people must be afraid — of the law? Of good? But it worries her that Thomas can't see the stain on her face. Even he can't see it.

With her hands in warm water her mind wanders. She thinks about the cemeteries that she has to choose from. Sage Hill. That's a good one. Bushes everywhere. But Mother didn't like bushes. She said they looked like permanent tumbleweeds. She said they stayed too fresh in winter, gave a false appearance to the dead scene around them. She liked trees, though. Maple and oak and magnolia. But not evergreens. Same as the bushes, they stayed too green and healthy-looking through the worst storms. Mother liked plants to show weathering, a passage of time. She liked to know that something alive had managed to live through the worst situation.

Winter is coming on strong this year, Hilary thinks. Soon it will be Christmas. Soon the snow will come.

After his shower Thomas calls Jonathan from the upstairs hall telephone. He pulls the phone cord into the linen closet for privacy and then sees the shelves crammed with preserves. He gags at the sight, mottled green and red and yellow jars, things floating within, like some sort of bizarre laboratory, and he moves back into the hall and whispers into the mouthpiece.

"Jonathan, hello."

"Thomas. How are things?"

"All right," says Thomas. "Sorry I didn't call last night. I was exhausted."

"How was the flight? You survived, obviously."

"It was pure hell. I might just stay here forever." Thomas smiles to himself. "Actually, I don't know which is worse, flying or staying here."

Thomas can hear Jonathan moving. He is carrying the cordless telephone and he is moving about their home.

"You should see this place. Hilary collects things."

"Collects what?"

"As far as I can tell, dolls, rocks, and preserves. There are also shelves in the basement full of canned food and toilet paper. As if she thinks the world will end soon and she's stocking up."

"Rocks? How do you collect rocks?"

"She's laid them out on the living room floor. Hundreds of them. You have to walk over them to watch TV."

"Really?"

"Yes, and the kitchen is unbelievable. Dirty dishes everywhere. I've actually got her scrubbing them right now."

Jonathan laughs. "Doesn't she have a dishwasher?"

"We can't decide where to bury Becka," Thomas says. "No one can agree on a spot. And Hilary doesn't want to sell the house."

Jonathan laughs again.

"Death is funny to you?"

"No, sorry."

Thomas rubs his chin. He needs something to eat. His stomach hurts from hunger. "I'm sorry, I'm just tired," Thomas says. There is a pause in the conversation.

"Are you sure I can't come? I'll hop on a plane today. We've been together for fifteen years, Thomas. It's about time they know."

"I haven't seen them in a long time. Why should I bring it up now. What purpose will it serve?"

"Jesus, Thomas."

"Just don't come here, okay?"

"Whatever."

"I just wanted to say hello. Tell you I miss you."

"Whatever," Jonathan says again. "I'll see you in a week, I guess."

"Yes, a week."

Thomas hangs up the phone. He walks down the hall towards his mother's room. It's the one room he hasn't been in since he's been home.

"She's dead," he says to himself. When he opens his mother's bedroom door Thomas feels his heart beat rapidly. He thinks he sees movement out of the corner of his eye, but it's just the curtain billowing in the breeze from the window which is open a crack to air out the room. "Christ," he says. Her bed is a mass of pillows and comforter. It looks for a second as if there is a body there. He remembers when his father left and how his mother stayed in bed for months. He was the oldest child and had to suddenly take care of everyone. And Hilary began to play the mother. She began to try cooking. She would do the dishes and wash the clothes. How did she know what to do? He remembers creeping up to Becka's bed to ask her for grocery money, to ask her to get out of bed and take care of them. He would plead and beg. And she would lie there with her eyes open, staring at nothing, seeing nothing.

And then he looks up at the whiteness of his mother's room, at the shine and gleam of everything, the polished wood, the mirrors glowing, the cold sun shining through the clean windows, and it strikes him, suddenly, how different this room is from the rest of the house. So clean and bright and airy. Almost holy. Like a shrine, a temple. Everything is sparkling. And then Thomas thinks that if Becka was one thing in her life, it was well loved. Well loved and doted on by her daughter. Hilary would have gone to the ends of the earth to make sure nothing harmed Becka. Thomas is sure of that.

4

Coming Together

Billy and Tess eat lunch at the sandwich store across from the strip plaza. They've just been to the grocery store to stock up on food, and the liquor store for beer and wine. You never know if Thomas might come by to eat, Tess had said, standing in her well-stocked kitchen, looking into her overflowing fridge. She'd need more groceries if she was going to feed all the Mounts in one sitting, wouldn't she? And so they wheeled the cart up and down the aisle of the grocery store and filled it full of party food. Pretzels, sausage rolls, olives, four kinds of cheese, popcorn, soda pop, Twizzlers, jujubes, and jelly beans — bulging large plastic bags in the back of their Oldsmobile.

"There might also be mourners," Tess says, sitting spread-out in the booth of the sandwich store. She often feels she has to justify her binge-spending at the grocery store. Billy complains but his voice is just a whine behind her left ear. She really has to justify it to herself. Tess always feels guilty when there is too much food in the house, but she also feels empty and horribly depressed when the cupboards are even the smallest bit bare, when she can see a gaping space in the freezer, a black hole, ready to suck her in. There's no fine line between the two and so justifying spending is easier to Tess than feeling depressed. Because when Tess is depressed she worries that she might stop eating and a life without food is a life not worth living.

"Becka had no friends," Billy says. "There will be no mourners."

"You don't know that," Tess says, taking a bite of her Meaty Man sandwich, her mouth leaking lettuce. "She might have had a secret boyfriend."

"Tess!"

"We don't know who she might have known, what she might have been doing."

"I lived there for nineteen years, Tess. I know exactly what she did every day."

"Did she drink in the middle of the night?"

"Of course she didn't, Tess, you know that." And then Billy realizes where Tess is leading. "I just had a couple of beers last night. I couldn't sleep. Hilary's house was such a mess, dolls everywhere. And then seeing Thomas again. He looks so much older."

"We all age, Billy. But we'll age faster drinking ourselves to sleep." Tess sucks mustard off her finger. "Does she still have those rocks on the living room floor?"

Billy nods. "And Dick Mortimer. Did I tell you we saw him? He runs the funeral home now."

"Little Dick Mortimer? The fat kid?"

"He's tall now."

"Still fat?" Tess looks down at her stomach.

"Not really fat. Just big."

Tess takes another bite of her sandwich. A little mustard catches on her lip, and as she licks at it another bit of lettuce falls from her mouth. She holds her napkin up to catch the spill. "That's the way it is with men," she says. "They're just big. Women are fat."

Billy watches his wife and for an instant he remembers how absolutely attractive he used to find her. The most beautiful woman in the world sitting there now with that mustard on her lip. Her large size used to be a comfort to him, something he relished, all that flesh to hold on to. But now he thinks she's just fat. And she seems to be getting fatter every day. No matter what she says, she's fatter than Dick Mortimer by a mile.

"When will they need you back at the photo shop?"

"After Christmas," Billy lies, looking down at his plate. He twirls a french fry around in ketchup. "They're just slow right now."

"I can't believe they're slow before Christmas?"

Billy says, "The economy is bad this year." He wonders again how he is going to make this work, how he's going to keep the lie going.

"And your security job too? What are you going to do until after Christmas? You're going to drive me crazy around the house."

Billy thinks about his daughter and her upcoming baby. "Our baby is having a baby," he says to his plate. He thinks about the cost of diapers, of having another mouth to feed.

Tess sighs. She looks at the clock on the sandwich-store wall. Sue will give birth in May and Tess will need all the energy she can muster to look after two children. She wonders if she should order another sandwich. She picks a fry off Billy's plate. "Everything will be fine," Tess says. "You'll see. Sue will go back to high school and we'll watch the baby. Everything will be fine."

"I don't know," Billy says. "It's hard to know anything any more."

"Don't be so down, Billy. Chin up. The sun is shining."

Tess motions out the window of the store and into the parking lot where, indeed, at that exact moment, a ray of sunlight lights up their car. The wind whips an empty bag around the parking lot until the bag catches on the tire of their car and flaps noiselessly. Tess takes that as an omen but she doesn't know what it's telling her.

"You weren't there last night, Tess. It seems like everything is getting worse. I think we're going to have to fight Hilary over sell-ing the house."

"How can things get any worse, Billy? Your mother is dead. What's worse than death?"

Billy shrugs. Living, he wants to say. Sometimes living is far worse than death.

"Although you never really saw her, did you, Billy? Maybe that's worse than death. Not saying goodbye to your mother." Tess pulls herself out of the booth and carries the tray over to the garbage. She dumps in the paper cups and sandwich wrappers. She wipes off her large shirt. "Do you have to pee, Billy? Because you'd better go now before we get in the car."

Billy looks into the eyes of the other diners.

They drive over to Becka's house to see Thomas and Hilary.

Up the chipped front steps, onto the porch, they walk right in. The front door is not locked.

The house is quiet. It occurs to Billy that he's been back to his childhood home twice in less than twenty-four hours. Death can change your whole life around, he thinks. Billy looks at the kitchen table. He thinks about the times he would come home from school and see his mother sitting there, her elbows on the table. Sometimes she wouldn't raise her head or say anything. The silence was deaf-ening. She sat there quietly, as if collecting her thoughts, as if prepar-ing to give a speech. When he was very young, Billy would rush up and kiss her cheek and she would make sounds comparable to a mother bird, cooings and twitchings and hummings. Making all the right movements. "Did you have a nice day at school?" she would ask. "Would you like a cookie and milk?" But there was nothing behind her eyes, a shadow had fallen over the brightness when his father walked out of the house. Damn him, Billy thinks.

In his bedroom Billy remembers that he would make sounds in his head, screams and hisses and bangs and hollers. All in his mind.

He would close his eyes, squinch his mouth and eyebrows, tighten his hands into fists. Drown out the silence, the sadness of his mother.

And now Thomas is across the country with his own successful architecture firm, and Hilary is all alone and half-cracked, and Billy craves just one more beer, maybe a couple. He makes his way to the fridge and pulls one out. It opens with a fizz. He's glad there were some left over from last night.

"Drinking already?" Tess says. "God, this place is a mess. We'll need to give it a good cleaning." Tess sighs. She pulls a candy bar from her purse. She runs her fingers over the kitchen counter, picking at the dried-on food spills. Then she washes her hands in the sink full of dishes. "These dolls give me the creeps."

"Eating already?" Billy says, indicating the chocolate bar in her mouth.

"Billy!"

Tess walks to the cupboard for a glass. Her legs rub together, making a slight swishing noise. The cupboard is empty so she washes a dirty glass in the sink. "At least drink out of this," she says. "It looks awful when you drink from a bottle."

"Where are they?" Billy pours the beer into the glass and sips at the foam.

They listen for Hilary and Thomas. Tess walks into the living room and looks at the rocks. She says, "Why can't I have a normal sister-in-law?" Billy is behind her. "You know the kind. Coffees together, talking about our kids and husbands. Bonding. Trading clothes." She shakes her head back and forth. The chocolate-bar crumbs fall in pieces on her large breasts. She wipes them onto the rocks below.

Billy laughs. "Trading clothes?"

"What's wrong with that?"

"They left the front door unlocked," Billy says. "They must be here."

Tess turns towards Billy and runs her fingers over his arm straight down to the glass of beer he is holding. "Honey," she says, "you have to tell me what's wrong."

"What are you talking about?"

"You know what I'm talking about. Something's wrong. You're drinking. You know —"

"Not here, Tess. Let's talk about this later."

"It's just that since Sue got pregnant we haven't . . . you know."

"Tess, for God's sake." Billy drinks his beer quickly.

"We haven't had sex."

"I know that," Billy whispers. "Don't you think I know that?"

"Is there something wrong?"

"No, I . . ." But Billy doesn't know what to say. "Why are we talking about this here? Why now?"

"Is it my size?" Tess smoothes her shirt down on her large belly. She blushes. She knows she is getting larger, it's just that with Sue pregnant and Billy so distant lately she's found such comfort in food. Besides, Tess thinks that some meat looks good on her, makes her look strong. Makes her face tight. She picks up one of Hilary's dolls which is lying on the rocks, naked. Tess smoothes her hands over the doll's hair. A dress is lying on the couch. Tess creeps over the rocks, surprisingly light on her feet. She tries to put the dress back on the doll. A blue satin one with a large bow in the back and a white lace collar. So pretty. But Tess's fingers are clumsy and big and she can't do up the buttons. She wonders how she'll dress Sue's baby.

"No, it's not your weight." But she's right. Her weight is bothering him. And ever since Sue got pregnant he can't bear to think about sex with Tess. It's nonsense, he knows, but if he stays away from the mother, then maybe the daughter won't really be pregnant. Maybe it's all just a big nightmare. He can't explain it to himself, let alone tell Tess what's wrong. The thought of being a grandfather makes him feel one step closer to the grave. It makes him feel old and weak and out of control. He goes into the kitchen and opens another beer. "Hilary, Thomas," he calls out, startling Tess who drops the doll.

"We're down here," Hilary suddenly calls up from the basement. "Come down the stairs."

Billy places his glass of beer on the counter. He opens the door to the basement. Tess follows.

"My, I didn't realize these stairs were so steep," Tess says as she holds on to Billy's arm and manoeuvres her bulk down. She puffs and pants. All movement is an exertion for her. All action is exercise. She belches up the taste of her Meaty Man sandwich. Onions and mustard. "Slow down, honey. Just slow down."

Tess and Billy make their way through some large boxes and shelves of preserves towards Thomas and Hilary who are standing by the furnace which is chugging loudly. Hilary is holding a sock up to her mouth.

"What are you doing down here?" Tess pants. Her eyes adjust to the dim light. "What's going on? What's that over your mouth?"

"Hello, Tess," Thomas says.

"A sock," Hilary says, her voice muffled. "There's mould everywhere."

Thomas bends to receive his kiss from the fat woman. She is panting and sweating.

"Hey, Thomas," Billy says, looking around. "I've been thinking. Why didn't you bring your girlfriend? What's her name again?"

"Girlfriend?"

"Marianne? Wasn't that it? Wasn't that her name, Tess?"

"Don't ask me," Tess says. "Ask Thomas. Why is there a sock in front of your mouth, Hilary?" Tess is trying to steady her breathing. She thinks about the bag under their car's tires flapping in the breeze, the moment of sunlight on her car, Billy not sleeping with her, Hilary's mouth covered with a sock.

"We broke up," Thomas says. "A long time ago. Listen, we're trying to decide where to bury Becka. You should be in on this."

"I'm sure it was Marianne," Billy says.

"There," Hilary says and points to black marks on the walls near the floor. "Mould. Everywhere. Asthma."

"What the hell is she talking about?" Billy asks. "Hilary, we can't hear you with that sock over your mouth."

"Are you going to bury her down here?" Tess smiles. "Now that would really be something. Next to all of these preserves. My God, Hilary, is this all you've been doing for the last twenty years? Preserving everything?"

"Not in the basement, Tess. Of course not," Thomas says. "We're just looking at the broken window and the mould down here. Hilary wants to have someone come to clean it all up." Thomas points to the window and then to where Hilary was pointing, at the black coating on the walls.

"That's mould?" Billy says.

"That's disgusting," Tess says.

"I can't breathe any more," Hilary says. "I have to go upstairs."

"Let's go upstairs then," Tess says. "I'll make some coffee and we'll have some sweet rolls. I've got some in the car. You look like you need some nourishment, Thomas. And Hilary, my Lord, you're all skin and bones. I just can't understand you Mounts — not an ounce of good fat to protect you from the cruelties of the world."

"Is that what it is?" Billy says. "Protection?"

"I'm probably already sick from the mould," Hilary says. "I probably have asthma and don't know it yet." Hilary takes the sock off her mouth.

Billy lingers in the basement while the others make their way upstairs to the kitchen. He looks at all the preserves stacked high. Blues and yellows and reds and oranges. He can see fruit and pickles floating in the liquid. Chutneys. Applesauces. Jams. It's an overwhelming sight. For some reason it reminds him of the funeral home and makes him think of death and body parts and how fragile his heart is encased in his chest. He roams around, tapping the sides of some of the jars. Or fetuses, maybe that's what they remind him of, dead babies. The black walls smell, a bitter, composty smell. Billy makes his way up to the kitchen where Hilary has shed her sock and is peering in the mirror above the sink.

Thomas bites hungrily into a sweet roll. He hasn't eaten anything yet and it's past lunch. He can't figure out how they are going to start cleaning this mess, where to begin. After rooting through the groceries in the back of her car, Tess has somehow managed to make coffee. Thomas still hasn't been shopping.

"We've got some time to decide," Hilary says, looking away from the mirror. "We don't need to bury her right away."

"Here's some cream, honey." Tess squirts cream into Hilary's hand. Hilary rubs it on her cheeks.

"We don't need any time." Billy laughs. "Why should it take time? We just decide and then we have the funeral and then we sell the house."

"Hilary, honey" — Tess pats Hilary's hands — "you really should go somewhere to get that hair fixed. Get it all chopped off. Get it out of your eyes. No one can see your pretty face." She pats her tight, short permanent.

"My pretty face?" Hilary echoes.

"Playing with your hair all the time isn't very attractive."

"Jesus Christ," says Billy, now drinking his fourth beer. "Let's just get this over with and get on with our lives. We've got to clean this place up, Hilary." Billy sucks on his beer bottle. He wants to sell the house quickly. That will solve all his financial problems.

"No," Hilary says. She says this flatly, with no emotion. "No."

"Hilary," Thomas begins.

"No."

"We have to sell. You need money to live on. The money Becka saved is almost all gone. I can't keep sending you money."

"No."

"Billy, Thomas," Tess says. "Leave her be. Her mother just died."

"She's our mother too," Billy says.

"But she's all Hilary had, Billy."

"What about Sage Hill? The cemetery there is nice."

Thomas says, "Fine with me."

"Too many bushes," Hilary says.

"I thought you liked bushes."

"Yes, but Mother doesn't. Not really."

"Didn't," Billy says. "She's dead. She must have liked bushes. She gardened all the time." Billy wants to bury her at Inglehaus because it's farther from his house and that gives him an excuse not to visit. He doesn't want to trim weeds and take flowers. His mother is dead and doesn't care about flowers any more.

"I think we should bury her somewhere special," Hilary says. "Somewhere we can visit all the time. Somewhere we can go to remember."

Tess picks up a doll from the table. She rocks it in her arms like a baby. She tries to remember when Sue was so tiny.

Thomas reaches for a beer from the fridge. He never drinks this early in the day but he's hungry and the sweet rolls are gone.

Billy calculates how many beers are left in the fridge. He quickly guzzles his and starts another. He'll have to start on the beer in the car and then stock up on more this afternoon.

Tess watches everything.

Hilary thinks of Mother moving around the garden outside, cutting the deadheads off the roses, pulling unsightly plants out of the dirt, bending over, her cigarette dangling from pale lips, plucking a dandelion from the high grass, trimming the bushes until they were all lopsided. But in the end Mother only wanted to look out at the garden from her bedroom window. And then in the last several months she stayed shut inside, listening to the sounds of the house, the groans and creaks surrounding her.

Hilary decides she'll bury her mother in the garden.

She'll do it no matter what Thomas or Billy say. Hilary wants to make her mother comfortable. Surely Mother won't want to be taken away from her home and planted in some strange park. Right now she's suffering at the funeral parlour, Hilary is sure of it. Somehow she has to get her mother back. Quickly.

"Cremation," Hilary shouts out. "We'll sprinkle her ashes in the garden. Have a lovely ceremony."

Tess pales. "Honey," she says, "you know what your mother thought of cremation. You know what she said about it." Tess turns her eyes to the ceiling as if acknowledging a host of heavenly angels. "She thought it was devil's work. She thought that fire consuming flesh was evil. God rest her soul." Tess crosses herself. Fat fingers moving from nose to belly button, from breast to breast. She hasn't been religious since she was a child, since she went to Sunday school every week and collected bags of candy for every verse she memorized from the Bible, and she didn't really know her mother-in-law, but it seems necessary suddenly to cross yourself when speaking about the dead in their own home.

"Mother never said anything one way or another about cremation."

"Yes she did, Hilary. We had a long conversation about it years ago. Your mother would flop over on her stomach at Mortimer's and hide her pretty face in a satin pillow if she knew what you were suggesting." Tess puts down the doll. She places it carefully on the table with the food and coffee and beer bottles and then she massages her large fingers, looking at the swelling.

"I agree," Billy says. "I don't like the idea of burning Becka. I've never agreed with cremation. It's a horrible thought. We'll bury her, Hilary."

Hilary thinks about Mother's death scowl, lips open, eyes wide, before the doctor came and moved her expression around, made it softer. He pronounced her dead of liver cancer. He said she died peacefully. To be scattered around her garden would do her soul a world of good. Hilary is certain of it. And when, Hilary thinks, did Tess ever sit down and talk with her mother? When Tess would visit she would push into the house, fill up the fridge with sweets and fattening foods, and then bustle off just as quickly as she came. But Tess always seems so sure of herself. Maybe it's her bulk. Weighty people seem to say powerful things.

Thomas laughs suddenly. "We could put her ashes in a preserve jar."

Silence. No one moves.

"You know what? I think we should all go play some minigolf," Billy says. He is still drinking. Warmth is spreading down his face to his neck and shoulders.

"What?" Thomas says.

"We should get in a round of minigolf at Greenhomes. The season is almost over."

"Minigolf? God, I haven't played minigolf in years."

"Cremation," Hilary says. "That's the only way."

"No," Tess says.

"No," says Billy.

Thomas shrugs. "I have no feeling about it one way or another."

"We are not selling this house either," Hilary says. "Just so you know."

Thomas sighs. "Let's go play minigolf. Let's talk about all of this later. I'm getting a headache."

"I'm staying here," Hilary says. "I have things to sort out. Besides, I'm not putting a foot inside Billy's car. It's unsafe."

"You can take me and the groceries home, Billy," Tess says. "I need to unpack them before the freezer items melt. I don't feel like golfing right now anyway. I think I might just bake some cookies."

"What I don't understand," Thomas says as he stands, "is why none of you talked to Becka about her wishes. She was sick for a while." Thomas shakes his head. "Why didn't you ask her where she wanted to be buried? Broach the topic, at least. It seems simple to me. Necessary, in fact. Just part of everything you have to do when someone is dying."

Billy swallows his beer in quick gulps. He burps. He looks at Hilary. Tess looks at Hilary.

"What I don't understand," Hilary whispers, "is why you didn't fly back here and ask her yourself? Why didn't you call her and ask her, for that matter?"

Thomas pales. She's right. Why didn't he call her and discuss matters with her? The odd time he did phone he talked mostly to Hilary and only said a few quick words to his mother. She always wanted to know if he was married yet. Thomas doesn't know why, it's not as if marriage ever brought her any happiness.

"Come on," Billy says. "Let's just get away for a while. We'll talk about this later."

"You have no idea, Thomas," Hilary says. "You weren't here. You didn't take care of her. You didn't lift a finger. Not a finger. You all have no idea."

"Let's go."

"Like I said before, you really should get your hair styled, Hilary," Tess says on her way out of the door. She pats Hilary's arm. "Maybe a permanent like mine."

Standing on the rocks in the living room, Hilary watches them load Tess into the Olds. She watches from the front window as Tess bends forward and her belly touches her thighs. Hilary can see Tess's mouth opening and closing like a fish out of water, panting from the work of bending, from the layers of fat pushing into her tiny lungs. Tess used to be a little girl, a petite girl. Hilary wonders if lungs grow when you get fat.

Having Sue made Tess swell up like a hot-air balloon. She never lost the weight. Now Sue is going to have her own baby and Hilary wonders if her thin body will expand out of control. Will she puff up and out like her mother? Hilary touches her belly and feels the flatness. She feels the bones of her pelvis sticking out.

How could she have asked her mother what she wanted done with her body after she dies? How do you ask someone something like that? You want to give them hope, don't you? You don't want them to give up. Because, at a certain point, hope is all there is left.

Hilary runs her fingers over her belly button. She wonders what it would feel like to have a baby nesting inside of her. Incubating. Hilary takes her favourite doll off the shelf over the fireplace, the doll her daddy gave her, and she holds it up to the light of the day. She looks at the doll's face and eyes and hair, she touches the dress, emerald green velvet, a yellow collar and ribbon for the back. The doll is wearing frilly underwear and polished black shoes. The broken eye sticks shut.

Hilary carries the doll over to the couch. The silence in the house is overwhelming. She turns on the TV. The sun is dimming outside. The air is cold. Hilary hugs the doll to her body but there is no warmth in its plastic frame. Her feet resting on her rock collection, she settles into watching a talk show about breast implants that have leaked and she thinks about burying Mother in the backyard right under the magnolia tree, its blossoms so pretty in early spring. Right there, Hilary thinks, just to the left of it to avoid the roots, and six feet down. She is never going to sell the house and move.

On TV a woman stands up in front of the camera and pulls up her shirt. The audience gasps. Hilary looks at the scar across the woman's chest, the scar that replaces the breast that should have been there. The woman says, "I just wanted to be healthy, to be whole," and Hilary looks closely at the scar and thinks that it looks a bit like the profile of her mother. Hilary can see the small nose, the thin lips, the curl of her hair.

Hilary shakes her head. She shakes the doll. She opens and closes the doll's eyes with her finger. It seems to Hilary that she is seeing her mother everywhere. As if her soul is hovering because she's not yet been put to rest.

"I'm being haunted," Hilary whispers and the doll's eye flaps open and then closes.

5

Greenhomes Minigolf Course

A large parking lot, a small clubhouse, and an iron gate lead into
Greenhomes Minigolf Course. It is a small minigolf course and each
hole is close together. Thomas played here when he was young. He
has travelled extensively by train and boat and car but he has never
again seen anything like Greenhomes Minigolf Course. The course
is designed to represent a selection of North American homes.
There are ten holes. There is a Tudor house, a bungalow, an apartment building, a condominium, a Gothic-revival mansion, a castle,
a stretch of subdivision semis, a townhouse, a low-rise building, and
a factory loft. The object is to get the ball through the front doors
of each building and to avoid the plastic pools and small cars that
run back and forth on tracks. Small plastic people move on their
own tracks out from behind bushes and from within the houses,
knocking the balls off course. The castle has a garden party in
progress. The subdivision has cars moving furiously around. The
condominium has people carrying groceries and laundry. The
Tudor house has a family picnicking on the lawn beside their pool.

The sign out front says,

GREENHOMES. ENTER THE WORLD OF BETTER LIVING.
NO OTHER GOLF PARK LIKE IT IN THE WORLD.
IDYLLIC SCENERY, FAMILY FUN.

Thomas thinks there can't be anything like it in the world.

The brothers park in the lot and walk together to the clubhouse. Billy stares at the heavy woman who rents them their golf clubs and balls. She has ringlety hair and a cherub face, round and full and pink. Her body is curvy. Billy can't take his eyes off her. She looks back at him and smiles. Her name tag reads "Grace."

"Not bad," Billy whispers to Thomas.

Thomas looks at the woman. "I should be grocery shopping," he says. "There's nothing to eat in the house."

"We'll go after. I'll take you. Shit, that's all I seem to do these days. Grocery shop."

The men move into the golf course. They are the only players. The wind is fierce, the sky is white and the air is cold. The glow of the floodlights on the course shine on them in the dimming light.

Thomas can't get his putt right. He bends down to the ground and closes one eye tight.

"What the hell are you doing?" Billy asks.

"Lining up my ball to the hole. Like pool."

"Oh," Billy says. "Did you learn that in university?" He laughs.

Thomas stands and presses down the turf with his golf club, forming a ditch that will lead his ball straight to the hole.

"That's cheating."

"It's not cheating. There are no guarantees."

"That's cheating."

"Besides," Thomas says, "you always win this game."

Thomas hits the ball and it bounces straight into the pool. He curses and waves his club in the air.

"Careful," Billy says, "you might hit someone."

"There's no one here."

"You might hit me."

"I can't stand this game. Why did I come here?"

Billy shoots his ball straight over the pool and into the hole. "Hole-in-one." He has never once knocked over a plastic person or damaged a tiny car. Between putts, Billy spends his time looking at Grace in the clubhouse. She looks back. They share smiles.

"She's looking at me," Billy says.

"You're married, remember. Soon to be a grandfather."

"Don't remind me."

"I really hate this game," Thomas says. "I've always hated playing minigolf. Squash, now that's a real game."

"Stop whining."

"I bet you can't play squash."

"I wouldn't want to play squash," Billy says. "Squash is a fag game."

Thomas ignores Billy and gets down on his knees and reaches his hand into the doorway of the Gothic mansion. His ball is stuck inside. Thomas's hand moves around searching for the ball. He knocks over a small plastic person as it ducks out from behind a doorway in the hall. He tries to prop it back up but it keeps falling over.

"Just leave that one," Grace calls from the clubhouse window. "It's been broken lately. Keeps falling over. Just leave it alone."

Thomas finds his ball and rolls it through the house and out into the garden. He stands and breathes deeply.

Billy waves at Grace. She smiles.

Billy imagines Grace in the nude, imagines her body, her lips, her beautiful round face. He's taken to doing that lately, imagining women naked. Even young girls. He caught himself imagining one of Sue's friends the other day and he felt sick to his stomach when he realized what he was doing.

"How is Sue?" Thomas asks, as if reading Billy's mind. "How's the pregnancy."

Billy says, "Sue's doing fine, I guess. Still don't know who the father is. She won't tell us."

Thomas is silent for a minute and then he says, "Why did you never visit Becka and Hilary?"

"I visited."

"Once a year?"

"Better than you."

'This isn't a competition," Thomas says.

"What is it then?"

Thomas takes a shot and misses his ball. He almost drops his club.

"I live across the country."

"I'm busy."

"And Tess?" Thomas asks, changing the subject.

"What about her?"

"How is she?"

Billy looks again at Grace. "You just saw her. You tell me how she's doing."

Thomas lines up his ball. "She didn't say much. She looks good."

"Good?"

"Yes." Thomas clears his throat. He is astonished at Tess's weight. She has ballooned enormously since he last saw her. Thomas feels she might burst. "You know," he says, "I play golf at home."

"Minigolf?"

"No, real golf. I have golf meetings and luncheons and golf parties. I can play real golf."

"Just not minigolf."

"That's right."

"Sure," Billy says, "you're a real golfer."

Thomas stares at his club. It feels heavy in his hand.

"You seeing anyone?" Billy asks. "Marianne?"

"No, not really. That was a long time ago." Thomas tries to remember Marianne, a lover's sister, the girl he paid to take to Billy's wedding. He remembers getting drunk and telling them all he was going to marry her. He tries to remember what else he said about her but he comes up blank. She sat silently at the wedding, staring at the wall. She wouldn't dance with him. She wouldn't talk with his mother. She said that would cost him extra. She got a free train ride across the country from it but that didn't impress her very much.

Thomas putts and misses again. "Goddamnit."

"Nice shot."

An hour later Billy takes the clubs back to Grace and she gives him such a sweet look that he pauses for a minute. He suddenly asks her if she would like to have a drink sometime. Grace nods and says yes, she would be happy to go out with him sometime. Billy says he'll come back someday soon. He takes his receipt and meets Thomas in the parking lot. On his way to the car he wonders if he should ask Grace if he could get a job at Greenhomes. A ball collector. Work behind the cash register. He could do that. Billy won't call on Grace, but the fact that she said yes, that she would go out with him, buoys his spirits. He slaps Thomas on the back and opens the door of the car.

"Want to go for a drink before heading back?" Billy climbs into the car and starts the engine. He pulls out of the lot.

"No," Thomas says. "I'm tired."

"You always sulked after playing minigolf." Billy laughs. "I'd forgotten that. You always sulked when we were kids."

"I'm not sulking, I'm just tired. Seeing Hilary, seeing the house after all these years, it makes me tired." Thomas rolls down his window and lets the cool breeze into the car. He hangs his hand out into the air. "It's just those dolls. They're everywhere. I can't move without seeing one staring at me."

"They're just dolls. She's always had dolls."

"But not this many. For Christ's sake, there was one in the shower with me last night."

Billy doesn't want to talk about that house. It gives him the creeps. "You're just a sore loser. That's why you won't go for a drink."

"No, I'm not. Really." Thomas tries to laugh, to lighten the mood. "It's the dolls." He rubs his eyes. "It's the mess. The house is a shit hole."

"You're telling me."

"What's happened there?"

Billy shrugs. "I guess we left," he says. "Hilary's been on her own for too long."

Thomas forms a gun out of his thumb and forefinger and shoots the trees as they drive past.

"Hit anything?" Billy asks.

Thomas smiles.

"We've got to sell that house," Billy says.

"Don't worry, we'll sell it."

"Yeah, Hilary will see those cute condominiums over on Trellis Street and she'll be the first one packing all her dolls," Billy says.

"She does seem stubborn. You might have to be patient, Billy. We might have to let her stay there for a while, get her used to the idea of living on her own first and then move her."

"I need the money," Billy says quietly.

"I told you, there might not be anything left for us. Let's just not push it right now. Let's wait until after the burial."

"Just go for a drink with me," Billy says. "One drink. A small one."

"No, thanks. Just take me back to the house. I'm going to go to bed early tonight. I'm going to close my eyes and try to forget about those plastic eyes staring at me."

"What about groceries?"

"Oh, shit. Can we stop somewhere quickly?"

They drive through the darkening streets towards Becka's house. Thomas tightens his neck muscles and back. He braces himself. He made it through one whole day and night. He wonders if he can handle six more.

Billy waits in the car at the all-night mini-mart. Thomas walks the aisles. He carries a small red-plastic basket in his hands. The boy behind the counter is watching a black-and-white TV. Thomas can't see what program is on but he hears a man say, "Got fourteen holes in it," and a woman reply, "Ain't no use no more." Thomas wonders if it's a repeat of "The Beverly Hillbillies."

Fruits, vegetables, and bread. Thomas takes his time picking out the produce. He likes being in a grocery store. His mind is only on shopping and nothing else. He likes the white lights overhead and the bright colours of the packages of food. Thomas wishes Jonathan were here with him. He misses him. Thomas noted the stacks of toilet paper and Kleenex and paper towels in the basement of Becka's house and so he walks quickly down the household-products aisle. The next aisle is the pastas and sauces and baking goods. Thomas stocks up on fresh noodles and gourmet sauces. He finds the coffee next to the cereals in the last aisle and he gets milk and cheese and butter from the fridge near the front counter. The boy at the counter hasn't moved since Thomas came into the store.

"Nice night," Thomas says.

"Yeah." The boy rings in his purchases. The commercial on the TV is about panty liners, about super absorbency, about fresh-as-a-field-of-daisies feelings. Thomas turns away. He looks out the window at Billy in the car. He can see the dark shape of his brother. Thomas is tired. He yawns. A boy in a black leather jacket enters

the store and nods at the one ringing in Thomas's food. He saun-
ters over to the counter and leans upon it.

"Fucking cold."

"Yeah," the boy behind the counter says as he bags Thomas's
groceries.

"Fucking freeze your balls off."

"Yeah."

"When you off?"

The boy looks up at the clock behind him. "John's taking over
in twenty minutes."

Thomas pays the boy, takes the bags in his hands, and leaves the
store. As he walks out he hears the volume on the TV increase and
the boy in the leather jacket says, "You gotta love that ass."

Thomas flatters himself by thinking that the boy was referring to
him. And then he remembers that he is, once again, that confused and
secretive boy who used to live with his sad mother in an old house.

"It's freezing in here," Billy says.

He starts the engine and begins to drive Thomas home.

"First stop at the liquor store," Thomas says. "I need to buy a
bottle of Scotch."

Billy nods. He completely understands.

"Mother," Sue says, "can't you get a grip? You're getting huge."

Tess is sitting in the kitchen of her home, eating a tub of ice
cream. She can't help herself. Sue has come down the stairs in full
swing. She is mad at Tess for everything under the sun: for vacuuming in the morning before ten o'clock, for making coffee when
she knows the smell makes Sue sick, for going out all day and not
saying where she was going, for refusing to buy Sue another pair of
cowboy boots, the ones with the purple fringe.

"Have some ice cream," Tess says.

Sue pats her growing belly. "My baby isn't going to have anyone to look after it if you die from overeating."

"What about you?" Tess says. "You'll look after it. You're the mother."

"Don't you have any self-respect? Don't you like yourself at all? Look at you. You're huge. You're gross." Sue points with her long, painted black fingernails. Her eyes are lined in black, her hair is dyed black. "Besides, I can't eat ice cream. I'm dieting."

Tess sighs.

When Tess was pregnant with Sue, she thinks, all she ever wanted in the world was a big tub of Neapolitan ice cream. She'd leave the strawberry because it tasted awful but she'd eat the vanilla and chocolate right down. "Why not just buy vanilla and chocolate ice cream?" Billy would ask and Tess would tsk and think, This man knows nothing about the world if he thinks brown and white are happy without a little pink to spruce up their cold, plastic existence. In a way, this kind of behaviour from Billy, this kind of thinking, is what made her fall deeper in love with him. Here was a man who needed to be watched over, taken care of. His mother had failed to ensure he saw sweet, colourful things when his head hit the pillow at night. As a result Billy still has trouble sleeping, always tossing and turning like he's on a storm-wrecked ship. Tess knows that if he just imagined a little pink dab of light here and there, beside the browns and whites of the world, he'd drift off quicker.

"Jesus, get your life in order, Mother." Sue drinks a glass of water. She marks off how many glasses she's had today on a list held up with magnets on the fridge. Seventeen glasses of water for a seventeen-year-old pregnant girl.

"Sue, you're going to lose that baby if you don't eat."

"I'm not getting fat. There's no way I'm going to look like you."

"But, Sue, the baby —"

"The baby, the baby, is that all you ever think about? What about me?" Sue leaves the kitchen. She stomps upstairs to her room.

Tess digs down into her ice cream. What happened to that nice little two-year-old? The shy one with the curly brown hair? Tess decides that she'll just eat a little something solid until she calms a bit. She reaches into the cookie jar and starts on the chocolate chips she made this afternoon.

Tess is waiting for Billy to come home from minigolf. She is looking out into the dimming early evening. Anxious. Tess fears for Billy. She is sure it hasn't quite hit home that his mother is dead and she knows that when it does the pain will come swift and hard like a good kick in the butt from God. When a person's mother dies, Tess thinks, no matter what she's like, that is when a person starts to realize that they themselves are not long for this world. Tess is sure there must be an attachment between a mother and a child that can't be broken by death and so, when one or the other passes, she thinks there will always be a hand poking up from the earth, ready to pull the living down.

Besides, Tess thinks, Billy's not been quite the same lately. Something is eating him.

"He needs some watching," Tess says to the dark outside. "He needs someone to watch over him."

"Are you talking to yourself?" Sue startles Tess. She is standing in the doorway of the living room. "Have you gone over the edge? What's wrong with you?"

It takes a lot of energy for Tess to imagine the bond between herself and Sue.

6

Annunciation

It is morning and the sky is dark and gloomy. Rain pours down.
Hilary is standing in the backyard with her thin arms wrapped
around her body, praying. Water streams down her face. She took
up praying when her mother was told she only had weeks to live.
Mother's liver was enlarged and the cancer had spread to her lymph
nodes. She was lucky to still be standing, the doctors said. After two
chemotherapy treatments, a week in the hospital, they told Hilary
to take her home and wait for it. There was nothing they could do
any more.

And they waited. And waited.

"A miracle," the doctors said.

And Hilary began to pray.

One day in the kitchen Hilary was helping her mother wash her
thinning hair in the sink when she heard a radio program about praying and how, when a person is dying and someone prays, that person
lives longer and sometimes even recovers. Studies have been done,
the voice on the radio said, among heart attack victims. All who were

prayed for recovered. They didn't even know that someone was praying for them. Most of the patients weren't even religious.

"Silly thing," Mother said. "Imagine that."

Hilary scrubbed her mother's head harder.

"Be careful. You'll pull the rest of the hair out." Mother leaned over the sink and gagged.

Mother's hair came out in chunks in Hilary's hand. She was weak, drained, turning yellow with the first signs of jaundice. Her kidneys were beginning to fail. Her feet were swollen and sore.

"Who ever heard of praying saving anyone," Mother said. "We all die. We can pray until our tongues turn purple and fall out but we still die." Mother stopped talking, the water in her hair dripped into the sink. "If praying worked," she suddenly whispered, "don't you think your daddy would have come back to me? Don't you think?"

This was the first time since Hilary was very young that she had heard her mother mention her daddy. Hilary felt electrified, as if everything in the kitchen was a live wire. She moved back from steadying her dying mother and she stood in the centre of the kitchen, afraid to touch anything.

"Hilary," Mother groaned, "hold me. I'm weak. I'll fall."

And her mother did topple a little, but Hilary caught her quickly and led her to a chair.

Hilary started to pray that day. She took the advice of the radio. She lined up some of her dolls in the upstairs hallway and pretended she was at church. She made her grandfather doll the minister. He was propped up at the head of the dolls on a toilet paper box and he stared down at them meaningfully. Hilary knelt amongst the faithful and she bowed her head and clasped her hands together. She prayed for her mother who sat downstairs in front of the TV.

Sometimes Hilary felt that if she stopped praying her mother wouldn't have to suffer so much pain. Hilary wondered if, by praying, she was punishing her mother, making her hold on to her aching life. It was only in the last few days of her mother's life that Hilary stopped praying.

Now Hilary wanders around the garden. She pats a tree, touches a bush, steps over cat shit. And she prays alone. Without her congregation of dolls. The rain falls hard and Hilary prays for her mother's soul which she assumes is hovering somewhere above her body at Mortimer's Funeral Home. And then Hilary prays for her own soul which she knows is stationed inside her cold body, right here on unstable ground.

She turns abruptly and goes into the house. She dries her face and hair on the stained dishtowel.

Hilary walks around the filthy kitchen fingering the crumbs on the counter, wondering if her mother is looking down from above.

There was a time, before the sick smell of death, when Hilary and her mother moved in sync, when the days rotated around their routine. Mother emerged from her room in the morning, timid and fragile. Hilary rushed the coffee, the toast, and her mother ate sparingly, standing at the counter. They would look together outside, at the weather, as if expecting to go out. And sometimes Hilary took a bus to the grocery store, the pharmacy. But mostly they settled in front of the TV, Hilary with her cocoa and her mother with a mug of coffee. They watched hours of TV. game shows, talk shows, commercials. Anything. Hilary then fixed lunch — grilled cheese, a tomato, water — which they ate in front of the TV.

And, inevitably, Hilary remembered, her mother would start to talk. She talked about superficial things — what needed to be done around the house, the preserves they should do next year. She talked about flying out to visit Thomas or maybe just dropping in on Billy, and she seemed to make herself believe that they went out every day, that they travelled and saw the world. She talked about cleaning, about the dust that was floating in the sunshine around her head.

And then her mother would become bored with the TV and she would begin to roam the house like a ghost, her mug of coffee in one hand, her cigarette in the other. She would stand by the front window for hours, looking out, watching the world pass her by. Sometimes she would take a mop and begin to clean, make a small effort. But then she would lie on the couch and remember that she really didn't like to clean.

The house really is a mess. Hilary strolls from room to room. She remembers when it was clean, when she and Thomas and Billy would spend every second Sunday with their sleeves rolled up. Billy in the garden doing heavy lawn work (mowing, raking, weeding), Thomas cleaning the bathrooms, his hands gloved, up to his elbows in the toilet, and Hilary wandering the house with her duster, her bucket, her vacuum cleaner.

Where is that vacuum cleaner? Hilary runs her hands over a doll resting on the windowsill in the hallway.

Hilary's dolls. Their little legs and arms so perfect, the rubbery or porcelain limbs. Hilary has always had a doll to hold in her arms, to snuggle, to cuddle, to pretend that it is real.

She enters the living room and stares at her rocks. For a moment, like a flash of lightning, she sees how strange they must look to others. But then she tentatively steps upon them, watching her footing, and she feels on edge and solid all at the same time. She feels steady and precarious. Even and tipped.

Hilary tiptoes back over the rocks and walks up the stairs to the second floor. She sits on the floor in the hallway with her dolls. She pretends she isn't all alone. She pretends that the house isn't so quiet around her. Hilary then stands and walks towards her mother's room. She opens the door. She peeks inside. The room is bright and clean. It was the one thing she knew she could do for her mother. Keep the sickroom clean. Her mother moaning in the bed while Hilary drowned out the sound with the roar of a vacuum.

Her mother was her largest doll, lying stiff and wrinkled, yellowed and swollen.

Hilary looks at her face in the mirror above her mother's dresser. Her damp, stringy hair

Hilary rummages in her mother's drawers. Hilary looks at her mother's underwear. She looks at her socks, her nylons. Everything well worn, holey, elastics gone. She thinks she didn't really take care of Mother as she should have.

She walks around the room.

She stands by the window, looking out.

What can she do? There is nothing she can do.

She leaves her mother's room and goes downstairs to the living room. She pulls a box out of the cupboard beside the TV. One of many puzzles she has collected over the years. She takes it into the kitchen and sits down at the table. She shakes out the puzzle pieces. A photograph of the completed puzzle on the box cover shows Leonardo da Vinci's painting, "Annunciation." Hilary loves this puzzle. She found it one day at a garage sale when she was coming home from school. She bought it for a quarter. She loves that look in the Madonna's eyes. What is it? Wariness? Apprehension? Hilary imagines that she would look that way if someone were to tell her she was pregnant right now. And the angel kneeling before the Madonna is beautiful but frightening. His eye in profile is blank, white, and the effect is terrifying. As if he has nothing inside of him. No soul. He holds his fingers out to the Madonna in a gesture that reminds Hilary of Thomas when he would lecture Billy. And the Madonna holds one hand up, saying "Stop," and the other hand rests crooked, arthritic looking, on a large book she is reading.

Hilary's mother used to work on this puzzle. When it was completed she wouldn't let anyone take it apart for days. She used to spend hours staring at the Madonna's face, her lips, her eyes, nose. If she had put it together on the kitchen table, they would have to eat on top of it; on the living room floor, they would have to walk around it. Then she would dissect it, piece by piece, and put it away for another six months, a year.

Hilary works from the left corner and soon completes the frame of the puzzle. Her hands are shaking. She steadies them by holding them together in her lap. She looks at the hallway, at the steps leading up to her mother's room and she holds her hands tightly. Thomas has taken the bus to buy cleaning supplies for the house, to pick up boxes. He said he was going to talk to Dick Mortimer and Hilary wishes she were there with them now. She would like to see Dick again. She still hasn't forgiven Thomas for saying those things yesterday, but she will try to forget. No one else took care of her mother. No one could. How could she expect Thomas to understand?

Hilary looks everywhere for the piece with part of the angel's wing. She finds it and adds it to her puzzle.

"The lady should have the wings," her mother said once about the Madonna. "What does a man need with wings?"

Hilary is cold and damp. She tries to concentrate but her hands are suddenly shaking and her eyes are beginning to tear.

Thomas is walking through the suburbs in the rain. He's been walking for hours. He decided not to take the bus and now he regrets his decision. It feels as if he can't get anywhere. He is passing house after house, strip mall after strip mall, but he can't get anywhere he wants to go. He is tired of holding his umbrella high. He thinks this is why he moved away from here. Where he lives you can walk one direction, any direction, and happen upon what you want. He wonders if he should go back to the house.

Thomas has been thinking about his father and why his father left them. He's been thinking, wondering, if he would have done that — left three small children and a wife. Thomas thinks he couldn't have done that. No matter how bad the situation.

Now Thomas is standing in front of Mortimer's Funeral Home. He wants to talk to Dick about finances. He wants to do this without the others around. Make some decisions. Get going on things. And suddenly he wants to see his mother. He wants to see her face. Last night he dreamt about the last time he saw her, at Billy's wedding, about how she struggled out of his arms when he tried to hold her tight because she said he looked too much like his father.

Thomas enters the funeral home and strolls down the long, polished hallways looking for Dick Mortimer.

"Hello?"

There is no one around. Just dead air.

"Hello?" he says again.

Dick Mortimer comes out of his office. "Hello. What can I do for you?"

Thomas looks at Dick.

"Thomas? Thomas Mount?"

"Yes," Thomas says. "I'd like to talk to you about finances, about the cost of my mother's funeral."

"Of course. How are you? I haven't seen you in so long."

The men shake hands.

"Come into my office."

"And I'd like to see her if you don't mind. I'd like to see my mother."

Dick stops walking into his office and turns towards Thomas. "What?"

"I'd like to look at her."

"Your mother?"

"Yes."

Dick is caught off guard. He left Rebecca Mount in the preparation room a couple of days ago, a sheet draped over her naked yellow body. He hasn't been organized lately. He's been distracted and busy. Besides, Dick figured he had time so he didn't put on her makeup or fix her. He didn't even dress her.

Dick motions Thomas towards a chair in his office. "Let's go over the finances first, shall we?"

"It smells a bit in here, doesn't it?" Thomas asks nervously. "But I guess that's part of the work, isn't it?"

"You're dead on," Dick laughs. "I've had some people compare the smell to burning or sulphur or burnt cabbage, maybe." Dick nods his large head up and down. "You get used to it with time. Sometimes I can't even smell it." Dick sits in his comfortable chair behind his enormous mahogany desk. He feels a little happy jab in his lower spine, almost a sexual feeling, a feeling of success. His body shivers with delight. No matter how many times he sits in his office, he feels this way. No matter how many people comment on the smell that lingers around him, he still loves his work.

Thomas feels suddenly tired. Walking through the suburbs in the rain has exhausted him. He feels as if he's coming down with a cold or a flu. He feels weak and drained.

Dick hands him a price list. "I'm sure you've gone over this with Hilary and Billy, haven't you? I sent one home with them."

"Well . . ."

"You really need to decide on a couple of things. First, the casket. Second, the service — where, when, how many."

"How many?"

"Viewings. Guests you might have. Third, the site of burial and all the extras that go with that."

"Such as?"

"Such as a grave marker, or if you want cement lining in the grave, or if you want the service to be continued at the site, that kind of thing."

"Do you have any package deals?" Thomas laughs.

"Yes, we do." Dick hands Thomas another piece of paper.

"I'd actually like to see her first," Thomas says. "Then we could sit down and talk. Would that be all right?"

"Have you ever seen a dead body before, Thomas?" Dick sits back in his chair and places his hands together as if praying. Fingers pointed high, spread apart, just touching.

"No."

"Did you see your mother at the end of her life?"

"No, I ..."

Dick raises his hand. "No apologies. I'm not here for that. What I'm getting at, Thomas, is that she is quite horrid to look at right now."

"That's all right," Thomas says. "I'm sure I can take it. I'm an adult, after all."

Dick sighs. "I'll be honest. She's yellow. She hasn't been made-up yet. She is naked."

"Yellow?"

"The jaundice from the liver cancer. Her kidneys gave out too."

Thomas sits silently. He looks at the floor. "I would really like to see her. You see, I didn't get a chance to say goodbye."

"That's what viewings are for, Thomas. Wait until her makeup is done, until she's dressed and prettied up."

The two men stare at each other for a minute.

"Please. I want to see her now."

Dick rises from his chair. Thomas rises too. "Come with me then." Dick has only shown two people their loved ones after embalming and before makeup and both incidents turned out horribly. Families crying, sobbing, howling. But Rebecca Mount was Thomas's mother and Dick has a policy to respect the families. Just because he has the body in his possession, it doesn't mean he owns it.

Thomas follows closely behind. His heart is beating rapidly. He follows Dick down the stairs to the basement where there is a labyrinth of hallways and doorways. Thomas breathes heavily.

"Just in there." Dick motions to a door. He unlocks it. Thomas enters. It is dark. Dick flips on the lights. After his eyes adjust Thomas looks around. He sees what looks like a medical room in a hospital, perhaps an operating room. There are empty steel tables and huge lights. Drawers in the wall full, presumably, of instruments. Machines. And there, against a wall, is a table with a sheet draped over the bulk that lies atop it.

Thomas looks in that direction.

"You just leave her there like that? You don't put her somewhere safe?"

Dick walks towards the table. He rolls the table to the centre of the room and flicks on the overhead light.

"The room is always locked."

"But she's just lying there."

"Where do you think I should leave her? You haven't chosen a casket."

Thomas stands motionless before the sheeted table. His arms hang low by his sides.

"You can do the honours," Dick says. He is a little angry. He wouldn't presume to tell Thomas how to do his job. Dick stands back, waiting for Thomas to pull the sheet off.

"I . . ."

"If you want to change your mind, that's fine with me." Dick looks at his watch. "It is your mother. I completely understand."

Thomas takes a deep breath. He feels like vomiting. He looks at Dick.

"What would you do?" Thomas whispers. "Would you look?"

"Oh, I've already seen her," Dick says.

"No, I mean —"

"Look at my own mother, you mean?"

"Yes."

"Yes, I would," Dick says. "In fact, I did." Dick lets out a large breath.

"I embalmed my own mother, to tell you the truth. I made her up and dressed her." Dick looks down at his shoes. He feels proud about this. It was one of his finest burials. "I didn't get the opportunity to preserve my father as I hadn't taken the embalming course when he died."

Thomas opens his mouth to say something but he simply can't think of a thing to say.

"It was comforting putting my mother to rest. But that is my job, isn't it?"

Thomas nods.

"I mean," Dick says, "I'm not an average person." He clears his throat. "I see dead — I mean, expired people every day. My mother. Well . . ."

"I understand," Thomas says.

"I'm not like you," Dick continues. He clears his throat again. "This is my job."

"I'm an architect," Thomas says and takes one large gulp of stagnant air and moves towards the table. "But I am her son. Aren't I?"

Dick nods.

Thomas pulls the sheet off his mother's face.

"Oh, God. She's so yellow," Thomas says.

She has no hair and this fact shocks him more than her colour, than the strange expression on her face, her closed eyes, the way her skin looks like wax.

"They lose moisture, you know," Dick says. "That's why she looks so small."

"Her face."

"You'll be surprised what a little makeup can do."

Thomas tries to look away but his mother's face keeps drawing him back. He regrets immediately that he wanted to see her like this. He knows that this is the image that will stay with him forever. Her lips are pinched tight, her eyes sealed shut. Everything about her looks forced, as if her death was something she was fighting.

Dick clears his throat. "I've heard that liver cancer is extremely painful at the end."

"Why is she stitched?" Thomas asks. "Did she hurt herself?"

"That's from the embalming," Dick says. "I'll cover those marks with makeup."

"What's this?" Thomas points a shaky finger towards Becka's neck, towards the marks there.

"I don't know," Dick says. "Bruises, I guess."

"Bruises," Thomas echoes. "On her neck." He puts his hands over his eyes and pokes his fingers into his sockets to stop the tears from flowing.

"Oh dear," Dick says. "I knew I shouldn't have let you see her."

Thomas drops the sheet and turns to leave the room. He feels overwhelmed.

"This happens every time I let someone see their loved one." Dick shakes his head. "I really should learn. But I feel that the bodies aren't mine to make decisions about. The bodies still belong to the families. . . ."

Thomas stands in the hallway. "I have to leave now," he tells Dick. "I'll come back and talk to you about everything soon."

"But —"

"I have to go now." Thomas starts up the stairs and then out the door into the rain. He feels as if he's walking against a wind. When the rain touches his face he feels alive again and able to breathe. He takes gulping breaths and looks around at the bright colours surrounding him: the green of the grass, the trees turning colour, the grey of the sidewalk. Everything seems to glow.

"Hey," Dick shouts out the door. "You left your umbrella. It's raining."

Thomas walks away in the rain.

"We really have to talk about the service," Dick shouts. "As soon as your family is available."

Thomas disappears around the corner.

Dick shakes his head. Serves him right to show dead bodies to people with weak stomachs. Then Dick smiles. He's certainly better than the average person. He looks Death in the eye, day in, day out. And it doesn't faze him a bit. He breathes deeply. Not everyone could do his job. Dick has lived in a funeral home his entire life. He couldn't ask for anything better.

He walks back to the room with the body of Rebecca Mount. His staff have gone home for the day. He walks over to her and stares at her face. Even after he set her face, she still looks scared of something. But what? Dick thinks death is natural. He is not afraid of it at all. It's inevitable. Why worry about something you can't change, he reasons.

Dick leans back on his heels. The thought of going upstairs to his apartment above the funeral home, having supper, and watching TV alone is more than he can bear right now. He's tired of having no one to talk to at the end of the day. He misses his mother. Sometimes Dick thinks he should try to locate his brother and strike up a conversation. Sometimes he thinks that they might get along now that they are the last of the Mortimers. But he knows in his heart that Steve wouldn't take his call. He wants nothing to remind him of where he came from. Dick stretches. He walks to the door and turns the main light out. Rebecca Mount's profile shines in the glow of the small light above her body. From the side she looks interesting, almost beautiful. Like some sort of twisted sculpture. He thinks her life must have been sad and lonely. He remembers that her husband left her. He remembers that she didn't go outside much. Dick steps back into the room and looks around. Everything is tidy. The air hangs heavy.

Dick circles the empty embalming table right next to Rebecca Mount. He wipes a finger over its metal surface. It is clean. And then Dick does what he has always done since he was a small boy. He climbs onto the embalming table and lies down. He crosses his hands over his chest and lies there, as still as he can be, his eyes closed, and he tries to clear his mind and think of absolutely nothing. He pretends he is dead. In this way Dick has conditioned himself to fear nothing. He lies on the table that has held so many other bodies and he is not afraid. Of anything. He imagines the embalming process, feels the cut on his clavicle, feels the solution cooking his body, tightening him. He is dead. He sucks in the odours, he lets himself become aware of the body beside him, and he opens up his mind to whiteness, to nothing, to an empty feeling of zero. A big hole. A chasm. If a body doesn't fear death, Dick reasons, then a body won't fear loneliness or pain or emptiness. It is in this way that Dick has grown strong, has pulled himself out of the fat-boy rut he was in back in high school. It is in this way that Dick has faced the world.

But it doesn't work today. Rebecca Mount stretched there beside him. She looks as lonely and uncomfortable as he is. And seeing Hilary Mount again made him remember parts of his past he would rather forget. And then Thomas's sadness. Dick's memories of his own mother's death. He can't concentrate. He sits up and eases himself off the table.

Thomas makes it home and walks immediately up to his bedroom. He lies on the small bed in his wet clothes. His eyes are closed. He tries to picture his mother and suddenly he can see her in his mind, standing clearly before him. She is dressed in a flowered terry-cloth bathrobe, her hair in a halo of curlers, a cigarette dangling from her fingers. She has just stepped out of the bath and Thomas can see the steam float off her neck and arms and calves. She stands there in a mist, her old bedroom slippers fuzzy and worn, one hand tucked into the robe pockets, her smile lopsided and nervous. She is younger than Thomas is now. Maybe Hilary's age, or even Billy's.

He must have been ten or eleven years old. Caught in the middle of reading a book with his flashlight under the covers. Becka was standing in his room and Thomas was not aware that she was there. Suddenly he felt her presence. She was watching him.

"Aren't you sleeping yet, Thomas?" Becka asked. She flicked her cigarette onto the carpet and stepped on it. Scrunched it with her slipper. She was never a fine housekeeper.

"No."

"And why aren't you sleeping yet?"

"I'm not tired." Thomas hid his book, flicked off his light, glanced over at Billy who was breathing deeply under his covers, a skinny bulk in his bed.

"And why aren't you tired, Thomas?" Becka whispered.

"Because I'm not tired."

"Then let's get up." And suddenly Becka took Thomas's hand and pulled him softly out of bed. "Get up, then, if you aren't tired. Don't waste your time in bed. Get up."

Becka pulled Thomas out of his bedroom and he remembers being cold in the darkness of the hallway, shivering in his pyjamas. He could hear Hilary sighing under her covers across the hall, almost snoring. He could hear Billy breathing heavily. Everything seemed to stand still and thus become magnified. Sounds echoed. His footsteps on the floor. Becka's shuffling, slipping walk.

"I don't really want to get up. It's cold out here."

A roller fell out of Becka's hair and the noise was like the pop of a BB gun. She giggled.

"Let go of my hand. I want to go back to bed."

"Come on. Let's dance." Becka lightly tugged Thomas down the stairs into the living room and she turned on the radio and began to dance. "Please." Thomas watched. He hugged himself to keep warm in his flannel super-hero pyjamas. Becka danced a waltz, grabbed a doll and pretended to lead. "No one ever dances with me any more."

"You're crazy," he remembers suddenly shouting. "You're stupid and crazy. Leave me alone."

Becka stopped dancing and looked at him. "Why won't you dance with me?" she asked.

But Thomas heard laughter — he felt as if people were always laughing behind his back. He heard it in his ears. All the time.

She extended her hand for Thomas.

Thomas ran out of the room, up to his bedroom, left her there, alone, by herself, staring at the doll in her arms.

He always left her. Just turned and ran away.

Why wouldn't he dance with her?

Now, still in his wet clothes, Thomas closes his eyes as he lies on his old bed surrounded by his childhood. He is so ashamed of himself, angry at the way he treated her.

And outside, in the cold, dark rain, Hilary begins to dig her mother's grave. Tess is right. Cremation isn't something Hilary would want either. Burning her body. The thought of hot fire on her mother's cold skin, bubbling it, melting it, makes her weak at the knees. At first Hilary uses a small garden trowel to dig the hole but the ground is too hard. Then she finds a shovel at the side of the house, half under the porch. The shovel is covered with spider-webs and dead gnats. Hilary grabs hold of it and, in her father's muddy running shoes, she marches with it out into the black garden and continues to dig.

She is angry because she couldn't find the Madonna's face. She spent the afternoon putting the puzzle together and she looked everywhere for the last couple of pieces that would complete the face. It infuriated her. She couldn't find the pieces. She wonders if her mother hid them somewhere.

The rain jets down around her, washes through her hair and eyes. Hilary can't tell if she's crying or if it's just rain on her face. The water stings the small cuts she made on her cheeks. Hilary digs at the surface of the ground until her muscles ache, feel stretched and raw, until her hands are blistered. She barely makes a dent in the soil and what she does happen to move turns quickly to mud and the mud fills the small hole she has created. Hilary digs out the muddy water, only to see more water fill the spot.

She has lost her mother.

All she wants is to get her mother buried good and deep somewhere as close to home as possible. All she wants is peace of mind, knowing she did the right thing.

Hilary stops digging and looks up at the dark sky and thick clouds. There is an intense ache in her gut, a feeling of emotional tenseness, every nerve on end. She drops the shovel and holds her stomach, she caresses just under her belly button. She feels the emptiness, the flatness.

Hilary picks up the shovel and digs again.

The Madonna lies faceless on the kitchen table.

Finally Hilary stops digging and looks down into the small, muddy hole. Her head feels thick with emotion, tight, awkward. It feels too big for her shoulders, for her neck. Hilary imagines her neck will break with the strain of holding her head up and so she lies sideways on the muddy ground and rests her ear to it, listens to the ping of the rain falling down, listens to the silence of a world under water.

Who is going to kiss her good night? Who is going to say "I love you"? Who will Hilary hold in her arms? The sudden knowledge that no one will touch her again makes Hilary's skin feel burned and raw. She gasps.

Thomas gets up from his bed. He wanders down the stairs, looking for Hilary. He sees her outside in the rain, lying in the mud. Thomas blinks his eyes. He opens the door and calls out quietly, so the neighbours won't hear, "Hilary, come in."

Hilary starts and then gets up quickly, shaking the rain out of her hair like a dog. She walks towards Thomas, her eyes swollen and red.

"What the hell are you doing out there? You'll catch pneumonia."

Thomas leads Hilary to the bathroom where she washes her hands and face and tries to comb the mud out of her hair. She wraps her hair in a towel like a turban and then she takes off her muddy clothes and puts on her mother's old bathrobe.

"What were you doing out there?" Thomas asks. He is sitting at the kitchen table when she comes into the room. "What's going on, Hilary? You've scratched your face."

Hilary drinks water from the sink using a soup can that is sitting on the counter, taking care not to cut her mouth. Hilary feels inside the pocket of the bathrobe and finds several of her mother's used Kleenexes. She fingers them. They are hard and dry. Crusted. The rain has stopped outside.

"Hilary."

"What?"

"What were you doing in the backyard? What were you digging?"

Hilary sneezes. "I think I've got a cold now."

"Of course you do. What were you digging?"

"I was just digging." Hilary looks out the kitchen window at the muddy backyard. Her small hole is filling up with mud and water.

"What were you digging for?"

"For?"

"Hilary."

"For Mother."

Thomas pauses. He takes a deep breath. "Do you want to see a doctor?"

"Maybe I should," Hilary says. "You're right. It might be pneumonia." Hilary coughs a little and then looks at her hands. "Don't you cough up blood with pneumonia? I'm not coughing up blood."

"I'm not talking about that. Do you want to see someone? Talk to someone professional?"

"Professional? I'm talking to you, Thomas. Don't be silly."

Thomas has a headache.

"Listen to me, Thomas," Hilary says.

Thomas nods.

"I want to bury Mother in the backyard. Right over there. I think that that is the best place for her. In her garden."

"But Billy and Tess don't want to cremate her."

"No, in a casket. Bury her body."

Thomas stands up quickly. Then he smiles. This is a joke, he thinks. He laughs.

"I'm serious."

"Hilary, that's crazy. It's illegal, for one thing. You can't bury a body in a backyard in the suburbs. You just can't do that."

"Why not?"

"Because that's the law."

"No one has to know."

"No, Hilary."

"Thomas."

"No."

Thomas remembers Becka in the garden. Cigarettes dangling from her lips or fingers, hair pulled back in a knot. He remembers her straw, floppy hat, the garden blooming behind her. He pictures that dead body he saw at the funeral home lying there on the grass and then he sees it melt down into the ground.

"Can't you see that it's the only place?" Hilary says. "You didn't come back to say goodbye, Thomas. You owe her something. Bury her in the right place."

"Don't give me that. You can't guilt me into doing something illegal."

Hilary says, "Can't you understand? I want to do something that will ease my heart."

Thomas takes the bottle of Scotch he bought off the shelf over the kitchen sink. He unscrews the cap and pours himself a drink. "Do you want one?"

Hilary shakes her head.

"Just suppose we could do it," Thomas says. "Suppose that it was legal. How would we sell the house then? You'd have to live here forever." Thomas pauses. "That's it, isn't it? You don't want to move."

"I didn't even think about that," Hilary says. "But yes, that's an advantage. I could take care of her here. I could grow flowers for her."

"This is morbid, Hilary."

"I'll do it by myself then. There's nothing you can do. You can't stop me."

Thomas sees Hilary as a girl, standing on a stool to fix their dinner, carrying a tray up to their mother as she lay in bed mourning the loss of their father. Once Hilary singed her eyebrows and eyelashes on the stove. Once she severely burned her palm on a casserole pan.

It would be easier to agree with Hilary. In the dark of the night it seems so simple, really. They could bury Becka in the backyard, quickly and quietly, and Hilary could stay living in the house and Thomas could go home and life would go on. It would be as if nothing had happened, as if no one was missing from the picture. Hilary would still be living with Becka. Death didn't happen. Thomas wouldn't have to say goodbye.

In her bathrobe, her hair up in a turban, Hilary looks a bit like Becka. Thomas feels overwhelmed. She needed so much out of him that he couldn't give to her. Thomas sits down.

Hilary leans towards Thomas. "I'll do it on my own," she whispers. Then she takes Thomas's head in her hands and pulls him close to her chest. She strokes his hair. "There, there, Thomas. Everything will be fine. You'll see."

7

The Boat

Billy is sitting at the kitchen table trying to remember some of the funny times in his life. Times where he almost pissed his pants he laughed so hard.

When was the last time he really laughed?

It is Saturday, just before dinner. He's had quite a few beers. Tess and Sue have been out all day. Separately. No note from Tess and his pregnant daughter skipped past him this morning and rushed out the door into the rain wearing something mildly see-through, something tight. Billy watched her light a cigarette at the corner juggling her umbrella and the lighter. He watched the thickness of her waist. He felt like crying. So now he tries to laugh but it is forced and controlled.

He got fired from both his jobs for showing up drunk. What's there to laugh at? Old man Paterson called him into the back of the photo shop, showed him the negatives he destroyed, left too long in the machine, showed him the empty beer bottles he found in Billy's desk drawers, showed him the list of financial losses Billy has caused the store over the past ten years. Paterson's face went red, he was embarrassed. Billy stood there smiling because he didn't know what else to do. And then Billy showed up at his night security job at the parking lot and Fred smelled his breath and said that was one time too many.

Billy puts his head down on the cool table and pretends that he is anywhere but in his kitchen, with a fat wife (obese, really — she's getting so heavy), a pregnant high school dropout teenage daughter, and no jobs. God, Christmas is just around the corner. The house is mortgaged up to the rafters. And he has to bury his dead mother.

His mother married his father just because she was pregnant with Thomas and look how her life turned out. And Billy married Tess because she was pregnant with Sue. Now, seventeen years later, he can't laugh when he wants to and, to make matters worse, he's thinking more about that woman at the golf course than he's thinking about his wife. And his goddamn daughter, with her black hair and painted face, is making his heart collapse. Sometimes he pictures his heart deflating like a slow-leaking balloon.

Tess comes home, puts some groceries in the fridge, pats Billy on the head, and moves into the living room to sit in front of the TV with a bag of potato chips and a large bottle of Coke. She doesn't tell him where she has been. He doesn't ask. Tess is trying to summon up enough energy to make dinner. She watches TV in the gloom, the outside dark from rain clouds. Billy stands in the doorway and watches Tess watch TV. He watches her mouth open and close, watches her chew and swallow. He sits down beside her.

"Tess," Billy says.

"What?"

"Maybe you should lay off those chips."

Tess turns to Billy. She looks at him. "Don't you tell me to stop eating."

"I just don't want you to get sick." He rubs his eyes. He can hear the buzz in his head getting louder.

"Sick? Don't you mean fat? Fatter?"

"It's not good to be so big." Billy tastes his tongue. It is dry and pasty. Tess turns back to the TV.

"You used to love my body."

She will eat until she blows up, she thinks. Until she explodes all over the living room. She feels like crying, like pounding her fists on the floor, like biting her tongue until it bleeds.

"You hate me because I'm fat."

"What?" Billy shakes his cloudy head. "Hate you? I don't hate you."

"You haven't slept with me for ages, Billy. You hardly talk to me any more. You just go off and work and drink all the time. You don't talk to me or Sue and Sue never stops yelling at me." Tess begins to cry. She puts her potato chip bag on the floor and places her head in her salty, greasy hands. "Oh God. I used to be thin."

Billy looks at the floor, at the bag of chips. He looks at his wife. He stands up and goes into the kitchen. He opens a beer, walks back into the living room and hands the beer to Tess. "Do you want a sip?" he asks. "It'll make you feel better."

"Oh, God, Billy. You drink so much."

Billy puts the beer up to his lips. "It's just beer."

"You're always drunk."

"What the hell are you talking about?" Billy suddenly shouts. "I'm never drunk."

"You drink too much and I eat too much," Tess shouts back. She picks up the potato chip bag and continues to eat. She wipes her tears on her sleeves and stares at the TV.

Sue slams the front door. She shakes out her umbrella. "Christ," she says. "I could hear you two fighting from outside."

"We aren't fighting," Billy says. He looks at his daughter. Her face and neck are coated in white makeup and her eyes are lined with black pencil. Billy shakes his head. "What is that on your face? You look horrible," he says. "You look like you're dead."

"Shut up."

"Don't talk to your father like that."

"Why would you want to look dead all the time? It will happen soon enough."

"Billy," Tess says. "Don't say that."

"He shouldn't talk to me like that, Mom."

Billy looks at Sue's belly. He can see a small bulge there. A baby growing inside. That just knocks him out. It terrifies him. Billy remembers the day Sue came out of Tess like it was yesterday. He remembers that wet thing, bloody and howling. He held her in his hands, the cord limp and detached, and he whispered into the air around her wet head, "You are so beautiful, my God, you are so beautiful." He couldn't stop saying it, over and over.

And now Billy curses himself for it. It's all his fault, he knows. If he'd only called her something other than "beautiful," if he'd only put notions of intelligence in her little mind instead of vanity, if he'd only known what she would do with her life, even called her "sweet" or "cute," because cute and sweet can be so many things that "beautiful" cannot be. Like not pregnant. Cute can be smart and nice but not pregnant. Beautiful is pregnant. Seventeen and beautiful and pregnant.

Billy stands up. He stumbles, almost dropping his beer.

Sue says, "You're a drunk. Jesus fucking Christ. All you do is drink."

And Billy raises his hand above her. "Don't you swear at me." He wants to slam his hand into her nose ring, break a bone, but a noise from the couch stops him. Tess mews like a cat. She makes a tiny noise that brings him back to reality. He lowers his hand. Sue stands beside him, glaring.

"Don't you hit me," she says. Her eyes are wide in their sockets. Black lines drawn in pencil around her eyes. White face, dipped in powder. Billy is looking the Grim Reaper in the face. He turns awkwardly, almost stumbling. Suddenly his house is much too small. He heads towards the closet in the hall and fumbles for his coat. "Don't you ever hit me. If you ever hit me, I swear I'll get you charged."

"Don't leave," Tess says. "Don't leave like this."

"Like what?" Sue says. "Drunk? If you wait until he's sober, he'll never leave the house. Just let him go. He's being an asshole."

"Sue, don't talk to him like that. Don't say those things."

Billy takes his coat off the hanger, drops the hanger to the floor with a loud clatter, bends to pick it up.

"Don't drive, Billy," Tess says. "You've been drinking. It's raining." She tries to rise from the couch but her weight keeps her in place. It's like there's a magnet holding her down. It would take all of the energy she has in her body to get up and right now she has no energy left inside of her.

"I'm just going out for a minute. I'm just going out," Billy mumbles. He slams the front door behind him and slides down the wet steps to the car.

Inside, Sue studies her reflection in the hall mirror. "I don't look dead," she says. She rubs at the lines around her eyes, smudges them, makes them thicker. "I look good. A little fat. This damn baby."

Tess stays on the couch, humped over her potato chip bag. She stares at the TV. Please don't let him die, she thinks. Please let him be safe. Sue sits down beside her mother and picks a potato chip out of the bag. She holds it up and studies it. Then she licks it. "These are greasy," she says. "I can only have one."

Billy drives slowly, his hands clutching the wheel, peering out the front window between the wipers, to Coco's, the little bar in the strip mall closest to his house. There are women and men on the dance floor and the tables are packed but the bar stools are free and so Billy plops down upon one and orders a beer. He watches the dancers and he rubs at the label on his beer. He peels it off. He thinks about how much money he has left, he tries to figure out what he's going to do with his life, but all he comes up with is a big white wall. He drinks his beer.

This is kind of funny, he thinks. His body is numb and his mind blurry. He is leaning onto the bar and he laughs slightly, half falling from his stool, laughs at nothing and no one. Everything is funny suddenly, the lights spinning on the dance floor, around him everyone is happy, and there's Dick Mortimer walking past outside, holding an umbrella high above his head. Billy rushes to the front door and calls him over.

"Hey," Billy shouts.

"Hi, Billy," Dick says, smiling out from under his umbrella. "How are you?" He looks up at the sign above the bar.

Billy likes the way Dick says that. Smooth, like ice, like a mirror. It's all in the way you look at the world, Billy thinks.

"Fine," Billy slurs. "Just great. Come in and have a drink with me."

"I don't know," Dick says. "I don't really drink."

Billy laughs. "You don't drink?" He claps his hands on Dick's shoulders and steers him into the bar. "That's a good one." Dick's umbrella jams at the door and the two men wrestle with it outside in the rain.

They finally get the wet umbrella inside the bar and they settle with it into a booth by the window. Dick looks down into the gin and tonic Billy ordered for him. It was Dick's father's drink. It seemed appropriate to get one for himself. He swirls the glass. Billy gulps his beer, orders another and a second gin and tonic for Dick.

"No, thanks —" Dick starts.

"Don't mention it," Billy says. "My treat."

Dick sips on his drink and suddenly feels warm inside. He looks at the other drink sitting beside him and he takes off his overcoat. Why is it that gin and tonics smell much better than they taste, he wonders.

"You couldn't give Thomas a deal on the coffin, could you?" Billy is saying. "How much you get those things for anyway? You must get them for a couple dollars. Can't you sell them cheaper than that?"

"Casket."

"What?"

"It's called a casket in the business. Not coffin."

"One deal. Not one lousy deal. What kind of a mortician are you?"

"Funeral director."

"What?"

"I'm a funeral director. We don't use the term 'mortician' any more. It's too depressing."

Billy laughs.

"That's funny?" Dick asks.

"What you do is depressing, Dick," Billy says. "No matter what you call it. You spend your life burying dead people."

"We cremate too," Dick says. "Besides, if I gave you a deal on the casket, the word would get out."

"I don't really care anyway," Billy says. "As long as Thomas is paying for everything."

They look down at their drinks. Before Billy pulled him inside this bar, Dick was walking in the rain with his umbrella, wondering if there was anything else in life that he would rather be doing. He was wondering if running his own funeral business for the rest of his life is going to make him completely happy. Now, sitting in the bar, drinking a gin and tonic, he suddenly thinks that maybe he would rather be a movie star. He would like to make people happy or scared or sad by the expression on his face. He's tired of the serious mask he wears day in and day out. Dick would also like to be famous. He had a touch of fame when he first expanded the business. On TV, his hand raised to the camera like a preacher, Dick did advertisements for his funeral home. He remembers a man in the mall recognizing him once. And two women buried their husbands at Mortimer's because of the advertisements. But he would have to be much better looking, have less hair on his back, be thinner. Movie stars make a lot of money. But Dick is doing just fine financially, he doesn't lack anything that he really wants. And his career does satisfy him. It gives him pleasure to put people to rest, to make people feel their loved ones have been taken care of. He wonders what Billy does. Then he thinks of Hilary and wonders if she has a job and wishes that he had stayed in touch with her after they graduated. Did she graduate or did she drop out? He can't remember. He does remember being head over heels in love with her for a couple of years. Sipping his drink he thinks that, instead of being a movie star, maybe he'd just like to be married, have a family.

"Where do you work?" Dick asks Billy.

"Photo store. And I'm a security guard."

"Two jobs."

Billy nods his head. He drinks his beer. Dick drinks his gin and tonic.

"That must be nice."

"What?"

"Working in a photo store."

"I don't want to talk about it."

"Developing pictures. Do you get to look at other people's pictures?"

"Look, I don't want to talk about it."

Dick sighs. He drums his fingers on the table. There are people dancing in the corner to pumped-in music. One woman is dancing by herself, swaying her large hips out of beat to the song. "I guess we've got the market cornered on caskets, don't we?"

"Fuck," says Billy. "Everyone's got me cornered these days."

"Why do you say that?"

"I don't want to talk about it."

"Listen," Dick says. "Is your sister seeing anyone right now?"

Billy laughs. "My sister? Christ, she hardly ever goes out."

"But is she single?"

"Haven't you seen her? Didn't you see her the other night?"

Dick drinks. Hilary seemed shy, but she was always shy. She was dressed funny with that old fur coat on, but Dick looks at his clothes and thinks that he isn't the most fashionable man around. And he does have to admit that she's awfully thin, but then he's getting fat so they would make quite a pair.

Dick rubs his eyes. Why is he thinking this?

"You shouldn't do that," Billy says. "The germs will get in your eyes. I watched a show the other day all about it. Rubbing your eyes is one of the easiest ways to catch a cold."

"What?"

"Never mind. I'm just watching TV a lot these days." Billy looks at his hands. "There are germs everywhere. Millions of them."

"Don't you think I know about germs?" Dick says. "I have to wear gloves all day long."

"Do you worry about it?" Billy asks.

"About what? Wearing gloves?"

"About diseases, germs, AIDS."

"Yeah, I worry." Dick looks at his drink. "I have to be careful. Being a funeral director is not all fun and games." Then Dick laughs. "I know that sounds silly, but my job can be fun."

"Fun?"

"Or at least exciting. Exploring the inner workings of bodies, watching how quickly the human shell begins to disintegrate. Seeing the grieving process work the same way over and over again."

"Oh, " Billy says. "That kind of fun."

"Well, there's the occasional funeral mishap. Like the viewing we had where an old woman threw herself on her husband's casket and the wheels on the frame came unlocked and the woman and her husband rolled across the room into the punch bowl."

Billy laughs.

Dick smiles. "I could tell you some things."

"I'm sure you could."

"Hey," Billy says. "Do you want to get out of here?"

"And go where? I'm enjoying this. Or do you know another bar that's better?"

"No, get out. Go outside."

"It's raining," Dick says. "It's raining quite hard. And my umbrella is small." Dick is feeling warm with the drinks in his body. Warm and content.

"You won't melt."

Dick looks down at himself as if he isn't quite sure Billy is telling the truth.

"Have you had enough to drink?"

"How much is enough?" Dick's head feels clear but his body feels heavy.

"Let's get out of here. Let's go get a boat and head out on the lake."

"But it's late," Dick says. "It's November. I have to work tomorrow. And it's raining and cold. Besides, I don't have a boat. Do you have a boat?"

"I have a boat. What have you got to lose?"

"My six-hundred-dollar suit?"

"Let's go," Billy says. "Come on."

"I don't know. The label says, 'Dry clean only.'"

"Fuck the suit. Wear your coat. It'll keep you dry. Besides, what else do you have to do? Have you got a date? Naked women waiting for you in a hot tub?" Billy laughs. "Come on. There's nothing waiting for you anywhere else."

"True." Billy does make sense. Dick does have naked women at home, he thinks, but they are dead. And besides, Billy's boat probably has a roof. It's probably one of those fancy new boats that he sees on the lake all the time. He could sit under the roof and watch the shoreline race by.

Dick follows Billy out into the rain. He struggles to put his coat on.

"You really paid six hundred dollars for that suit?"

They stand beside Billy's car. "I'll go get my own car," Dick says. "It's just over there." Dick points down the street to where his car sits, dark and lonely, in the funeral home parking lot. Dick knows he is too drunk to drive but he doesn't care for some reason. Billy doesn't know he is too drunk to drive and so he drives very slowly and swervingly down the road, heading out towards the small lake on the edge of the suburbs. Dick follows in his own car.

But there is no boat with a cover, there is no speedboat. As a matter of fact, Dick discovers that Billy doesn't even own a boat. When they get to the lake Billy steals a rowboat that was tied to a footing at the pier. The rain lets up for a minute and Billy convinces Dick to climb in, to live a little, to take a chance now and then. And then they are floating quietly out into the lake and the rain is falling again. Dick's umbrella is in his car. They are soaked, cold, and very drunk. The boat is carrying water. Billy's jeans are drenched because he waded into the water up to his knees before he saw the boat tied there, waded out to feel the water on his body. Billy passes Dick a bottle of rum and Dick drinks from it.

"Quiet," Billy whispers.

"I didn't say anything."

"No, I mean it's quiet out here."

"Yeah." Dick's coat is stuck to his skin. He's uncomfortable and he has to pee. "I've got to take a leak. And it's freezing out here. You said you owned a boat. How the hell did I let you convince me to get into this thing?"

"No, I didn't say I owned a boat, I said I could get a boat."

"No, you said you owned a boat."

"Well, that's not what I meant to say."

"Nice try. I thought this would be a real pleasure cruise. Heat. A roof."

"At least I thought of bringing something to drink. What did you bring?"

"What did I bring? Jesus, Billy." Dick sits quietly for a minute. "I've really got to piss."

"So?"

"So, where do I go?" Dick looks around. He sees nothing but black water and a few lights on shore.

"In there." Billy points down into the blackness.

"I'll have to stand up. I can't stand up in a boat."

"Haven't you ever pissed off the side of a boat?"

"No," Dick says. "I've never been in a rowboat before. My father was always working. I've never even been fishing." Dick kneels in the boat. He clutches at the sides and the boat tips and rocks a bit. "There's no way I can stand." He tries to get up and the boat shakes violently. "Shit."

"Just steady yourself."

"We'll probably die of hypothermia if we fall in. Do you know that?"

"Do you think we'd get a cut rate at your place of work then?"

Dick stands. He holds his hands out to balance himself. When he catches his balance he opens his fly.

"Steady," Billy says.

"Jesus Christ."

"Balance. It's all about balance."

"What's about balance?"

"Pissing off a boat."

Dick can't concentrate because of the swaying of the boat. His coat keeps getting in the way. Billy grabs the gunwales and steadies the boat with his weight. "Balance," Dick says. He sighs happily. "What else is about balance?"

Billy scratches his head and the boat tips a bit.

"Goddamnit," Dick shouts. "I've pissed on my pants."

"Keep your voice down. You've only pissed on three hundred dollars. What are you complaining about?"

"Very funny, Billy." Dick kneels in the boat and tries wetting down his pants with water from the lake but the motion almost rocks the boat over and he thinks that he's washing with water he just pissed in and Billy tells him to sit down and stay still. Billy feels level-headed out on the water. It's the only place he feels real.

"Chequebooks, I guess."

"What?"

Billy says, "Chequebooks are about balance. So are teeter-totters."

"Aren't you deep," Dick says. "No wonder we didn't hang out together in high school." He looks at his shoes. He's pissed on those too. He can smell it coming off him. He smells like a bum. He pulls his shoes off and tries to dip them in the water. They've moved forward some so he reasons that his piss is behind him.

"Face it," Billy says. "You were a loser. That's why we didn't hang out together."

Dick wants to say, Who's the loser now? But he remembers that everyone is a potential customer. "Christ," Dick says. He loses a shoe. Billy leans over to watch it sink. The boat tips slightly.

"Goodbye, shoe," Billy says. "At least you've got another."

Dick's foot is cold and wet now. "Balancing the good and the bad."

"What?"

"Balance."

"And the ugly. Get it." Billy laughs. "The good, the bad, and the ugly."

"Jesus." Dick is suddenly angry. He is trying to say something.

He doesn't know what. But what he's trying to say is not funny. "You're such an idiot."

"Don't you ever call me an idiot." Billy stops laughing.

They are quiet for a minute. The water laps up against the rowboat. The lake is swollen from the rain.

"Look, I'm sorry," Dick says.

"Forget it."

"I didn't mean to call you that. It's just that I'm wet and I lost my shoe."

"I said forget it."

Dick drinks from the rum bottle.

"So Hilary isn't seeing anyone?" Dick says. He pulls his coat around him.

"Face it, Dick, you're going after the wrong fish."

"What do you mean by that?"

"She's not normal."

"She's your sister."

"That doesn't mean she's normal."

Dick clears his throat. "I can't believe I lost my shoe. This is an expensive pair. And my coat and suit are wrecked."

"Serves you right to be wearing nice clothes in a boat in the rain."

They laugh.

Dick says, "I thought I'd be home by now, back from my walk in the rain with my umbrella. Hey, where is my umbrella?"

Billy shrugs.

"This is crazy," Dick says. "I think the boat is taking on water. We're going to sink."

"Crazy like Hilary," Billy says.

"Yeah, right." Dick drinks again. He feels ill. "Do you know when the last time I made love to a woman was?"

"A live woman?" Billy laughs.

Dick pauses. A nauseous feeling comes over him and just as quickly disappears. "Funny, Billy," he says. "Very funny."

"No, really, go on."

"It was when I was in college. Vera Trudle."

"Trudle?"

"She was in my embalming class. We had to wear suits to school, black suits, and Vera showed up one day with a bright red skirt on. The teacher wouldn't let her sit through the class."

"You had to wear suits to school?"

"I remember seeing her in the cafeteria after she got kicked out. I bought her a coffee."

"You had a cafeteria at your school? What do funeral directors eat for lunch?"

The rain is hitting down hard now.

"You're not thinking of sleeping with my sister, are you?"

Dick swallows rum. He coughs. He wipes the rain out of his eyes. "No, not really."

Billy rows farther out into the lake.

"She used to pick up rocks on the way home from school every day," Billy says when he stops to rest.

"Who?" Dick says.

"Hilary. She would carry them home in her pockets, weigh herself down with them."

"So?"

"She put them all over the living room floor after my mother got sick. She just dumped her boxes out one day. I came over to see if they needed anything and the entire fucking floor was covered in rocks. And now she won't move them. She likes them there."

Dick doesn't say anything.

"The point is," Billy says, "the point is, Dick, that I think she's not right in the head."

"People do funny things, Billy. You don't have to put her in a hospital for it."

Billy thinks that if they do put Hilary away, perhaps he can split her third of the house sale with Thomas and come out ahead. He could even buy that boat he's been pining after. And, of course, he'll need lots of money for diapers for Sue's kid. Christ, he has a headache. He puts the oars down and takes the rum from Dick.

"She was always different in school," Dick says quietly.

Billy snorts.

"Why did your father leave you guys?" Dick asks.

"Who knows," Billy says. "He just went out one day and never came back."

"Shit," Dick says. "Was he fighting with your mother?"

"No," Billy says. "It was weird. He just left. We never really found out why." Billy suddenly realizes that he is shaking. "I don't want to talk about it. I'm freezing."

"Did he take clothes? Did he pack anything? Was it all planned?"

"Look, I said I don't want to talk about it. It's none of your goddamn business."

They are silent.

"Let's get out of here," Dick says. "You're shaking."

Billy would like to stay out longer even if he is freezing, but he takes up the oars and begins to row them back to shore. Problem with hanging around with funeral directors, he thinks, is that they really aren't very much fun. Everything becomes so personal.

"Hey," Billy says. "What does my mother look like now?"

"What is it about you Mounts?"

"What do you mean?"

"Thomas was in today, looking at your mother."

Billy stops talking to think. Thomas was there, looking at Becka? This thought puzzles him, intrigues him. "Well," he finally says, "what does she look like?" He thinks he might like to go see her tomorrow. Maybe he should make an appointment with Dick.

Dick tries to think about this. How do you describe a dead mother to a son?

Should he tell Billy how he wheeled his mother's body into the embalming room on Thursday afternoon and worked on her for three hours? Should he explain how he pulled up the carotid and the jugular, drained her, filled her, sealed her again? Cut above the belly button? Pumped out the organs, filled the chest cavity with fluid? Dick should probably tell Billy that he used a non-formaldehyde-based solution because formaldehyde reacts with the jaundice and would have made her dark green. Maybe he should tell Billy about those marks around her neck. Strange, but then liver cancer sometimes leaves marks. Perhaps he should tell him how Rebecca Mount was swollen right up, edema from kidney failure. The liver gives and then the kidneys, as if all the organs are good friends and can't bear to live without each other. He could say how he was careful not to push on her skin too hard. Careful not to leave thumbprints. One hard touch and the skin won't bounce back. Dented skin.

And then she dehydrated and now she's small, shrunken.

Stitches near the clavicle and on the belly, he could say.

Naked, he could say.

Yellow.

Face heavily creamed to protect her from burns if the chemicals leak (cream which, luckily, he wiped off several hours later, before Thomas saw her).

Dick still has to finish work on her. He'll apply cream-based makeup to her hands and face, he'll shampoo her wig and set it, give her a manicure, dress her, place her hands on rubber blocks to position them. Make her look just fine. Nose spray to keep the flies away.

But instead Dick says, "She looks great."

"Bullshit." Billy stops rowing and looks down into the water.

They pull the boat up under the dock and Billy climbs out. He looks down at the inches of water in the bottom of the boat. He scratches his head and then he helps Dick onto the pier. They sit for a while, looking down at the boat. Dick wonders if his shoe will be a home for fish, if they'll live in there, be safe from predators. His stomach churns. It's been a long time since he's had so much to drink. He knows he'll feel sick in the morning.

Billy stands and walks to the other side of the pier. He vomits into the water. The noise he makes is quiet and controlled.

"Fuck," Billy says when he's finished. "That feels better."

Dick shakes his head. He can smell Billy's sour stomach odour. He wonders how you could fall as low as this man has, this Billy Mount. Dick thinks that once you fall down like that, it's impossible to crawl back up.

8

Decision Made

Sunday morning and the small hole Hilary dug has filled up with mud and water. She is standing in the backyard wearing only a housecoat, staring at the hole and shivering, when Dick pulls up to the house. Dick climbs the front porch and peeks in the window. He knocks. No one answers. He decides to walk around the house to see if anyone is outside or in the kitchen. He comes upon Hilary in the backyard.

She is startled. She clutches her robe around her. She can feel her small breasts and thin hips jutting nakedly against the fabric of the robe. She is bare under this material, naked.

"Sorry," Dick says. "I didn't mean to scare you."

"No, I . . ."

"Did you just wake up? Really, I'm sorry to bother you," Dick says. He looks at Hilary's hair, skewed and messy, caked with mud from the night before. Like a rat's nest. It looks to Dick as if she's just had a night of passion. He smiles to himself. But then he sees the lines on her cheeks from where her fingers have been scratching and his heart goes out to her.

"I just was looking at the ground," Hilary says. "I was thinking about the hole."

Dick looks at the hole in the ground. It is about two feet wide and not very deep. "Oh," he says. He itches his scalp. "Planting something?"

"Sort of."

"I was just wondering," Dick begins. "I just came over to see if you've thought of any place to bury your mother," Dick says. This wasn't why he came. He just had an urge this morning to see her. Stand close to her again like he used to when they were young. Nothing Billy said last night scared him away from wanting to see her again. His head aches from drinking and his stomach is raw.

Thomas walks out of the house, freshly showered, still rubbing sleep from his eyes. Seeing Dick brings up the image of his mother lying dead on the table at the funeral home.

"Hi," he says.

Dick turns to him. "Hi."

"Listen," Thomas says. "Thanks for yesterday. Really. I'm sorry I had to run out so quickly."

"What?" Hilary says.

"No problem," Dick says. "I have your umbrella at my office."

"Great," Thomas says. "Thanks."

"I understand these things," Dick says, looking at Thomas. "It's hard."

"Can I get you a coffee?" Thomas backs into the house.

"Yes. That would be nice." Dick follows Thomas. Hilary follows Dick.

"What are you talking about?" she says. Behind Dick she feels like a mouse again. She wants to reach high and touch his shoulders.

"Nothing, Hilary."

Thomas fixes coffee. Dick sits at the kitchen table and looks at the puzzle of "The Annunciation." "Where's her face?" he asks. His head is pounding. He collapsed on the floor just inside his bedroom door and woke up in his damp suit and coat early this morning with a huge desire to speak to Hilary.

"I can't find the pieces." Hilary feels angry about it. There is the Madonna, about to be told that she is pregnant, and she has no face. Imagine what that would feel like, Hilary thinks. "Mother did the puzzle last. I think she lost the pieces."

Thomas makes coffee and joins Hilary and Dick at the kitchen table. Dick looks at the dolls in the kitchen. He can see into the dining room from where he's sitting and the entire dining-room table is covered with dolls. He jiggles his leg nervously.

What are you planting out there?" Dick says. "I thought it was too late in the year to plant anything."

Thomas looks at Hilary. Last night he agreed to bury Becka in the garden. Her body, not her ashes. The more time he spends with Hilary, the more he realizes what Hilary's life must have been like — taking care of her reclusive, then dying mother. But in the plain light of day the idea of a home burial strikes him as absurd. How will they sell the house with a grave in the backyard? If it were discovered, they could go to jail and he is sure that Hilary would end up in a mental hospital. Besides, Dick Mortimer has Becka's body. Thomas doesn't know how they would get it back from him. Thomas opens his mouth to say something but Hilary interrupts.

"I'm not planting anything. I would like to bury my mother in the garden," Hilary says. "Right there. I was digging a hole to bury her." She points out the sliding-glass doors towards her hole. Dick watches the curve of her thin arm, her face filled with concentration. Thomas nervously studies the puzzle on the table.

"In the garden?"

"Yes."

"Oh, cremation," Dick says. "Sprinkling the ashes. We've got some great urns and lockets. Keepsakes. You can wear a touch of her ash around your neck or in a ring. It's not really a good idea to bury the actual urn in your garden because if you ever sell the house, someone else might dig it up."

"No. We want to bury her whole. Her whole body. In the garden. In a coffin."

"Casket," Dick says. And then he smiles. "Her whole body? This is a joke, isn't it?"

"No."

"But it's illegal. You can't just bury a body in your backyard. You need a graveyard, often a vault or a cement liner. There are areas set up for the dead. You can't just bury them anywhere. Imagine," Dick says, "if everyone buried their loved ones here and there. Just imagine." He laughs. He looks at Thomas but Thomas avoids his eyes. "No one would know where to step."

"I think the plague started that way," Thomas whispers.

"No one has to know about this, Dick." Hilary is staring hard at him, trying to read his soul. "We would keep it a secret."

"That's impossible, Hilary."

"Secrets are easy to keep, Dick. You know how to keep secrets, don't you? I've done it for you."

Dick's face pales as he suddenly registers what she is talking about. He feels his throat constrict.

When Hilary and Dick came upon Dick's father embalming that young woman, when he turned to them and told them to get out of the room, what Dick tries to forget, what he has spent his life suppressing, is the large bulge in his father's pants and his father's hand on the dead girl's breast.

"He didn't —" Dick begins.

"I'm sorry, Dick," Hilary whispers. "I shouldn't have said anything. I've kept it a secret."

"What are you talking about?" Thomas asks.

"I'm sorry." Hilary looks at her hands. She feels faint. "When I heard she was going to your father's funeral home I was worried, I got so —"

"We can't bury your mother in the garden. I would get arrested. I would get my licence revoked. I would be ruined." Dick puts his head in his hands. His father, Christ, his father.

Hilary says, "But when I saw you there I knew she would be fine. Dick, secrets are fine. Sometimes people need to keep secrets."

"I don't want to think about it," Dick says.

"What?" Thomas asks.

Hilary turns away from Dick. "I just want to bury my mother in the garden." She begins to cry.

Dick moves to comfort her. He pats her hand. "I'm sorry. It's not your fault."

Thomas studies the puzzle. He stares at the angel Gabriel kneeling before Mary. He has an urge to rip off the angel's wings, throw them in the garbage. Are angels afraid to fly? he wonders. Thomas doesn't know what Dick and Hilary are talking about and he doesn't want to know.

"You don't really have to be a part of it," Hilary says. "We'll do it. We just need her back, please. And we need a casket. An inexpensive one. Will you do that?"

"But —"

Hilary stands. She brushes the tears from her cheeks.

Dick looks at her thin legs, her long neck, her knotted hair. Her bathrobe is slightly open. She looks wild. Dick is spellbound, speechless.

"Surely," Hilary says, "people buy caskets from you all the time. Surely there must be people who store them in their basements, just to be sure they have them for the future. No one will think twice about it if you sell me a casket. No one will miss her body. Just give us back her body."

"But the paperwork, the death certificate. . . ."

"Can't you work around that, Dick?"

Thomas gets up and leaves the room. "You two figure this out," he calls back. "I'll pay for everything, but I don't want anything to do with the planning."

Dick stands. He walks up to Hilary. He looks down at her. She is standing by the kitchen sink. His fingers suddenly ache to take her skinny neck in his hands and caress it. He wants to run his hands over her bathrobe, under her bathrobe, over her body. What's happening to him?

"Can we go out?"

"Now?" Hilary looks outside. "I'm not dressed."

"No, tonight. Can we have a date?"

Hilary looks up at Dick. "A date?" He is standing close. She can feel his breath on her.

"Dinner or something."

"Oh," Hilary says. "I don't know."

Dick looks down at his shoes. "I'm not like him. I respect the bodies."

"I know." She clutches her bathrobe around her. Her hands flutter to her neck.

"I would never hurt someone."

"I'll have to wash my hair if we go out," Hilary says. "And take a bath."

Dick says, "I try to forget about that. I try to remember him the way he was. I know he was a fine mortician."

"I'm sure he was," Hilary says. "Really. We all have our weaknesses, I guess."

Dick nods his head slowly. "When would you need your mother's body?"

"Oh," Hilary says. "Really? Would you? Wednesday night, I think. I think I can get organized by then. And a casket too. Something nice but simple. Something inexpensive."

Dick nods. "I'll see you tonight then? Eight o'clock?"

Dick leaves through the sliding-glass doors. On his way out he looks at the muddy hole in the yard. "You'll need to dig deeper than that," he calls to Hilary. "And be careful with the neighbours. Don't let them get suspicious. You can't let anyone know about this." He walks to the side of the house. The sun is on the ground. His hangover has lifted. "Do you know how deep to dig? Do you know how to keep the walls from caving in?"

"I'll learn," Hilary calls from the back door. "I can learn anything I want to learn."

"Yes," Dick says, "I'm sure you can."

"Dick," Hilary calls out, "we should just try to remember our parents in the best possible light."

Dick nods. He disappears around the front and climbs into his car and shakes his head. He can't believe he is jeopardizing his entire career for Hilary Mount. For this funny woman with the wild hair and stick-thin body. This woman who lives with the dolls. Dick is nervous but he feels like he is young again. His heart is beating wildly. He opens his window, turns on the music loud enough to forget about his father, and drives fast all the way back to the funeral home.

Hilary rushes upstairs to her mother's room to find a dress. Her hands are shaking as she sorts through her mother's closet.

"A dress, a dress." Hilary pushes her mother's clothes aside, inspecting one after the other. "Dress, dress, dress." She looks at herself in the full-length mirror on the back of the closet door.

"Purple? Green? Flowers? Stripes?" Hilary begins to take the dresses off the hooks. The smell of cigarette smoke lingers in them, so thick Hilary can practically taste it. She throws the dresses on the floor. Each dress holds a memory. Her body stings. She thinks she may be getting a fever. Maybe she got a flu from being in the rain last night. Hilary holds up a red dress and stares at it. She remembers her mother wore this several months after her father left them. She wore it to the grocery store. Got all dressed up fancy, lipstick on, and went to the grocery store. That was after she stayed in bed for a while, when she got up the nerve to try and face the world again. And this green dress was the one she wore several years ago when Hilary walked her halfway down the block and then, at the corner, she turned and rushed back home, pounded on the locked front door, "Let me in, let me in."

Hilary inspects the red dress. She takes off her bathrobe and tries it on. It hangs on her like a sheet. Her mother was thicker, shapelier, she had breasts and hips that jutted out. Hilary's small, thin body is flat and straight. But when Hilary pulls in the belt around the waist and looks again at her reflection, she thinks that she looks fairly pretty.

The man who will sew her mother's gums shut is coming over to her house tonight to take her out. His father touching that dead woman. His hand resting on her white breast. The nipples erect. Part of Hilary thinks that maybe that will be the first time someone will touch her, when she's dead.

"What are you doing in here?" Thomas is standing at the door, looking in.

"I'm trying on dresses."

"Oh?"

"I'm going out tonight." Hilary smiles. Hilary's face, lit up like that, floods Thomas with the memory of their childhood, with a picture of the girl she was before their father left. Thomas feels overwhelming sadness for where Hilary has gone with her life.

"Where are you going?"

"I don't know. A restaurant. Dick Mortimer is taking me."

"What did you two decide about Becka?"

"Dick's bringing her over Wednesday night."

"We're going to bury her in the garden?"

Hilary smiles.

"I don't like this," Thomas says. "Not one bit."

Hilary turns away from Thomas and slips the red dress over her head. She begins to put her bathrobe back on. He sees her back, like a concentration camp victim, the lines of her ribs pushing through the white skin. Her hips jut out, stabbing her underwear. Her legs don't meet at the top.

"God, Hilary, you're so thin."

"Don't look at me when I'm changing."

"Why are you so thin? Why are you scratching your face raw?"

Hilary shrugs. She ties the belt tight at the waist. "Can't you see the marks?"

"What marks? There are just scratches on your face."

Hilary whispers, "I'm stained. I can't get the stain off."

"What are you talking about?"

"Don't you get it?" Hilary turns to face him. "Don't you know what it has been like around here? How can you not know?"

"But I sent money for a nurse."

"Mother didn't want a nurse."

"Mother didn't want a nurse," Thomas echoes. "She wanted you. A slave."

Hilary takes the red dress and leaves the room. From the bathroom window she can see the neighbour cutting down his tree. He is peering over the fence between the houses, studying Hilary's small hole in the ground.

Thomas stands in the doorway to Becka's room. He tries to steady his breathing. He purses his lips and smacks the wall with his hand. The sound is loud and hollow.

Billy is sitting at the kitchen table nursing his hangover. Tess moves soundlessly around him. Sue is standing by the fridge counting out how many calories she is allowed today. Billy looks at Sue. She looks nothing like her mother.

"Can I have twenty bucks?" Sue asks. "I need some things at the pharmacy."

"What things?"

"Don't talk to your father right now, Sue. He's not in a good mood."

"Just things."

"Is there more coffee?" Billy asks. "I need more coffee."

"Have a sweet bun, honey. Have some oatmeal. Have an egg. Fill up that void." Tess pours Billy more coffee.

"I need new lipstick, for one," Sue says, turning towards her parents. "And some deodorant."

"I'm not hungry," Billy says.

"You're never hungry," Tess says. "You have to eat. Keep your strength up."

"I need some birth control pills."

"What for?" Billy says. "You're pregnant."

"For after."

"Christ," Billy says. He looks down into his coffee cup. He tries to steady his hands but they are shaking too much to hold still. "Can't you learn from your mistakes?"

"I have money in my purse," Tess says.

"Don't give her money."

"What do you think I'm doing," Sue says. "I'm learning from my mistakes. This time I'm not going to make a mistake. This time I'll be ready."

"You don't need any money. I gave you money yesterday."

"Fuck you." Sue says this quietly.

"What?"

"Sue," Tess says, "why don't you watch some TV."

"Just fuck you both," Sue says. "I'm sick of your fighting and drinking. That's all you ever do." She walks out of the kitchen. Billy stands. His hands shake. He wants to throttle that girl. Tess moves to stand between Billy and Sue's receding figure. Billy and Tess stare into each other's eyes and neither of them blinks when the front door slams shut.

Last night Billy peeled off his wet clothes and rolled into bed next to Tess. He watched the car lights on the ceiling. He moaned a bit because his stomach hurt from vomiting several times, but Tess stayed heaped away from him, facing the wall. Her body is a mound of skin and fat and muscle and bone, a large doughy hill that he just can't climb. And he wanted to last night. He actually wanted to make love to her like they used to a long time ago when everything was good. Billy lay there on his back and watched the lights and thought of his life, of his mother's death, of his brother and sister and daughter, his lost jobs, the woman at the minigolf course, and his unborn grandchild.

"We have to talk," Tess says.

"Not now." Billy sits down again. He sits on his hands. He puts his head down over his coffee mug and sniffs. Maybe he can wake himself up with the smell.

"Now." Tess sits down beside him. The chair groans under her weight. "I need to know something, Billy."

"What?"

"I need to know how you are feeling inside."

"My stomach hurts."

"No, how you're feeling emotionally."

"Oh, for Christ's sake, Tess. You've got to stop watching those talk shows on TV."

"Everyone dies, honey. There's nothing you can do about it. But you can't hang on to a person, hold on tight, when they are dead. You have to let them go, help them go, really. Billy, you're holding on so tight to your mother that she's sucking you into the other world."

"What the hell are you talking about? The other world?" Billy's head is pounding.

"She's pulling you down with her." Last night Tess decided that this is what all the signs are pointing to. Ever since Becka died, Tess has been seeing hidden meaning in everything. Just yesterday she noticed Sue was wearing the same earrings, a matching set. This never happens. And the day before, when Tess put ketchup on her scrambled eggs, her late-night snack, the plastic squeeze bottle didn't squirt at her like it always does.

"What does my mother have to do with anything?" Billy says.

Tess crosses her legs. She manoeuvres her large bottom around the vinyl chair. Billy hears the sucking sound of nyloned thighs, the swishing sound of polyester rubbing vinyl. "I think it's your mother, Billy. You've got to get her buried soon. And buried deep. She's haunting you, honey."

"Give it up, Tess. Haunting me?" He laughs.

Tess looks at her hands. She studies them. "Then it must be me," she says.

"What?"

"Then it must be me. Why else won't you make love to me? Why else don't you love me any more? Just because I'm getting fat? I've been fat for years, Billy. Why all of a sudden?"

"What?" Billy's head aches. He feels queasy. "Listen, Tess . . . I —"

"Tell me, Billy." Tess sits up as straight as she can, her belly protruding.

Billy doesn't know what to say.

"What did I do to deserve this?" Tess asks.

"I lost my jobs, all right? I got fired. Are you happy now?" Billy shakes his head.

"You lost your jobs? Both jobs? When?"

"A couple of days ago, a couple of weeks ago."

"Why didn't you tell me?"

Billy shrugs. "What should I have done?"

"You should have told me. Oh my God, Billy, why didn't you tell me? Why did you get fired? I thought they just gave you a long holiday at the photo shop. Isn't that what you said? That's what I thought you said. Lord, what are we going to do?"

"I don't know why they fired me."

"You don't know why? Did it have something to do with your drinking?"

Billy sips his coffee.

"What are we going to do now?" Tess asks. "How are we going to live?"

"I'm working on it."

"You're working on it? You're doing nothing but drinking."

Billy stands. "I have to get out of this house."

"Billy, we should talk about this."

"I've got my mother's funeral to worry about too, you know."

"Billy, we don't have any savings. Sue is having a baby. I haven't worked in years."

"Don't you think I know that? I have to go. Becka needs me."

"You never even visited her when she was alive. Why is your mother so goddamn important now?"

Billy walks out of the kitchen. He climbs the stairs to the bathroom. His stomach feels heavy, full of lead. His mind hurts.

Billy soaps himself all over. His lean body is white with bubbles. He has an urge to hum a tune but he can't think of anything meaningful. Something mournful and wilting. Something you'd play on a harmonica. Or bagpipes. Billy wishes he knew how to play an instrument. He wishes he had some sort of talent. Something he could fall back on when times were bad.

Billy thinks that everything seems to be about everyone else — what will Tess and Sue do now that he lost his job? How will Hilary feel if she is forced to move? But it all really comes down to you, doesn't it? Just you. You enter the world alone and you go out alone. The people you snag along the way are just comfort, just warm bodies to help you pass the time. He thinks about Grace at the Greenhomes Minigolf Course. Maybe it is about bodies. Maybe it's all about the journey, the passing of time, the getting from here to there, from birth to death, surrounded by bodies. Other people's bodies.

Billy dries himself roughly. He wants to ache some thought into his skin, create some pain to focus on. He dresses himself and leaves the house without saying anything more to Tess.

Tess sits at the kitchen table eating the breakfasts that Billy and Sue didn't touch.

"Waste not, want not," she says as she eats. She feels like crying.

9

Flat-chested Models

It is early evening. Dick scrubs himself in the shower with a hard brush. His skin stings all over. He is desperate to get the smell of the funeral home off of him. While he's in the shower he looks his body over, tries to admire it. He tries to look down on it with love. But it doesn't work. All he sees is hair, lots of it, and rolls of fat, along with wrinkles and bulges and stretch marks and a shrivelled little penis and moles and pimples and more hair. He can barely see his toes, for Christ's sake.

Dick's mother used to love his body. She loved it to death. That's what she would say, "I love your little belly to death, Dick Mortimer." Now she's dead and no one loves his body the way she did.

Dick wonders if Hilary might like his body. He wonders if she's partial to men with lots of hair and baggy skin. He thinks about lying down next to her small, thin body, ruffling up her already-scruffy hair, and touching her softly all over. Dick watches the warm water going down the drain. He watches the soapy water snake down into the little holes which are stopped up with bits of hair. What if she thinks he's too hairy?

Then he thinks of his father touching that dead body. Squeezing her breast like a cantaloupe. Erect and drooling. Was he drooling? Dick remembers a lecherous face, a drooling, sick face turned towards him, shouting, "Get out, get out." He backed up quickly and ran. Hilary's footsteps echoed behind. But when his father came home that night for dinner nothing was different. He clapped Dick on the back, asked Steve how school was, sat down in his chair by the radiator, and smoked his cigar.

Was it really him that they saw?

What must Hilary think of funeral directors?

When Dick gets out of the shower he hears a pounding at his door. He wraps a towel around his bottom half, holds on to it tightly, and opens the door. Billy Mount is standing there, panting, looking pale and sick.

"Hi," Dick says.

"Hi. Can I come in?"

Funny, Dick thinks. You live in the same area with people your entire life, they don't even bother to say hello to you if you pass them on the street, and then you take in their expired loved one and they are suddenly pulling you into bars to drink with them, stealing boats and knocking at your door at all hours. When people experience death, Dick has noticed, they seem to feel a natural attachment to the person who sells the casket, who stores and embalms the body and organizes the burial.

Billy wanders into Dick's apartment. "I wondered if you wanted to go minigolfing," he says. "Are you busy?"

"Yes, well. . . . I have a date this evening."

The phone rings. Dick answers it and holds his hand up to stop Billy from talking. It's one of his assistants. Seems they are all out of eye caps downstairs. They need the eye caps now or the eyes won't stay shut on the two people they are embalming. "There's a new box in the basement," Dick says. "Beside the furnace."

Billy walks around the apartment above the funeral home. It is sparse and small. He hears the buzz of machinery below, the chugging of the furnace, the hum of the lights. He smells the chemical odour of prepared death. He looks at the pictures framed on the walls: Dick's father opening his business, a picture of the first casket they sold, the first dollar bill they ever made. There is a picture of Dick shaking the old mayor's hand at the ribbon-cutting ceremony at the opening of the new, improved funeral home years ago. Dick looks proud, the sun beaming down upon his face. The mayor looks tired and drawn. It seems to Billy that the mayor died shortly after the opening and Billy wonders if Dick gave his family a deal on the casket.

"Are you sure?" Dick asks into the phone. "By the furnace. In the corner. Check again."

Billy looks at Dick's bookshelf. Books on embalming, on the dangers of formaldehyde, on the construction of caskets, on the history of the funeral industry. A couple of novels Billy remembers reading in high school; he thinks that high school was probably the last time he read anything worthwhile.

"All right," Dick says, still clutching his towel, balancing the phone. "Put them in and finish embalming and then go home. Dress and makeup tomorrow. It's been a long day, Darren." He hangs up the phone. "Billy?"

"I just wanted to know if you wanted to go golfing."

"Golfing?"

"Did you say you have a date tonight?"

"Yes, with your sister." Dick can't help but let out a little laugh.

"My what?"

"Your sister. I'm taking her out for dinner." Dick walks over to a mirror and smoothes down his eyebrows. The towel slips a bit and

Billy sees the top of Dick's large, hairy ass. His skin looks sore and raw.

"Shit," Billy says. Now Hilary is dating the funeral director.

"I can't play golf tonight. Maybe tomorrow?"

"No problem. I just wondered. . . ." Billy doesn't even know why he wanted to do something with Dick in the first place.

Dick stares into the mirror. Thank God he doesn't look anything like his father. "Hey," he says, "can you help Hilary dig for Wednesday? She needs someone strong to dig." Dick pulls at a hair growing out of his nose.

"Dig?"

"And support the walls with wood." He rubs his nose, trying to get the hair to go back inside. "I'd prefer she used cement but there isn't enough time. Plus it would look suspicious, don't you think?"

"For what?"

"To dig the hole in your mother's backyard." Dick looks in the mirror at himself. He wonders why he has so much hair growing everywhere — in his ears, on his shoulders. But none on his ankles where his socks are. He's completely bald there.

Billy's face registers nothing. "Is Hilary having plumbing problems? Why didn't she call me first?"

"For your mother's grave," Dick says. "Didn't anyone tell you about it?"

"What?"

"Hilary and Thomas," Dick says. "They are burying your mother in the backyard, under that big tree, the magnolia." Dick turns towards Billy. "I thought someone would have told you."

"What?"

"Just like I said."

"Cremation?"

"Her whole body. Casket and all. It's illegal, of course, so we'll have to be quiet about it." Dick raises his right index finger to his mouth in a hushing gesture. He feels like he is talking to a child.

"When?"

"On Wednesday night. If you help, the digging will go faster."

"Shit," Billy says. He looks at the floor. Maybe if he stares at it long enough he could see straight down into the funeral home, right to his mother's body. "Why?"

"I'm bringing your mother over on Wednesday night. We'll do it quietly. No one can know. This is important. Billy, are you listening?"

"Shit." It seems that's all Billy can say. His mouth is dry. He needs a drink.

"Are you all right?"

Billy nods. "They can't do that," he says. "They can't bury her there. How are we going to sell the house?"

Dick turns back to the mirror. He shrugs. He thinks about what he's going to wear to see Hilary. A suit or something casual? "It's what Hilary and Thomas want," Dick says. "You should talk to them. Your sister has already started digging."

"Fuck," Billy says. He walks quickly out of Dick's apartment. He leaves the door open and hurries down the stairs.

"I'm sure if you talked to them," Dick begins, "they'll be reasonable about — Billy?" Dick doesn't notice that Billy is gone until he feels the cold breeze from the open door. He walks over and shuts the door and wonders if anyone walking by on the street below saw his naked, hairy back. Then he wonders if his father touched all the corpses or just the women. Then he wonders if his father went farther than touching. Dick stares at himself in the mirror. His eyes look frightened.

"Father went farther." He plays with the words. His voice startles him.

Jonathan climbs up the stairs to the front door of the house. He knocks. He notices the rusty baby carriage lying at the bottom of the steps. He looks down at the street and sees candy wrappers in the gutter. It is early evening. Jonathan's plane was delayed and then the taxi got lost in the suburbs. Jonathan understands why. All the streets look the same. Strip mall after strip mall. Everything so flat. He is tired and frustrated and worried.

Jonathan couldn't stop himself from coming. He worried all last night and straight through the plane ride about Thomas's reaction but there was some force drawing him close. Something he couldn't control. He's been with Thomas for fifteen years and he knows nothing about Thomas's roots and, no matter what Thomas says, it's about time he discovered them for himself.

Hilary calls out for Thomas to get the door but Thomas is in the shower and doesn't hear her. Thomas is soaping his chest and thinking about Hilary's protruding rib cage. He wonders if he should take her to a doctor. He thinks about anorexia and bulimia, everything he knows about eating disorders. It was like looking at a skeleton.

Hilary straightens herself. She is wearing the red dress. She wishes her mother was alive to see this. She runs down to the door and opens it.

"Hello?" Hilary is taken aback. A well-dressed black man is standing on the front porch holding an overnight bag and a bottle of Scotch. "Are you selling something? Because if you are, we don't need anything." Hilary moves to shut the door.

"No," Jonathan says. He blocks the door with his shoe. "I'm here to see Thomas. Thomas Mount? God, please tell me this is where Thomas Mount is staying." He pauses. "You must be Hilary." He looks at her in her red dress. "It's wonderful to finally meet you."

Jonathan puts his hand out and Hilary opens the door wider and shakes it. "Who are you?" she asks. His hand is beautifully dark. A rich darkness, creamy. The palm is pale pink lined with dark. Hilary thinks it is a wonderful hand.

"I'm Jonathan."

"Oh?"

"Jonathan Brandley."

Hilary looks at this man, this Jonathan. She feels as if she's staring into the face of someone special, as if she's just met a movie star or a politician. He is striking.

"Thomas is in the shower."

"May I come in?"

Hilary nervously ushers him into the living room.

"Look at that," Jonathan says. "Thomas told me there were rocks on the living room floor. Can I walk on them?"

Hilary nods.

He steps carefully across the rocks and sits on the dent in the couch.

"They look great."

Hilary stands before him twirling her hair around her finger. She smiles.

Jonathan sits politely and waits for Hilary to tell him what to do.

"I have a date tonight." Hilary stands in the doorway.

"A date?"

Hilary smiles.

"With whom?"

"Whom?"

"Your date."

"Oh, Dick Mortimer."

"And who is Dick Mortimer?"

"He's a funeral director." Hilary says this with such conviction, with such pride, that Jonathan sits up on the couch, straightens his back.

"A funeral director."

"Yes." Hilary smiles. "A funeral director. He owns his own funeral home."

"How nice," Jonathan says. He looks at the rocks below his feet.

There is a knock at the door. Hilary's face suddenly turns red, her hands shake.

"That must be your funeral director," Jonathan says. "Where is Thomas's room? I'll wait for him there."

Hilary nods her head. "Upstairs," she says. "Second door on the right."

Jonathan stumbles over the rocks and makes his way up the stairs. The dolls watch him walk past. "Christ," he whispers as he stumbles upon a little boy doll who is hiding in the shadows.

Jonathan opens the second door and comes upon Thomas in his bedroom getting dressed.

"Jesus," he says. "You're right. This place is a mess."

Thomas starts. Almost falls over, with one foot in his pants. "What the hell are you doing here?"

"I wanted to see you."

"I told you not to come. Christ, Jonathan, don't you ever listen to me?"

"I wanted to come."

"Jesus."

"It's time I was part of your life, don't you think? Don't you think fifteen years gets me an admission ticket?"

"It's too complicated," Thomas says. "It's too much."

"Listen," Jonathan says. "I just wanted to be here to support you."

"This isn't support, damn it. I told you not to come. Supporting me would be doing what I told you to do, or not to do."

Jonathan looks out the window. He looks out at the backyard and sees the muddy hole that Hilary was digging.

"I guess I could fly home," he says.

"Jesus," Thomas says. "Do you know how much money you wasted on the tickets?"

"It's my money."

"I know, but —"

"I don't want to leave," Jonathan says.

"Jonathan."

Thomas zips up his pants and moves to the window to join Jonathan looking out.

"You're just going to complicate everything even more. I didn't want to have to explain. There's so much going on you don't understand."

"If you would talk to me, then maybe I would understand."

They watch the neighbour coming and going from the side of his house, carrying branches from a freshly trimmed tree to his woodpile.

"What's that?" Jonathan asks.

"The neighbour."

"No, what's that dug-up part there? That hole?" He points down.

"Oh." Thomas turns from the window. He scratches his scalp. He rubs his chin and his eyes. "A grave, I guess."

"What?"

"That's where we are burying my mother."

"Burying your mother? In your backyard?"

"It's Hilary's idea. Seems the funeral director doesn't mind."

"The guy she's dating?"

Thomas nods.

"Oh, shit," Jonathan says. He laughs. "There's no way you are getting rid of me now. Now I've really got to stay."

Downstairs Dick is standing at the front door holding flowers in his large hands. The flowers are shaking. Hilary opens the door and lets him in.

"You look great," Dick says. "Red is my favourite colour."

Hilary says nothing. They look shyly at one another. Dick looks at the living room floor and sees the rocks Billy was talking about. He looks at the dolls everywhere and he feels shivers move up and down his spine.

"Someone is walking on my grave," he jokes. "Or I'm about to get some money. No, wait. That's itchy palms."

Hilary is confused.

"Shivers," he says. Dick wonders for an instant if Billy was right, maybe Hilary is a bit crazy. The dolls are lined up everywhere. They look like baby-sized adults.

Hilary feels uncomfortable with Thomas and his friend being upstairs. She feels as if they are spying, watching her. She keeps looking towards the staircase.

"Are you alone?" Dick asks.

"No." Hilary moves towards the kitchen with the flowers. "Not alone."

"Who's home?" Dick looks up at the hallway ceiling. He hears nothing. He wonders if she thinks the dolls are alive.

"Thomas and his friend, Jonathan," Hilary says. "Come into the kitchen."

Dick walks into the kitchen without removing his coat and he perches uneasily on a chair and watches Hilary put the flowers in an empty pickle jar. She fills the jar with water after she's arranged the flowers. The kitchen is still a mess but Dick tries to ignore it. After all, he reasons, they just had a death in the family.

"Thank you for the flowers."

"No problem." Dick clears his throat. "I'll buy you a vase next." He looks at the puzzle on the table. "You still haven't found her face, have you?"

"No. She's faceless."

"You'll find it, I'm sure."

"Thomas keeps saying it's just a puzzle but I think it's more than that."

"More than a puzzle?"

"Yes," Hilary says. "Much more. Don't you?"

Dick shrugs. He doesn't know what to say. Dick whistles a tune under his breath. Hilary smoothes her hair down.

"You look nice," Dick says. "Really nice."

"Thank you." Hilary blushes. "It's my mother's dress."

"I wouldn't have known that," Dick says. "It looks brand new."

"Should we go?"

Dick helps Hilary with her coat at the door. His hand touches the back of her hair. Hilary feels heat travel down her body. Dick feels electrified.

"Your car," Hilary says, when she gets outside. "It's new?"

"A couple of years old."

"It has air bags?"

"Yes?" Dick scratches his head.

Hilary holds her breath, sucks it in hard, and then climbs into Dick's car.

They drive for a while in silence and then Dick mentions beef teriyaki and he stops the car at his favourite Japanese restaurant. He opens the car door for Hilary. Her legs are stiff from tension. Her hands hurt from gripping the car seat. They sit at a table by the window surrounded by couples, the men in business suits, the women with finely sprayed hair, manicures, and high-heel shoes. Hilary looks at the view, a strip mall parking lot. A Donut King just beside the restaurant. A muffler repair shop. A pet food store — Paws 'n' Claws. She looks at the cars coming and going. The exhaust pipes spew smoke, the car lights glow into the cold air, and Hilary orders chicken and looks out the window.

Dick comes here a lot. He smiles at the Japanese waitress. He feels strong and proud.

"Funny how we lost touch," Dick says.

"Things happen." Hilary looks at her chopsticks. She picks them up and studies them.

Dick clears his throat. "I missed you. You were my only friend in school."

Hilary looks up at him. She says nothing. They sit silently for a while, watching the people around them.

Dick tries again to make conversation. "Have you started to dig yet?"

"Nothing more than what you saw," Hilary says. She plays with her chopsticks. She doesn't know how to use them.

"You'd better get a move on," Dick says. "The ground is frosty now. It'll be hard work."

"Yes," Hilary says. "Hard work."

Dick reaches out to touch Hilary's hand suddenly. She pulls back. No man has touched her before. Mother's touch felt like sandpaper. Rough. Thomas's touch is smooth. Billy doesn't touch.

"Do you see many naked bodies?" Hilary suddenly asks. She puts her hand back on the table. His touch was warm and dry. She reaches tentatively towards his fingers. She pulls away again.

Dick chokes on his drink. "What?"

"In the funeral home?"

Dick thinks about his answer. "They are all naked, Hilary. I have to dress them."

"Yes," says Hilary. "I guess that's right."

Dick feels warm all over. He is sweating. He takes off his sweater and Hilary notes the sweat stains under his armpits. She smells a strong chemical smell coming off of him — the funeral home. She sniffs deeply. Dick's face turns red.

"I showered," he says. "I just can't get the smell off of me."

"I know," Hilary says. "It's not bad. It reminds me of . . ."

"Of what?"

"School. Biology class. You."

They eat their dinners silently. Hilary wrestles with her chopsticks. Copies Dick. Mostly uses her fingers.

"Did you ever finish high school?" Dick asks.

"No."

"Maybe you can now," he says. "Maybe now that your mother is gone you can go back to high school."

Hilary looks up from her plate. "No," she says.

Dick swallows his wine. "Have you ever seen your father again?"

"Why are you asking me all these questions?"

"I thought we could get to know each other again."

"You shouldn't be asking me these things. I'm not asking you about your father."

"I'm sorry."

"Are you finished?"

Dick looks at his unfinished dinner. He is confused. "I guess." He wants dessert.

"I want to go now," Hilary says. "I want to go to the funeral home."

"To see your mother?"

"No," Hilary says. "Of course not. I just want to go there again. Like we used to."

Dick calls for the bill.

Hilary steals herself for the car ride. She takes deep breaths. Each time, she thinks, it is getting easier.

It is dark outside and Tess is pacing in front of the living room window, eating a Snickers bar. It isn't very satisfying. She has been pacing all afternoon, waiting for Billy. She looks at Sue who is curled up on the couch watching TV, eating unbuttered, unsalted popcorn, and drinking Diet Coke.

Tess sighs.

Sue takes a sip of her Diet Coke. "Get a load of this outfit," she says. "I could wear that."

Sue is watching a fashion show and Tess looks over at a stick-thin figure she supposes is a female parading down a runway wearing a

sheer, see-through bra and tight hot pants. She doesn't have breasts.
Just two dark, erect nipples floating in the loose material of the bra.
Flat chest. Tess blinks. She moans. She suddenly sinks to the ground,
her polyester tent-dress covering her legs. She hunches over on the
floor. Two erect nipples — is that what her Billy is doing? Is he
having an affair? — and her world comes crashing down.

"What's wrong?" Sue stands. "Fuck, Mom. What's going on?"

"Help," Tess says. "Help me."

Sue clutches under her mom's fat armpits, trying to raise her.
"Get up," she shouts. "Get up."

"Call someone," Tess says, "call the police."

Tess thinks, The signs: the bag in the wind, the ketchup, the
matching earrings. It's all come down to this. Her arm feels numb
suddenly and there is a crushing pain in her chest. She feels as if
someone is sitting on her, squishing her.

"Indigestion?" she whispers. "Maybe it's just indigestion."

Sue is on the phone calling an ambulance.

The pain rips through Tess again and she feels faint and can't
breathe and the world spins until her nose hits the carpet and her
mouth tastes of peanuts and chocolate.

"Get a fucking ambulance here now," Sue screams into the
phone. "No, I won't calm down. My mom's dying." She lights a
cigarette with shaky fingers. "She's throwing up on the living room
floor." She isn't allowed to smoke in the house but she doesn't care
right now. This is an emergency.

Tess smiles to herself before she passes out. Listening to Sue's
angry voice makes her realize that someone cares. At least someone
cares, she thinks.

IO

What We All Want

Billy peers through the dark into the Greenhomes Minigolf Course clubhouse at Grace. He is stepping on the bushes under the window, watching her. There are only two cars in the parking lot besides his and he watches as a young man counts money from a tray on the front counter and Grace fiddles with her coat. He stares at her, summoning up his courage. Billy has been drinking in the car since he left Dick's and now he has to pee. He looks around. He opens his fly and waits for the urine, and then sighs as it comes splashing out into the bushes and against the wall. When he looks up again Grace is gone and the young man is turning off the lights. He watches the young man leave the clubhouse, get into his car, and drive off into the darkness. The lights in the parking lot flicker and go out. Billy looks up at them. He looks back into the window. It is dark now, the lights are off. There is silence. Nothing. An eerie black space. But the other car is still standing in the lot.

Billy suddenly hears footsteps.

Michelle Berry

Grace is standing just to the left of Billy. His heart speeds up. He steps out of the bushes and smiles at her. "What do you want?" she says.

"I thought I'd take you up on your offer."

"My offer?" Grace looks confused. "Oh, when you asked me out." She smiles.

Grace is much shorter than Billy and she cowers a bit under his gaze. He looks down on her mass of coiled, dark hair.

"It's cold tonight, isn't it?"

Grace starts to walk towards her car.

"Can I buy you a drink? Actually, I have some beer in my car."

Grace stops walking. She turns towards him. She weighs her options and looks at her watch.

"Aren't you married?" Grace says. "I've seen you around with her. Your wife. You used to come in a lot with her, play a couple of rounds."

Billy nods.

"You shouldn't be dating other women then, should you?" Grace shakes her head but Billy can see in the darkness that she is a bit pleased. "That's not nice."

"I can't help myself," Billy says, and in saying this he feels like he's just popped a balloon — a little burst of adrenaline, a gasp of air, and it's out in the open, the protective covering isn't there any more.

"Well. . . ." Grace turns back to her car. "What do you know about that?"

Billy kicks his foot on the ground, stubbing his toe, making pain a more intimate part of him than this conversation.

"You're one of those men who likes women big, aren't you? A big handful, something to pinch and hold on to."

Billy sucks in his breath.

"Well, come on then," Grace says. "I'm not all that big but I'll do, I suppose. You can come home with me."

The wind rips out of Billy. He feels weak at the knees.

162

"Just be quick about it," Grace says quietly. "I haven't got all night."
She climbs into the driver's side of her car and unlocks the passenger
door. "Come on then," she calls out of her window. "Get in."

And Billy does get in. He grabs a case of beer from his car and
locks the doors, and he walks with large strides towards Grace's car.
He climbs in. He can't stop shaking. He keeps his hands in his coat
pocket and his ball cap on and he shakes and twitches and his teeth
chatter. All of the times he's wanted to do this have come crashing
down into this moment.

"My," Grace says, "you're frozen. Let's get some heat going."

Grace pulls the car out of the lot and drives in the opposite
direction of Billy's house. They drive in silence, sharing an open
beer. Grace lives on the outskirts of suburbia, where a new hous-
ing development is being built, but where, for now, most of the
other neighbours are factories and highways. She lives in her childhood room in a virtually deserted house. Her mother rocks
endlessly in front of the TV, cane out to poke the channel selector,
a bowl of peanuts in her lap. She is half blind and fully deaf. Since
Grace's father died last year and Grace moved out of her apartment
and into her mother's home to take care of her, she has sold the
furniture around them, keeping only the kitchen chairs and table,
only the toaster oven and microwave, only the rocking chair her
mother sits in. In Grace's bedroom there is only the bunk bed.
Grace says her mother sleeps in the chair in front of the TV. Grace
will sell the house once her mother dies. She will use the money
to move to the city and buy an apartment. She will find a new job.

Grace makes Billy tiptoe into her room behind her mother. She
takes her mother to the bathroom, refills her peanut bowl, adjusts her
cane-to-TV ratio, and joins Billy in the bedroom at the back of the
house. He is sitting on the bottom bunk. She locks the door. Grace
lies down on the bottom bunk. Billy listens to the hum of the TV
set and he waits for his heart to stop violently beating. He sips on

the beer he brought in from the car. He does nothing. Grace waits.

"It's difficult," Grace says, "to afford taking care of her, buying her medicines, on my salary. So I had to sell some things. My father's pension dried up."

Billy thinks about money and jobs and such. "Hey," he says, "do you think you could get me a job at the golf course?"

Grace thought they were coming back to her place to have sex. She's had several men in like this, men she just gets a look at, a whiff of, in the minigolf clubhouse. She has them back to her house, tiptoes them past her mother, and they make love on her bunk bed, usually on the lower bunk. She knows they are mostly married, wanting a quick thrill, the feel of something different under their bodies. But this man, this Billy, is different. He hasn't touched her yet. And he is making her nervous. He is full of pent-up energy and he seems to just want to sit. Grace was more in the mood for sex. She fixed her hair and even sprayed some imitation Chanel No. 5 on her wrists while she watched her mother pee in the toilet.

She touches his back and he stiffens. "Don't you want to fool around?" She sits up and takes a gulp of his beer.

Billy clears his throat. Grace gets up from the bed and stands in front of him.

Billy thinks about it all. He finishes his bottle of beer and places it on the floor. He thinks about her horrible little room, how depressing the whole thing is. The whole situation reminds him of his sister and mother, of lives wasted. What he really wants now is a job at the golf course. He wants that much more than he wants Grace.

Billy touches her waist. It feels strange to him to touch actual hips, not just fat. Grace touches his shoulders, runs her hands across them. This feels good to Billy but not as good as he thought it might feel. Nothing is happening to his body and this begins to worry him.

Grace lifts her shirt off in one sweep and her large breasts dangle down the front of her chest. Billy wasn't expecting that. He expected a bra, at least, but there is no bra on now (removed through the armholes of her shirt in the bathroom while her mother was wiping) and her nipples are huge and unnerving. Billy can see a few tiny black hairs around each nipple. He is that close.

"Oh God," he says.

"Yes," Grace says. She caresses her nipples, making them erect. She has her eyes closed.

Billy reaches up to touch her breasts with both hands but nothing happens. It feels as if he's touching two balloons filled with warm water. He's too drunk. Grace moans.

"Shh," Billy whispers.

"She's deaf," Grace says. "She won't hear a thing."

Billy stands up.

"Where are you going?"

"I can't," Billy says. "I just can't. I'm sorry. It isn't you."

Grace wonders, for a moment, why she does this, why she has these men in to her home. She watches Billy stumble to the bedroom door and unlock it.

"I have to go," Billy says. "I'm really sorry. Maybe some other time."

"No problem," Grace shouts. "No problem at all." She throws a pillow at Billy as she watches him move away from her and rush past her mother and out the front door.

Grace is thirty-seven years old and not getting any younger. It occurs to her that all she's doing is waiting, waiting for someone to be nice to her. That's what we all want she thinks, a little kindness, a little loving, the feel of a warm body close by.

Dick doesn't think he's going to have any fun in the funeral home. Bringing Hilary here was a bad idea. Her bad idea. He turns on the lights and starts to give Hilary the tour but then Hilary turns off the lights and reaches in the dark for his hand. She finds it. Her touch is warm and damp.

Hilary is shaking.

"Like we used to," she whispers. "Remember? When we were kids?" With the lights off it seems easy to hold a man's hand. Hilary suddenly feels larger in the dark.

"I don't know," Dick says. "This doesn't feel right."

"Come on. Please."

They walk through the building together. Hilary has her eyes closed. Dick leads the way. He is sure-footed and stepping lightly. He squeezes her small hand in his.

"Hilary," Dick suddenly says. And then all she can hear is her name being whispered around her head as they walk. Over and over. *Hill-aaa-reee*. Hilary. With each step he whispers her name.

Whisper.

Hilary walks down the stairs to the basement and opens her eyes. But it is so dark that there is no difference between her open eyes and her closed eyes. Open. Shut. Open. Blackness.

"Hilary."

Her red dress is silky and soft and Hilary uses her free hand to touch it, smooth it over her belly. Dick's whisper is gentle, like light rain. Like a tear falling off a cheek onto a table. Wet. Liquidy. Something lurking, a catch in the throat, a tightening of the "aaa" in Hilary.

"Is this the embalming room?" Hilary says.

"Yes."

Dick leads her into the room. He doesn't know why he brought her into this room. Why he didn't take her into his office or into the furnace room. He supposes it is because they often came to this room. Before they saw his father. This was the tempting room, the room that symbolized death, the room that gave them both courage.

Dick shuts the door. There are two bodies lying on the tables. One of them is Hilary's mother. Dick is afraid Hilary will want to turn the lights on but she says nothing, she holds his hand and he leads her to an empty table. The darkness is complete. No matter where she moves her eyes all she sees is black.

"Lift me up on it," she says. "You used to kiss me here, do you remember?"

"Yes," Dick says. And he lifts her tiny body, so light, so angular, onto the table.

Sometimes when he would kiss her, she would forget all about the laundry, the dishes, the housecleaning. She would forget about her father and forget to wonder why he left them. And then the kiss would end and she would go home feeling lighter.

"Will you kiss me now?"

"What?"

"Will you? Just pretend we're young again." In the blackness her small voice is strong. She is amazed at her boldness. She doesn't feel shy at all.

They never kissed anywhere else. Only in the embalming room. Only in pitch blackness.

Dick leans in to where he expects Hilary is sitting on the table. He can't see anything. But she isn't sitting. She is lying down. Hilary can't tell if her eyes are open or closed. She blinks. Dick touches her face with his hands. He wants to kiss her but he feels frozen. He can't move.

God, his father made him sick. And he feels suddenly sick again. The Japanese food churns in his stomach.

He tries to look at Hilary. He peers into the darkness but he can't see anything.

"Kiss me," she says again. Erase time, she thinks. "Please."

Instead of kissing her, Dick puts his hand on her stomach and slowly moves it around. He hears her breathe in sharply. He feels her hip bones and rib cage. She's so thin. And then he moves his hand up between her breasts and runs his finger along her clavicle, traces the line he would cut if she were dead.

"My father," he whispers. "I'm sorry he did that." His hands move around her neck.

Hilary sits up quickly.

"Don't touch my neck," she says. "Please don't ever touch my neck." She jumps off the table. "I want to leave now."

"I'm sorry. I didn't mean to —"

The room is utter blackness. "I'm frightened," Hilary says. "Please."

Dick moves to comfort her. He follows the sound of her breathing. She is stumbling in the dark, closer to her mother's body than Dick would like her to be. He touches her arm, then puts his arms around her and pulls her close. "Do you think my father . . . do you think he — was it often?" he whispers.

Hilary says nothing, her face buried in his smell.

"God, Hilary. They were dead."

"Worse things have happened in the world." Hilary whispers as she pulls herself away from him. "There's nothing you can do to change things once the person is dead."

"Which person?"

"Your father," Hilary whispers. "My mother."

Dick leads her out of the room without turning on the lights. In the hallway he turns on the lights. "I'm sorry," he says. "About the kiss."

"I don't like my neck being touched," Hilary says, quietly. Her face is flushed. "I've never liked my neck being touched."

They walk slowly back up the stairs and they stand together outside of the funeral home in the cold night.

"Will you come upstairs?" Dick asks. "I could make coffee."

Hilary follows Dick up the rickety metal stairs to his apartment. Dick makes coffee. He takes it to the couch and then turns on the TV. Hilary sits and puts her feet up on the coffee table.

"This feels comfortable," Hilary says. "It feels so familiar."

"I don't know what to say about my father," Dick says.

Hilary nods. "Sometimes I studied with you over there by the window," Hilary says. "Do you remember?"

"You used to cheat."

"You were smarter than me. I had to save myself." Hilary pauses. "It all seems so useless now."

Her mother below her. Hilary above, having coffee. She thinks about her home, about her dolls and her puzzle and the loneliness that will hit her hard when everyone leaves. She wonders where the Madonna's face is, where she lost those puzzle pieces. Where could those puzzle pieces have gone?

"Can I hold your hand?"

Hilary nods.

Dick takes her hand.

He wonders what the rocks on Hilary's living room floor mean, he wonders about all the dolls. He wonders how it happens that horrible things can be buried so deeply in your soul. The memory of his father's sickness came crashing down on him today. The impossibility of it all, the horror he experienced from watching it and then the quick burial of it in his subconscious. Always there, lurking, just not on the surface.

Hilary thinks of how her mother's death took forever and yet was over in seconds.

Dick watches TV but he can't focus on what is going on. He is holding this woman's hand.

She's below me now, Hilary thinks. Right underneath me. Hilary moves close to Dick. He lets go of her hand and puts his arm around her shoulders. He turns the volume up on the TV.

Like a married couple, Hilary thinks.

Maybe the rocks are covering dirty carpet, Dick thinks, or scratched-up linoleum, or unfinished wood. Maybe it's a practical solution to an expensive problem. He thinks that Hilary's dolls are perhaps a collection of antiques, perhaps they are valuable, maybe even an inheritance.

The doctor said that her mother would soon lose consciousness. He said that she would drift into another world. He said that she would stop crying out all the time, begging for morphine, begging for release. But she didn't. And Hilary couldn't stand the sounds.

Dick's arm around her is warm and forgiving. She feels safe.

Hilary prayed all Thursday morning long, prayed until her arms hurt from holding them up and clasping her hands together, prayed until her faith stopped. Until something in her body gave, like a dry leaf breaking in half, a bitter, crackling sound to Hilary's ears.

Hilary leans into Dick. She is so tired. She looks up into his face. He has fallen asleep and she didn't notice. There was no relaxing of muscle, no heaviness of the arm on her shoulder. Hilary stares at the TV, at the flashing images. A man runs across the screen but Hilary can't seem to focus on what he is doing. She closes her eyes. She shuts everything out.

Back from the Dead

Hope is all Billy needs as he sits in the hospital waiting room with his pregnant daughter and a large cup of coffee straight from the machine, lukewarm and watery. He feels as if his actions last night led to this. If he hadn't gone home with Grace . . . if he hadn't touched her breasts . . . then none of this would have happened. Tess would be fine. Billy is itching for a drink right now. He wishes he had something strong to put in his coffee.

"She's had this coming," Sue says. "She's just so damn fat."

"Shut up, Sue."

"But it's true."

Sue says, "Where did you go last night? You came crawling in this morning looking like shit."

Billy stands up. He wants so badly to raise his hand and knock some sense into his daughter, teach her a little respect, but he sees the people around them in the waiting room looking at him, staring him up and down. He has never before hit his daughter but something in him is growing and he is afraid of what he might do.

The people in the waiting room are also looking at Sue, at her garish makeup and black clothing, at her piercings. Billy wonders when Sue has the time to put on all that makeup or if she, perhaps, sleeps wearing it. He thinks of her pillow in her bedroom and what it must look like covered in makeup and he realizes that he hasn't been in her bedroom for months and months. For quite some time. Maybe, Billy sighs and sits back down, maybe if he'd just go into her room every once in a while, show some interest, none of this would have happened. Maybe she wouldn't be pregnant.

Billy spent the night in his car in front of the Greenhomes Minigolf Course. In the parking lot. He slept sitting up and now he's stiff and uncomfortable and his breath stinks.

He wonders if he should pray. He tries to remember when he prayed last. Billy remembers going to Sunday school when his father lived with them. But all that stopped when his dad shut the door behind him and disappeared.

Billy remembers praying for the Oldsmobile and he got it.

He prayed for the house and he got it.

He prayed that Sue would be born with all fingers and toes and he got that (he should have prayed for a brain for the girl, he knows now).

But he gave up praying recently when his two biggest wishes, that he would find another job and that his daughter wasn't really pregnant, didn't come true.

"I'd pray," Billy says to Sue, "but praying is for the gullible. Praying is for idiots. It doesn't get you anything." Billy taps his forehead. Sue looks at him. "Real life is for the smart ones."

"So?"

"I should have left a long time ago," Billy says. "I should have moved away from home. I should have started my own photo-finishing shop. But I stayed here, damn it, and life went around in circles and now I'm too old, too far in debt, to skip out and move on."

"Why are you telling me this? Why are you telling me that you wanted to leave us?"

"I'm telling you this because it's not too late for you to learn something about life, Sue. Soak it up now, because soon" — Billy points to her belly — "you won't have time to concentrate on anything but that baby."

"I'm not leaving," Sue says. "I'm going to stay right here with my friends."

"Your friends? Jesus, Sue, your friends won't mean anything in a year or two."

"Mr. Mount?" A nurse pats him on the arm. "Will you come with me, please?"

"Is she okay? Is Tess all right?"

"Come this way, please. The doctor would like to talk to you."

"I'm coming too," Sue says. "I'm coming."

The nurse looks Sue up and down. She shakes her head. Sue gives the nurse the finger behind her back. She follows her father and the nurse down the long, white corridor of the hospital which is strangely empty. Shining. Gleaming. A young man, a doctor, in a white coat meets them in front of Tess's room in intensive care. He takes Billy's arm from the nurse and smiles openly at Sue. Sue scowls. Billy thinks it's strange that so many new people have touched him lately.

"Let's sit here for a minute," the doctor says.

"Oh, God," Billy says, "she's dead."

"First thing's first," the doctor says.

"Is she dead? Oh, God."

The doctor looks at Sue. "Your mother" — he looks at Billy — "your wife, is fine. Just fine."

Billy feels like crying. He swallows loudly. He releases a gush of air, a choking sound.

"She's had a mild heart attack."

"I told you," Sue says. "She's too damn fat."

"Sue." Billy glances at the doctor. For a minute there his life almost turned completely upside down. For a minute there he almost lost something. Now he feels right-sideup again and sitting straight. Now he feels solid.

"She's right, in effect," the doctor says. "Mrs. Mount's heart can't take all that weight."

The doctor says she needs rest. He says she needs to lose weight, stay away from fatty foods, exercise, stop smoking . . .

"She doesn't smoke."

. . . eat properly, get plenty of sleep, have no stress, be able to sit down and put her feet up for a while, take time to smell the flowers, be quiet and peaceful, do yoga, perhaps, or Tai Chi, something, anything, to make her live a long and happy life.

But for a little while she needs to stay in the hospital and be hooked up to machines to monitor her heart. They need to make sure she is fine, that she won't relapse, that it won't happen again. Just for a while. She can go home on Wednesday. It was a small heart attack, a blip on the screen, nothing to worry about this time.

Billy thanks the doctor. He shakes the man's hand.

"You can see her now," the doctor says. "Just for a bit. Try not to upset her."

Billy pauses at the door to Tess's room, he hangs back a bit and watches Sue slouch up to her mother's side. He stands at the door and takes it all in. Tess strapped to machines, looking pale and drawn, looking sick of the world. Sue stands beside her mother, not knowing what to do, fidgeting, looking like the child she once was. Billy stands back.

"Come here," Tess says. She pats the bed. "Billy, come here."

Billy walks into the room. He feels moisture on his face. A sudden coolness.

"My God," Tess says. "Are you crying?"

"No."

"Yes, you are," Sue says. "Feel your face. Look in here." Sue holds up a makeup mirror she finds in her purse.

Billy moves to the mirror. Takes it from Sue. He stares at his reflection. His face is contorted, squinched like a bawling baby. His eyes are red and leaking tears, his nose is running. "I didn't think I was crying," Billy blubbers.

"You're crying, honey." Tess pats her bed.

"I think he's feeling guilty that he didn't come home last night," Sue says.

Tess sighs.

"Are you feeling all right, Tess?" Billy asks. He tries to compose himself. He blows his nose into a Kleenex and dries his eyes.

"I feel all bruised. I feel like a truck ran over me." Tess tries to laugh.

"I told you that you have to lose weight," Sue says. "Even the doctor says that. Doesn't he, Dad?"

Billy nods. He reaches for Tess's hand.

"Lose weight? Is that what this is?" Tess swallows hard. "How?"

Billy sits on the side of the bed. He starts to cry again.

"Why are you crying?" Tess says. "You're not the one who has to diet."

"Exercise too, Mom," Sue says. "Maybe we could do aerobics together. I've got some great videos."

"But the baby. You shouldn't be exercising."

"Exercise is good for the baby. God, Dad, stop bawling. Pull yourself together. I'm going to get some water to drink and I want you two to smarten up by the time I get back." Sue stomps out of the room.

"What's wrong, Billy?"

Billy sniffles. "I don't know. I just can't stop."

Tess reaches for Billy's hand. She takes it. She squeezes hard. They sit together on the bed, Tess staring out the window, Billy sobbing. Finally Sue comes back into the room and takes her father home.

Dick walks Hilary to the front of the grocery store near the funeral home.

"I'll call you later, if that's okay," he says. "Have fun shopping."

"Yes," Hilary says. "We need groceries." She feels headachy and stiff from sitting up all night in Dick's arms, staring at the TV set. She didn't want to move for fear of waking him. She didn't want to wake him because she felt warm and protected and strong. Because she thought he might make her go home. She didn't want to go home last night because she wanted to be near her mother. Sitting in Dick's arms she was there, right there, upstairs from her mother. Close to her.

Dick woke up startled when he saw Hilary sitting beside him. His eyes quickly focused and he remembered suddenly where he was. He made Hilary coffee, he made her breakfast. They talked politely about the weather. And then Hilary reached up to him as he was standing next to the sink doing breakfast dishes, and she pulled his head down to her level and she kissed him on the lips. Hard. Ever since that kiss Dick has been animated and excited. Happy and nervous. Hilary feels the same way she did before the kiss.

"I'll be working on your mother this evening, getting her presentable. Making her beautiful again. I'll be thinking of you. When can I see you again?" Dick wants to hold this tiny woman in his arms and not let her go. He knows she's a little eccentric but he's decided that doesn't matter. He likes her just the way she is. He woke to her soft hair on his shoulder this morning.

Hilary says, "You'll come to the burial, won't you? You'll help?"

"I wouldn't miss it."

Hilary watches him walk down the street and then she ducks over to the side of the store and waits until he is gone, until he turns the corner. Then she walks down the street towards the funeral home. Follows in his footsteps.

It is early afternoon and Hilary sits in the park across from the funeral home. She waits and waits and waits. She is cold. The lights in the funeral home grow brighter as the sun begins to set, the sign illuminates, glows: MORTIMER'S FUNERAL HOME. At one point Hilary sees Dick leave the funeral home and go up to his apartment. Then, after an hour, she sees him come out of his apartment and walk down the stairs back to the funeral home. Dick stops and looks around, as if he knows he is being watched. He scratches his chin. Then he enters the funeral home and Hilary sees a light glow from the hallway window, the stairwell window, and then the basement. In the park Hilary hides behind a tree. A car passes on the street and a light rain begins to fall. Dewy almost. A touch of cool moisture.

Hilary crosses the street and hides in the bushes beside the funeral home. The street is deserted in the early evening rain. She watches the basement windows and then she moves over towards a lit one and crouches, still in her red dress, a heavy coat covering it, she hides in the greenery. The windows are mottled but Hilary finds one that has a crack in it, a sliver pulled out of it, and she leans down and presses her eye close. She is shivering in the damp cold.

Dick is washing his hands at a sink. He is looking carefully at his fingers, searching them, as if he feels they aren't his. He pulls on latex gloves. He snaps them, but Hilary cannot hear the sound. The room is sterile and clean. A silver table in the middle. A wall of drawers and glass cases. Instruments. Embalming machines. Dick sets up a smaller table by the large one with bottles, jars, pencils, a hairbrush, lipstick. A white-blonde wig rests on a Styrofoam head.

Dick places a picture of Rebecca Mount on a clipboard beside him. He studies it. It is of Rebecca standing in the backyard when she was much younger, her hair blown a little in the wind, her arms folded in front of her, a cigarette in one hand. She is laughing. There is the shadow of Hilary falling just to the right of Rebecca, elbows cocked out to hold the camera, looking as if she is trying to fly away. A bird woman suspended in the darkness of a shadow.

Dick walks out of view. He comes back rolling a table and on this table is a body draped in a sheet. Hilary holds her breath. She closes her eyes. When she opens them her mother's body lies there before her.

Dick lifts up Rebecca's chin and studies her neck. Hilary holds her breath. There are marks on Rebecca's neck, bruises, purpley-brownish marks. Dick puts her chin down again. He stands there, thinking.

Hilary is suddenly above her body. She sees herself down there, looking into the window, watching what is happening to her mother's body, the rain picking up and soaking her hair, the tears moving down her face as if her eyes are leaking out her soul. She can see her mother but she feels like she is watching a stranger, that that isn't her mother, that can't possibly be her mother.

Dick takes a small bottle of spray and squeezes it up Hilary's mother's nose.

Hilary settles down on her calves. She rests her small bum on her shoes, she leans into the windowsill. It's like watching TV, she thinks. She scratches her cheeks.

Dick begins with the makeup. He coats Rebecca's face in whites and then beiges and then pinks. He does her shoulders and the scoop of her neck. He paints her hands. He paints thick over the marks and a sewn-up line on her right clavicle. Then he applies eyeshadow and bright red lipstick. He tweezes her eyebrows and combs them up in a surprised fashion. He brushes on a touch of mascara and places earrings in the holes in her ears. He fiddles with the wig for a bit, looking back and forth at the picture before him. Then he cuts her fingernails, polishes them, a dusty rose colour. Dick works quickly and sensibly, carefully. He doesn't pause or look as if he's thinking about anything in the world except what he is doing. It's as if he were working on a mannequin, something plastic.

Hilary thinks her mother might just jump off that table and stand up and smile.

Dick pulls on Hilary's mother's underwear, bra, nylons, and purple dress. It is awkward, his face is red, straining. He is sweating, wiping at his forehead with a paper towel. Hilary holds her breath. Dick moves towards Rebecca to adjust some makeup on her face and then he stands back again and looks at the picture before him and then at Rebecca Mount.

He smiles.

He slips off his gloves. He stretches tall. He yawns and looks at his watch and then writes something in a notebook beside him.

And then Dick leaves Rebecca Mount waiting and walks out of view, down the hallway of the funeral home to the casket and supply room. He wheels out a Blue Diamond casket — the carbon steel with shaded, brushed finish; the light blue regal velvet interior with swing-bar hardware. A mere three thousand dollars. Not quite top of the line, but not the lowest of the bunch either. And even though he knows Thomas should be able to afford it, he won't charge anything. He wants to do this for Hilary, give something to her. He pushes it ahead of him quickly, whistling under his breath. Dick opens the lids and blows on the pillow, making sure it is dust-free, and then he struggles with Rebecca Mount a bit until she is lying in the casket. He adjusts her arms and legs and torso and neck and head. He uses props to make her look comfortable — a head-rest, an arm-and-hand positioner, and a repose block for the shoulders. He straightens her dress. He touches her wig a bit, brushes it, smoothes it down where it got all mussed up, and then he shuts the bottom half of the Blue Diamond casket and stands back for a third time. Dick closes his eyes and then opens them. He pretends he is seeing this body for the first time.

Perfect.

Lovely.

But Hilary is not there to see this. She is walking, head down, in the rain, towards home.

She is wondering about her father and where he might be right now. She wonders if he is still alive and she hopes he is dead, dead, dead. And then she thinks about Dick and what he does every day, about what he faces, and how that makes him special.

Death. She is thinking about death.

That heart-and-breath-and-movement-stopping fear of death. Her mother is there now, dead. Hilary is still living. She is walking in the cold towards home. The street lights shine around her but she feels like she's walking in the dark.

When Hilary enters into the house she is surprised by the sound of the TV, by the warmth of the furnace, by the movements of life around her. Thomas is sitting on the couch with Jonathan.

"Where have you been?" Thomas looks at his sister. "We were worried sick about you. And look — your face is bleeding again."

"Out," Hilary says. She wipes the small line of blood from a scratch with a Kleenex she finds in her pocket.

"You're wet," Jonathan says.

"Out all night? All day? Twenty-four hours?"

Hilary shrugs. She tiptoes across her rocks and sits in the armchair beside the TV. She looks at Thomas and Jonathan.

"You should dry yourself or you'll catch cold. Here, take your coat off."

"I was out with Dick."

"How did it go?" Jonathan asks. "It must have been a good date if you're just getting home now." He smiles.

"Did you know Tess is in the hospital?" Thomas says.

"Why?"

"Heart attack."

"Is she all right?"

"She's fine now. I just went and visited. Billy's all shook up."

Hilary looks closely at Thomas and Jonathan. There is something about them, about the way they are sitting, so close together, on the couch. She scratches her hair and then pulls a strand into her mouth and chews on it. She takes her coat off and crosses her arms in front of her, she hugs herself. Her mother's mouth is sewn up now.

Thomas clears his throat. "Stop staring."

Hilary says to Jonathan, "If you're going to stay here, maybe you can help us dig the hole for the grave."

"The more the merrier," Jonathan says.

Thomas looks at the TV. He crosses his arms in front of him. He watches the glow without seeing the shapes within. Blue lights from the TV move throughout the room, flashing on the walls and ceiling.

12

Out

Tess is sitting up in the hospital bed eating her breakfast with as much vigour as she can summon for a piece of dry whole-wheat toast, a glass of orange juice, and a cup of decaffeinated coffee with sugar substitute and skim milk powder. She is starving. Anything would taste good just about now. She even thought of popping open her roommate's IV bag just to taste the sugar-water solution suspended within. When Billy calls she wants to ask him to bring donuts or cinnamon buns or Danishes, something sweet, something she can fill up on. But she knows she can't. There's a hole in her stomach that is hankering for starchy food. No wonder people die in the hospital, she thinks. It's the food. Or lack of food. Tess's life is on a downward spiral now. No food equals no lust for life. She thinks she might as well have died.

Tess thinks of Billy and his sobbing yesterday. In those wet eyes Tess saw something sliding up over her Billy's trusting twinkle, something besides tears dimming the shine. Tess now, in the sunny morning, eating her breakfast, being alive to the world, starving and afraid to die, wonders if she saw what she wanted to see or if she saw what was really there.

Tess knows that if she were to die, if she had died yesterday, the world would go on without her. The sun would rise and set and Sue would have her baby and Billy would breathe air and swallow food. Life would move on and she would be dead in a casket, shut up like a turtle in its shell. This thought frightens her. Even with all her bulk she doesn't really add up to much in this world. Things have got to change.

Tess feels faint and tired of it all. She is so very hungry. She has licked the crumbs on her plate, has run her tongue around the inside of her orange juice cup, has swallowed all her skim milk powder. Tess moves her tray away, lies back down on her pillow, adjusts her bed to a comfortable level, and tries to close her eyes. Tries to block out all these thoughts about death. She has to focus on living now and what she's going to do with herself when she's one-hundred-and-thirty-pounds-slim-as-a-rail. And what's she going to do when Billy comes clean? Because she knows something happened the night she almost died, and the minute Billy tells her what it was Tess's whole reason for being will change. But her roommate is waking up now and coughing and spitting and groaning and all Tess can do is listen to the woman's sounds and feel afraid inside and out.

"My God," the woman moans from behind the curtain that is pulled around her bed.

Tess looks over. She can see the IV stand poking out from the curtain. It shakes a little.

"Help me."

Tess rings the buzzer for the nurse. She sits up and waits. The nurse enters the room, gives one look at large Tess, sitting cross-legged on her bed like a Buddha, pointing a chubby finger at the other bed, and then disappears behind the curtain. The woman's groaning suddenly stops.

Tess closes her eyes. Her chest hurts. She feels bruised.

"Hush," Tess can hear the nurse scolding. "There's nothing wrong with you. Sit back down."

The nurse noisily pushes back the curtain. Tess opens one eye and looks carefully at her roommate. A shrivelled old woman, small and frail. Her IV bag larger than her upper arm.

The nurse ties the curtain. "Come now," she says. "Have you two been introduced? Have you met your roommate, Mrs. Rankle?"

The old woman shakes her head.

"I'm Tess Mount," Tess says. "Heart attack."

"This is Hilda Rankle," the nurse says loudly, looking at a clipboard on a shelf beside the bed.

The old woman says, "I don't know why I'm here. They brought me here and left me to die."

The nurse laughs. "You two will be great friends." She leaves.

Tess smiles hopefully. The old woman lies back down in her bed on her side and faces Tess. Her eyes are rheumy and pale blue.

"My son in law left me here last week. Just brought me here in the middle of the night, told the nurses that I was unconscious, but I was really sleeping. They've operated on me twice since then. I think," she whispers this, "they are trying to take my organs out. I think they are going to sell them."

Tess smiles. "I'm sure that's not the case," she says.

Hilda then begins to list her complaints. She starts with the top of her head; dandruff, split ends, eczema, scabs — and moves slowly down to her toes — athlete's foot, ingrown toenails, bunions, warts, corns.

"All these things," Hilda says, "and they still want my organs. Imagine that. I guess the inside of me is better than the outside."

"Oh, I'm sure they aren't taking anything out of you," Tess says again.

"What do you know?" Hilda scowls. "You better watch out too — your inside looks like it's probably better than that fat outside."

"That's not nice," Tess says. "That's an awful thing to say." Tess's eyes begin to water.

"I'm not a nice woman," Hilda says. "I don't have much time left. I'm not about to waste it being sweet." She turns over and faces the wall.

Tess can see the old woman's naked back. She tries to think of happy things, beautiful things. But all she can think about is her hunger and her stomach growls.

And then Billy is standing there in the doorway, a sheepish look on his face, relief etched into his features. Tess looks up at him and through him and over him. She looks around him, trying to judge the way she feels, trying to see the aura around his body. The glow of his being, who he is. There is something lurking in the shadows.

Billy comes to her and holds his hand out. He holds it out as if paying for something, looking down into his hand, looking anywhere but in Tess's eyes. Tess takes his hand, feels his palm's smoothness, the callused bumps on his knuckles, the gouges where he picks at the skin around his fingernails. She gives a tight squeeze and lets go.

"Are you okay today?" Tess asks.

Billy nods.

"When will I be out of this hospital? I've got a horrible room-mate," Tess whispers.

"Wednesday," Billy says. "They are doing more tests. Just moni-toring you. Checking you out. How are you feeling?"

"I'm hungry," Tess says. "I'm so hungry I could eat a horse. I wish we had insurance for a private room."

Billy smiles.

"I wanted to ask you to sneak something in, a cake or something, some Kentucky Fried Chicken, but then I remembered my death sentence." Tess's eyes begin to tear.

Billy shakes his head. "It's a life sentence, Tess. It's just a new way of looking at life."

"Christ, Billy. I might as well have died. You might as well kill me." She begins to cry. "I can't live without food. I just can't do it."

Hilda grunts, "If you ask me, you could stand to lose something. You're as big as an elephant."

Billy closes the curtains between the beds. He can feel Tess's sadness thickening. He can reach out and touch it.

Tess sobs. "I saw those skinny models on TV, saw their bellies, ribs like ladders, saw their flat breasts. My heart just gave in. Those skinny models, those girls. . . ."

"What models? What are you talking about?"

"Why didn't you come home the other night? Where were you?"

Billy opens his mouth to say something. He doesn't know what he's going to say. He's been with Tess forever, it seems. Since they were kids. And they have been happy. Off and on. There have been moments, especially lately, when Billy would like to just get up and leave everyone behind him. Disappear like his father. But he hasn't. He's stuck through it all. That must mean something.

He didn't really do anything with Grace.

But he wanted to do something.

Or did he?

"I was out," Billy says. He feels itchy all over, especially his genitals. He wants to scratch but he knows that he would be drawing attention to his guilt. His face turns red, blood-hot red all over.

"I have no one who loves me," Hilda says from behind the curtain. "Feel yourselves lucky."

Billy picks at his fingers with his nails. He bites his lip.

"And my stomach aches," Hilda says. "They've stolen my organs. My liver, my kidneys, my appendix. They took my appendix and they've probably given it to someone who will clone me. I saw that on TV."

"Rest," Billy says to Tess. "You'll be home soon."

"You can't walk out now," Tess says. "You can't leave me like this. You can't leave me with her. We have to talk."

"There's nothing to talk about," Billy says. "I was just out, that's all, having a drink."

"Drinking, Billy. Jesus."

"You eat, Tess," Billy says. "I drink." And saying this astonishes him. It can't be the same thing. He leaves quickly before she can say anything else.

Billy's footsteps disappear down the hall and Tess tries to imagine the sound of the engine starting and the short drive to her house. She pictures her kitchen, her fridge and stove, her food cupboards. So many years of looking into those food cupboards, ignoring what is going on around her, eating, always eating. And then her mind moves up the stairs of her house and settles lightly on her cotton, floral pillowcase in her bed. She wishes she were there, her head on the pillow, resting gently. And then she wonders, if she were there, if her head were resting on her floral-covered pillow, would Billy be lying there beside her. She has to take hold of herself, make some changes, get things straightened out. She nearly died, goddamnit.

"I think we should escape," Hilda says. "We should get out of here as soon as we can."

Thomas, Hilary, and Jonathan are eating breakfast silently in the kitchen. Jonathan has cleaned up the dishes and Hilary is astonished to be eating off plates and bowls, using real glasses. Hilary is eating scrambled eggs and toast and drinking new coffee with real cream. Thomas has been back and forth to the grocery store, has stocked up the fridge and plugged in the old freezer in the basement. He filled it with hot dogs and hamburgers, frozen dinners and bread, quick food. Hilary looks around the kitchen. Her puzzle has been carefully moved to the dining-room table which looks dusted. Her dolls have been placed on shelves and tables and look clean and shiny. Until Hilary saw the shine she didn't realize how dusty everything must have been. She admires the furniture, her grandmother's — given to her mother when she married her daddy. Hilary thinks the furniture is hers now, passed on from woman to woman, down the line. Unless, of course, Billy decides to take it, along with everything else she owns.

"It's so clean," Hilary whispers.

"What happened to your puzzle?" Jonathan says. "The face is missing."

"I can't find the pieces," Hilary says. "But I haven't really looked everywhere yet. I'll look more today."

"I think that puzzle was always missing pieces," Thomas says. "I think I remember that."

"No," Hilary says. "No. I remember her face clearly. I remember those pieces."

"Probably from the picture on the box. You probably just think you remember."

"No, I remember. I remember holding the pieces in my hand. I remember Mother doing the puzzle. The face pieces were her favourites."

They eat carefully, quietly. Every chew seems to reverberate in the cleanliness.

Jonathan gets up for a cup of coffee. He refills all the mugs without asking if anyone wants any more.

"So," Thomas begins.

"We have to dig today," Hilary says. "And maybe buy things for the party."

"The party?"

"The funeral. People will come. Billy and Tess and Sue." Hilary stirs sugar in her coffee and then blows on the steam like a child. Loud puffs, her cheeks filled with air.

Jonathan watches. "I think it's admirable that you're burying your mother in the garden, Thomas. If you can get away with it, I would like to be buried in our garden someday. You could put me under that iron bench, beside the bird bath."

"Jesus, Jonathan, it's illegal."

"Your garden?" Hilary echoes.

Jonathan and Thomas look at each other.

"It will just make things worse," Thomas says to Jonathan.

Hilary sips her coffee, watching her brother and his friend. If Hilary could only find the puzzle pieces for the Madonna's face. She wants to see the eyes clearly, the lips, the set expression on her face. What would it be like to be told you were pregnant when you didn't want it, didn't expect it, didn't even make love to anyone to get it? Hilary remembers from the Bible, from the years her daddy made them go to Sunday school, that Joseph was going to set Mary aside, not marry her, because she was pregnant. But he got an angel too, didn't he? Someone came down from Heaven and said, Marry that woman because she is carrying God's son.

Hilary's mother got pregnant just out of high school. She didn't want Thomas, didn't expect him. But Daddy married her. Without an angel telling him to do it. She was safe within the rules, Hilary assumes. Hilary thinks that she would like to be pregnant now more than anything in the world, and if some angel came down from the sky and told her that she was pregnant, she would dance for joy. She would even consider throwing out some of her dolls to make room for cribs and playpens. She would make the living room floor a soft place for the baby to crawl.

Thomas clears his throat. He looks at Jonathan, runs his eyes over his lover's face. This is the man he has spent his life with. This is his life.

"Do you know I'm gay, Hilary?" he asks.

"Gay?" Hilary says.

"Jonathan and I live together. We've been living together for fifteen years."

"Fifteen years?" Hilary looks at the two men sitting before her.

"I'm just telling you because I think you should know." Thomas feels shaky. He has moved his new world into his old world now and the feeling is not good. It's a stomach-dropping feeling. Thomas fidgets around on his seat as if he has fleas.

"But," Hilary starts, "you've had girlfriends."

"No, Hilary, all that was just pretend."

"How can you pretend girlfriends?"

"I made them up."

"But you brought one to Billy's wedding. How can you make up a girlfriend?"

"That was a sister of a lover."

Hilary stands. She looks at the two men. "Gay," she whispers. "Together? You, Thomas?"

"Yes."

She laughs. "Oh my God. What would Mother have said?"

"It doesn't matter now," Thomas says.

"Is that why you didn't come home? God, that's why you didn't come home."

"No, of course not." Thomas looks at Jonathan. "I'm afraid to fly. I have a busy life. I —"

"That's why you didn't come home. I knew there had to be a reason. It wasn't just us, it wasn't that you didn't love us."

"No, Hilary, of course not — the point is — Jonathan is my lover."

"What does it matter?" Hilary says. "Really? What does it matter?"

"I thought it might matter."

"When are you going to learn, Thomas, that nothing really

matters." Hilary walks out of the kitchen and into the living room. She walks across the rocks and looks out the front window.

Jonathan comes up behind her and puts his hand on her shoulder. She jumps.

"You startled me," Hilary says.

"I'm sorry. Are you all right?"

"I'm just looking out the window," Hilary says.

"I thought we'd clean first."

Hilary looks at Jonathan.

"I just cleaned the kitchen and a bit of the dining room. The rest of the house needs a vacuum and dust. The bathroom needs cleaning," Jonathan says. "I know I don't know you and you don't know me but I think we need to clean your house before the funeral."

Hilary looks at her dolls lined up on the couch.

Thomas comes into the living room.

"Do you really love each other?" she asks.

"Yes," Jonathan says.

Thomas nods.

"Fifteen years together," Hilary says. "I didn't know."

"I'm sorry, Hilary."

"No," Hilary says, looking away from Jonathan and Thomas to the window again. "I don't know much of what is going on in the world." She presses her face to the cold glass, presses her nose flat. The sensation is both claustrophobic and cooling on her cheeks. She pulls away. "Sometimes I feel like I've just been born."

Jonathan puts his hands on Hilary's shoulder again. She shrugs it away. "Let's have our showers and get ready for the day," he says. "We've got a lot to accomplish. I'm going to vacuum this room and I have to figure out how to do that without disturbing the rocks."

"Can't we pick them up?" Thomas asks.

"No," Hilary says. "They have to stay there."

Jonathan shrugs. "She's right. It would take all day just to move them."

Hilary presses her face to the glass again.

Thomas looks at her. He can feel something stuck in his throat, his saliva won't go down. His eyes well up as he turns to go upstairs, to get dressed for the day.

Driving home from the hospital, turning the corner before the mall, Billy sees Sue walking along the road. He stops to pick her up. They begin to yell at each other as soon as she gets in the car.

"Aren't you going to see your mother today? She's your god-damned mother."

"But I have things to do," Sue says. "She won't miss me for one day."

"What could be more important than seeing your mother at the hospital?"

"Things. I have to meet Sandy."

"When did you get this way, Sue?"

Sue looks out of the window.

"You used to be something special. You used to be someone."

"Christ, Dad." Sue slumps down in her seat. "You can drop me off here."

"Now all you do is scream and holler. I bet you gave your mother the heart attack. Were you fighting with her?"

"You wouldn't know, would you? You were out."

"I. . . ." Billy looks at his hands on the steering wheel. His knuckles are tight.

"You don't have to tell me what you were doing," Sue says. "I can smell it a mile away. Stop the car. I have to meet Sandy."

"What do you mean by that?"

Sue sighs. "When Samantha slept with Joey, everyone in school knew she had done it. Intuition, I guess. Women can guess these things. We know."

"What are you saying?"

"You fucked someone else, Dad. I know. Mom knows. Live with it."

Billy pulls the car over to the side of the road. "Get out," he hollers. "Get the hell out of my car." He reaches over and slaps Sue on the shoulder. "Get out."

Sue slams the door.

Billy rolls down his window and screams, "I wasn't unfaithful."

"Whatever." Sue starts walking back down the road. She is rubbing her shoulder.

Billy leans on his steering wheel, his forehead resting on his hands, and he begins to cry. His mind is so whirlingly crazy he doesn't know what to do. Twice in two days he is crying. A man who hasn't cried since he was a small boy. What's gotten into him? He reaches under his seat and takes out one of the beers from the pack he's been drinking all morning. He opens it and swallows it quickly, letting the bubbles burst inside his belly. He burps. He sobs and burps and drinks. He hit his little baby. He watches her through his rear-view mirror as she disappears down the road. He drinks more beer. And the more he drinks, the more he thinks about Grace and the less he thinks about Tess and Sue. He thinks about how he wants to try again, how he wants any woman's body that will just lie there and let him do what he has to do. He doesn't want a history with anyone, he doesn't want this tenseness, this uncontrollable sadness. He just wants a good screw. He just wants to think with his body, not his mind. He wants to explore things other than feelings. He drinks more and the empties pile up beside him.

Billy turns on the car. He drives swervingly down the road towards Greenhomes Minigolf Course, towards Grace. He doesn't notice that he's driving so slowly that several people move out to pass him. Billy doesn't notice that he has the air conditioner going in the car, instead of the heat. He sees an older man walk out in front of his car and he brakes just in time. The older man raises his hand to stop the car from hitting him. The man peers at the Oldsmobile and then walks stiffly away. Billy suddenly remembers his father coming to his baseball games and sitting in the stands with a proud smile on his face.

Billy drives into the Minigolf course parking lot. There are a few cars scattered around, parked haphazardly. Billy can see into the clubhouse window and he sees the young man from the night before talking to a customer. There are three or four people playing on the course. Billy drinks the final beer and then gets out of the car. He has to piss badly and he thinks of the other night when he pissed in the bushes and he wishes it were dark out. The cold is palpable. Billy feels the air whipping him. He hunches his head into his shoulders and walks, hands in pockets, into the clubhouse. The bell on the door rings and everyone looks at him. The young man smiles. Billy glances around, looking for Grace.

"Can I help you?"

Billy shrugs.

"Are you here to play some holes?"

"No," Billy says, "I'm looking for Grace."

"Oh." The young man walks to the back of the store and hollers into a doorway. Grace comes out, wiping her hands on her shirt. She sees Billy. She looks at him.

"Hi," he says.

"Hi." She has something white on her upper lip. It looks like sugar.

"Can we talk?" Billy feels horrible. His voice is slurred and his mind is wandering.

"About what?"

Billy looks around. Everyone in the clubhouse is silent, listening to the conversation between Billy and Grace.

"Come here," Billy says.

"I'm busy," Grace says. "I'm having a break. I only get one break a day. I need to take it."

Billy looks at the other customers. He is nervous. He beckons her. He whispers, "Can't we go outside and talk?"

Grace looks at the young man. He nods his head.

"I've only got a minute," she says. She follows Billy out into the cold. "Shit, it's cold out here." She hugs herself. Her teeth chatter.

"We can sit in my car."

"Fine." Grace runs to Billy's car and waits for him to open it. She sits in the back seat because of all the beer bottles on the front seat. The car reeks of beer. Billy sits behind the wheel and watches Grace in the rear-view mirror.

On Sunday, after Billy ran out of the house, Grace climbed into the top bunk and listened to the mumblings of her mother's TV set and thought about her life and what she's going to do with it. Billy hadn't even said goodbye or "See you again," he just left. And when he left, as when all the men who come over to her house walk out, Grace felt an overwhelming sense of relief. She knows that each time she lets a stranger into her home she is taking a monumental risk. And when that stranger leaves, relief floods her system.

"So, what's up?" Grace asks. She licks her lips. She was in the middle of a snack and she can still taste the coffee and donut she was eating. Her coffee is probably getting cold in the back room of the clubhouse.

"I don't know." Billy looks at Grace in the rear-view mirror. He tilts it to catch her reflection. He can't figure out what he found attractive about this woman the other night, what made him want her. In the light of the day he sees the pimples on her forehead, the red mark on her lip where she bites it. There is ink on her hands and her nails are bitten down and chipped.

"Well, it was nice seeing you again." Grace makes a move to get out of the car.

"Stay," Billy says. "Just for a second."

"Why?"

"I don't know."

"Christ," Grace says. "You're drunk."

Billy looks at the bottles on the seat beside him. "I've had a few," he says. "That doesn't mean I'm drunk."

"You shouldn't even be driving. Why are you driving when you're drinking?"

"Shut up," Billy says. His eyes go cold.

"I'm getting out of here," Grace says.

"Listen," Billy says. "I'm sorry. It's just . . . my daughter . . . I'm being henpecked from all corners. I just thought I might like a little comforting. I thought maybe you and me, we could, you know, go back to your house."

"No," Grace says. "I don't think so."

"Why not?"

"I have a rule," Grace says, running her fingers up and down the car window which is fogging up from the heat of their bodies. "One night only. No matter what."

"That's not a good rule," Billy says. "How will you know if you've ever found the right person?"

"I'm not looking for the right person."

"What are you looking for?"

"Same thing as you, I guess."

"What's that?" Billy really doesn't know and he hopes to hell she will tell him.

"Sex."

"That's not it," he says. "There's something else."

"Yeah, well," Grace says, "that's all I'm looking for. I don't need all the shit that comes with relationships."

Billy nods, knowingly.

"I just need sex once in a while. That's all it comes down to. We're all animals, you know, deep inside these human skins."

"But don't you hate to be alone?"

"Nope," Grace says, putting a stick of gum from her pocket into her mouth and snapping tiny bubbles against her tongue. "Being alone is great." She opens the car door. "Besides, I'm not alone. I've got my mother." She laughs. "Sorry about that," she says. "I'd really like to sleep with you but I have my rules."

"Yeah, sure." Billy really has to pee. He can't concentrate. "So, is there any chance of getting a job here?"

Grace turns to look at Billy. She gets out of the car.

Billy sits in the car and watches Grace walk back into the club-house. He should consider himself lucky, he thinks, lucky that she's not chasing him. Imagine if she came looking for him and Tess found out about everything. Billy shakes his head. He opens his fly. He takes an empty beer bottle and he aims with his penis and tries to pee straight into the bottle. He fills the bottle quickly but can't stop the flow from coming. He pisses all over his pants and the car. The odour permeates the air. Billy feels sick. He feels as if he's fallen from a great height, and that he's getting awfully close to hell.

It is evening and the house is fairly clean. Jonathan can't convince Hilary to get rid of any of the preserves although he does manage to better organize them. He carries the preserves in the linen closet down to the basement. He puts the pickles together, the jams side by side. After he has moved the jars he tries to get rid of the mould on the walls in the basement. He scrubs but the job is too big. He organizes the dolls into some sort of haphazard pattern, the newer ones in the living room, the older ones in the other rooms — sitting and standing on shelves and beds and tabletops. He is glad to be finished with the dolls as several of them, when moved, say things like "Mama" and move their eyes independently. Jonathan finds them unnerving. In Becka's room he cleans up the broken glass under her bed and straightens everything in the room, throwing out the bottles of pills and needles and other medicines.

Hilary follows Jonathan around. She follows him like a lost puppy. If she had a tail, Jonathan is sure it would be wagging. When Thomas, who has been out grocery shopping, comes back, Jonathan is pleased to see him. He wondered briefly if Thomas had deserted him here and if Hilary, this strange sister, would somehow keep him locked up in her world of dolls, dust, and preserves.

"Where have you been?"

"Shopping."

"I found her eyes," Hilary says.

Thomas looks at Jonathan. Jonathan shrugs. Thomas takes the bags into the kitchen.

"The Madonna's eyes. The puzzle. I found it resting on a preserve jar while Jonathan was vacuuming the basement."

Thomas looks at Jonathan. "You vacuumed the basement?"

Jonathan shrugs again. "I even tried to clean the mould."

"Lucky me," Hilary says. She leads Thomas to her puzzle in the dining room and there Thomas sees the strangest pair of eyes he has ever seen looking back at him. They are attached to a bit of the forehead and a touch of hair. The eyes are watchful, uneasy, not quite real. The eyes remind him of something but he doesn't know what.

"Now I just need the piece with half of the nose on it and the mouth piece with the chin," Hilary says.

"The house looks incredible," Thomas says.

"I told you we had the pieces for the face," Hilary says.

Jonathan shrugs. "There's only so much a person can do. She won't let me get rid of anything."

"No, it's clean. It's so much cleaner. The basement?"

Jonathan smiles. "It's still pretty gross down there. You'll have to paint over the mould, I guess. Hide it."

"Jonathan's a saint," Hilary says and she means it. She really means it. "I don't know which one, but he is definitely a saint."

There are footsteps on the front porch and then the door rattles open and Billy walks in. He is swaying. He is wet. He smells like piss.

"Christ," Thomas says. "What happened to you?"

"Nothing. Who's this?" Billy asks. He smacks Jonathan on the shoulder.

"A friend," Thomas says. "Jonathan, this is Billy, my brother. God, you stink. You smell like piss."

"Hello," Jonathan says. He puts his hand out to shake Billy's hand but Billy looks away.

Billy says, "A friend from the Caribbean. The house looks different somehow. Why's it look different?"

"Jonathan's been cleaning," Hilary says. "Now we have to dig the grave."

"Jonathan is not from the Caribbean," Thomas says.

"Dig the what?" Billy says. "Oh, Jesus," he laughs. "Dick Mortimer told me. You're joking, aren't you?"

"Why do you smell like piss?" Thomas asks.

"It's getting late," Jonathan says. "Shouldn't we start on that tomorrow?"

"No," Hilary says. "We have to start tonight. It's going to snow tomorrow. I can feel it in my ankle."

"In your ankle?"

"You've got to be joking," Billy says. "You aren't burying my mother in the backyard. How the hell will we sell the house if there's a dead body in the backyard?"

"Billy, go take a shower. Clean yourself up. You can borrow some of my clothes."

"Fuck," Billy says. "I forgot to go back and visit Tess. What time is it? I should go now." He looks at his watch.

"You can't go there like this, Billy," Thomas says. "Take a shower. Or lie down. Why don't you lie down on the couch."

"Why?"

"Not until he showers," Jonathan says. "We just cleaned."

"Just do it."

Thomas takes Billy's arm and leads him into the living room. Billy stumbles on the rocks, knocking them around, twisting his ankle slightly. But he doesn't feel the pain. Thomas puts a blanket under Billy and Billy lies down on it.

"Do you ever think about him, Thomas?" Billy says.

"Who?"

"Dad?"

Thomas doesn't say anything.

"Because I do. I sometimes think about him a lot." Billy rests his head and closes his eyes. "I almost hit an old man on the road and I thought about Dad coming to watch my baseball games. Just like that."

"He should have showered first," Jonathan says.

Hilary leans down and straightens her rocks, puts them back in place. "He smells horrible."

"We'll get the blanket dry cleaned," Thomas says. He turns to Jonathan. "I'm sorry about this."

Jonathan smiles. "I've been black all my life. I'm used to it."

Hilary says, "I think you're beautiful." She says it quietly, testing it on her tongue.

Jonathan takes her hand. "I think you're beautiful too."

"Really?"

Thomas is staring at Billy's sleeping figure.

"We need shovels," Hilary says. "There are several of them in the shed out back."

When, Thomas thinks, rubbing his eyes, did life get so complicated? He wants to go home with Jonathan. He wants to go to work and design buildings. He wants to live a peaceful, ordinary life.

"I think about him," Hilary says suddenly. "I think about Daddy all the time. Do you?"

They dig most of the night.

The cold ground keeps collapsing around them in chunks.

"Sand," Jonathan mutters. "It's all sand. And it's frozen stiff."

Hilary thinks, after several hours, to remind Thomas about the supports he should build.

"Something has to hold up the walls," she says.

"What are we going to use?" Thomas's hands are numb with cold.

"Wood?" Thomas follows Hilary past Billy, who is still sleeping, down into the basement. From the window Hilary can see Jonathan still digging in the backyard. She helps Thomas rummage for rotten lumber in the basement. She tries not to look at the mould, she tries not to breathe very much.

"What's this from?" Thomas asks.

"The tree house Daddy was going to build."

"He was going to build a tree house?"

"We were going to have picnics in it. We were going to have a club. I was going to be the only girl allowed in."

Thomas sits on a box. He looks at his sister. "You remember the good things," he says. "I mostly remember the bad."

"I remember the bad too," Hilary says.

"Wasn't it all bad?"

"No," Hilary says. "Not everything."

Thomas carries the lumber, piece by piece, up the stairs. He brings up a saw. They use the pieces of the chair that Thomas broke when he first arrived, the pieces that were piled in the dining room, near the buffet. Thomas goes back to the basement for rusty nails and hammers, his father's unused tools. Jonathan helps as Thomas measures out the space and builds supports. Billy sleeps on. The night is black and cold.

"What are you doing?"

Hilary looks up. The neighbour is standing on the ladder he used to trim his tree. He is peering over the fence.

"Building," Hilary says.

"In the dark?"

Hilary has never spoken to this neighbour. He is new to the neighbourhood. The house was sold about a year ago and the young family that lived there before moved out and this single man moved in.

"It's the only time we had to build anything," Thomas says. He tries to laugh. He looks down at the hole and the supports. It looks just the right size for a dead body, he thinks. Surely the man will know what is going on.

"What are you building?"

Hilary, Thomas, and Jonathan stand still. Jonathan's hammer is raised, mid-swing.

"We're starting an entrance to the basement," Jonathan says. "We want to be able to get into the basement from the backyard."

"An entrance?" Thomas says.

"Oh," the man says. "Aren't you building that awfully far from the house?"

"We'll have a tunnel with storage under the ground," Jonathan says.

Thomas puts his hands over his eyes.

The neighbour looks at the three of them standing there. He shrugs. "That's crazy," he says. "I've never heard of that."

"Well," Hilary says, "we do things differently over here."

"Do you have a permit?"

"You don't need a permit to make an entranceway," Jonathan says.

Thomas stands still. Speechless. The architect in him wants to argue these facts.

Jonathan starts to hammer loudly. He drowns out the man's voice. They continue with the gravesite and the man stands on his ladder and watches. Billy sleeps off the alcohol in the living room. Snow begins to fall softly on the heads and shoulders of Jonathan, Hilary, and Thomas. They don't notice it. They build and dig until the neighbour goes inside, until the ground holds somehow and the hole is dug and the supports are in place. The final resting place.

I 3

Blood

Dick suddenly can't wait to see Hilary again. He doesn't know what's gotten into him. He can't wait to see her slender body, her small feet, those lovely eyes. Even her chapped cheeks.

He feels born again. He feels thrown up into the air. He feels as if his heart has lifted high. Lighter than he's ever been before. A weight, something heavy, has been taken off his shoulders, his head, his neck, his arms, his legs, and Dick feels he can stand so tall he can touch the tops of the trees.

He wonders if Hilary feels the same way.

He can't stop whistling.

He whistled while he made up Hilary's mother (a lovely tune, through flat lips, through his front teeth).

He whistled in the shower.

He whistled all day at work yesterday.

Dick is whistling opera, show tunes, rock 'n' roll, even some disco. He's got ABBA and the Beatles and Vivaldi and Meat Loaf and Ella Fitzgerald and a Spanish guitar song he once heard at an embalming convention pouring out of his soul. Not to mention the prayer-songs and hymns and mournful pieces that are inevitably part of every workday. All jumbled up and tumbling out of Dick Mortimer's mouth. He can't help himself.

Dick whistles one low, long whistle, as if calling for a dog or noticing a lovely woman on the street. He has the urge to spin around, hold his arms out and twirl.

So he does. A big, hairy, lumbering man, he holds his hands straight out, his arms heavy, and twirls quickly, whistling a tune. He is dizzy. He looks around. It is lunchtime and the staff is at the McDonald's across the street. No one has seen him. All is quiet in the funeral home.

Billy drives past the funeral home on the way from his home to pick up Tess at the hospital. The snow is falling heavily, has been falling all night, and the cold streets are sheets of ice. Billy drives slowly. The mat at his feet is wet from where he dumped a pot of hot water on it to wash off last night's piss. His clothes are in the washing machine at home and he has a fresh shirt and pants on and has showered and shaved.

This morning he woke up on the couch at his mother's house to the sound of garbage trucks coming down the street. His ankle was sore from twisting it on the rocks. He limped into the kitchen and rummaged in the cupboards until he found a bottle of Scotch. He drank a glass and then poured some in the bowl of cereal he managed to scrape together. He knows something is happening to him but he isn't quite sure what.

Billy is driving to the hospital, sipping the Scotch that is resting between his legs and thinking, Tess knows I tried to sleep with Grace. And Billy reasons in his drunken mind that if Tess knows that he was indiscreet once, just once, then he will be fine, then she will forgive him. But if she finds out that he went back, that he tried to get Grace to have sex with him again when Tess was lying in the hospital, then he thinks Tess will walk out of his life and never come back. Does he really want that? Does he want to be all alone without a job, without a family? Billy doesn't know. The question is whether to come clean and tell Tess about Sunday night, to confess everything about Grace, or whether to avoid the subject until it all blows over. Just tiptoe around it.

"Tiptoe," Billy whispers into the hush of the car. He likes that word. It sounds good on his tongue. "Tiptoe through the tulips."

Or should he just walk out? Just leave and never come back. Why does he want to stay with her? With Sue? With the new baby? Besides, he didn't do anything. Tess has no right to be as mad as he thinks she will be.

Today is his mother's funeral and he is going to help bury her in his own backyard, the yard he hid in when he was just a child, the yard he sometimes watched his mother garden in. He starts to sob. Tears stream down his face. His nose runs. He sips at the Scotch, standing between his legs, and he cries. How could he have judged her? Billy thinks. He didn't even know her.

"Look at me now," Billy says. "Billy Mount. Look at me now. Crying all the goddamn time. Like some woman."

He pulls into the hospital parking lot and parks beside a large truck. Billy rests his head on the steering wheel and clutches the bottle between his legs.

"Things are getting worse," Billy says. "Everything's falling apart." He rolls his head back and forth on the steering wheel, relishing the feeling on his forehead.

"Job, wife, kid, mother," he says. "At least I have you." He opens the Scotch again and takes a final swig. He rolls it under his seat. Billy wonders if men hit some sort of menopause, if maybe that is what's happening to him. Mood swings, sobbing, feeling lost and confused. A mid-life crisis. That's what it's called.

Billy gets out of the car, straightens up slowly, and limps up to the hospital and through the main entrance and straight up the stairs until he is standing in front of Tess's room.

"Here goes," he says to himself. He blows into the palm of his hand, smells the Scotch on his breath, checks his pockets for mints which he doesn't have, and then enters the room.

Tess is fully dressed. She is sitting on the side of her bed, her face less swollen (in fact, she is looking less all over somehow), wearing a blue tent-dress and a touch of lipstick. She has brushed her hair and curled it. The candystriper helped her.

"Nice to go home feeling better and prettier," the candystriper had said. And Tess thought that maybe half a make-over was better than none.

Billy stands there looking at her. "Ready to go?"

"I guess," Tess says. "You're wet."

"It's snowing. You look nice."

"Thanks. Snowing?"

"She looks like a whore," Hilda says, coughing, from behind her curtain. "A fat whore."

Tess whispers, "It makes me happy that she's staying here and I'm going home. I dreamt last night that she died."

"Just ignore her," Billy says.

"I'm going home now," Tess calls out. "It was lovely to meet you."

"Without some of your major organs and with a cheating husband," the old woman says. "Lucky you."

Billy looks down at his feet. Tess stands. She holds on to the bed to steady herself.

"Whoopee," Hilda says.

Tess walks over to the curtain and pulls it back. Hilda is lying there in bed, a shrivelled, nasty woman, and there are tears coming out of her eyes and wetting her wrinkled cheeks.

"Poor you," Tess says. "I think I might even miss you." She takes

Hilda's hand in her own moist palm. She squeezes. She wipes the old woman's face with a Kleenex.

"Go away," Hilda says. "Get out of my space."

Tess pulls the curtain across Hilda's bed again and walks to the door. Billy carries her overnight bag. He holds out his hand. Tess takes it for balance. She leaves the room and walks down the hall. She feels like a prisoner being released from the death sentence.

"Why are you limping?"

"A small accident. I don't remember really. Hilary's rocks, I think."

"Where's Sue?"

"Didn't come."

Tess swallows hard. When Sue called the ambulance, when Tess heard the fear in her daughter's voice, she thought that maybe things would change, she thought that perhaps Sue was just pretending to be loveless and cold.

"I asked her yesterday."

"Busy?"

"Yes."

Tess feels as if her heart could break again and she holds her chest, thumps it a bit, tells herself that her daughter really is busy, that coming to the hospital is one chore too many. Tess can smell the liquor coming off Billy. It's leaking through his pores. But now is not the time to talk about it. Now is not the time for anything but watching one foot lead in front of the other, making its way forward, walking out of the hospital and bringing her back to life. A good life. A bad life. A bit of both. But she's walking away from her death and now she's ready for anything.

Billy stumbles when he's outside.

"I'll drive," Tess says.

"No, no, no," Billy says. "You're sick."

"You're drunk. Which of us is more dangerous, do you think?"

Billy watches his wife get into the driver's side of the car and he climbs in beside her. The half-empty Scotch bottle rolls out from under her seat when Tess turns the corner, the windshield wipers thumping noisily. She looks down at it. Billy doesn't notice. He is leaned up against the window, staring out.

"Tonight is my mother's funeral," he says.

"You never drink Scotch. Why does it smell in the car? It smells like pee. Did you have a dog in here?"

"We're burying her in the backyard."

"Our backyard?" Tess glances at her husband.

"Her backyard. They dug all night. How are we going to sell the house now?"

"Dug? They?"

"Sometimes I drink Scotch. Just when I'm in the mood. Besides, there was no beer at Becka's house."

"Who's digging?"

"Jonathan, Thomas, and Hilary dug Becka's grave in the back-yard of her house last night. We are burying her tonight. I don't think you should question me about my drinking."

"Who's Jonathan?" Tess stops at a red light. Her stomach aches. She is so very hungry. "God, it stinks in here."

"I'm not an alcoholic."

"You're not?" Tess whispers. She sees a drive-through donut store. She wants to pull the car up to the window and order a six-pack of donuts, all mixed. "Who's Jonathan?" she says again.

"Thomas's friend. He's black."

"Black?"

"Something funny between them. You can see it in the way they look at each other. It makes me feel sick somehow."

They drive towards home. Billy watches Tess. It is still snowing heavily.

Sue is standing on the front steps when they get home. She is crying.

"What's wrong, honey?"

"Blood," says Sue. "Lots of blood."

Billy looks around, he searches the new snow, looking for blood. He can't focus. He feels bleary eyed and tired.

"Where?"

"Oh God," Tess says. "The baby."

Sue sits on the top stair in the snow. She is shaking. She has her arms wrapped around her tight black clothing. A tear hesitates on her nose ring and then falls to her lap.

"Where?" Billy asks, knowing he's asking the wrong thing but not being able to focus. "Where's the baby?"

"Come inside," Tess says. She helps Sue up. "Come out of the cold."

Sue and Tess limp together into the house.

"I don't want to lose the baby," Sue cries. "I never wanted to lose the baby."

Billy looks up the stairs at his wife and daughter as they disappear into the bathroom. He hangs up his coat and takes off his boots. He roots in the fridge for beer but there isn't any and so he puts his coat and boots back on, walks to the car, and retrieves the half-empty bottle of Scotch. He mixes it with water to make it last. He drinks all of it. He falls asleep in front of the TV and he doesn't wake up when Tess shakes him half an hour later, when she shakes him hard to tell him that she's taking Sue to the hospital. He doesn't wake up when the front door slams, when the car starts, when a fire truck passes the house, siren wailing. Billy sleeps for several hours.

He finally wakes up when Sue and Tess come home. The clock on the VCR glows three o'clock. Tess's face is white from strain and exhaustion, Sue's face is red from crying. Blood, Billy thinks. He looks up into their faces and he thinks he sees something there, something far away and sad and loving. He reaches his hand up and tries to touch them but they fade in and out of view and his head splits and then they are gone. To bed. They both go to bed to have a nap.

"Wake us when we have to go to the funeral," Tess says to Billy. Her voice is distant and controlled. "It was close but she didn't lose the baby."

Billy tries to open the door to his bedroom but Tess has locked it. He can hear the mumble of her voice as she talks on the telephone to one of her friends. He sits down by the door and stares at the hallway around him. He stares at the carpet and the staircase, at Sue's closed door and the open door of the bathroom. He knocks his head against the wall quietly, carefully, in rhythm with the pounding he can hear, the thump of his heart, his blood.

It is late afternoon. The white sky is darkening. Billy stands and walks downstairs. He finds the empty bottle of Scotch and places it beside the front door. He settles in front of the TV. He will take the empty Scotch to the funeral and he will bury it next to his mother. He will get rid of his habit, bury it with her. And then, later tonight, he will tell Tess about Grace and they will try and sort things out. He will try and find another job. And if they don't sort things out, then Billy will face the consequences of his actions. He will accept his fate and somehow life will go on. It always does.

The TV glares harshly before him. There is a man on the screen, his arms up, his trench coat waving out in the wind. He is calling for someone (Billy can't hear who because he has the sound off), and his face is contorted, sorrowful. Billy watches his face, watches his hands, the way his feet are placed. Billy forgets that the whole thing is staged, that the man is acting, and Billy feels the man's pain, senses his loss. He turns on the volume and settles into his chair.

"There's the piece," Hilary says. She bends down and picks up a puzzle piece from the floor of her mother's closet. "I've been looking for this piece. You must be good luck." It is the side of the Madonna's face and half the nose. "Now I just need the mouth with the chin."

"Let me see," Jonathan says. He is looking through Hilary's mother's drawers. They were watching TV when they decided to see if Becka left anything, any notes to do with her funeral service. Hilary didn't think so but Jonathan never passes up the opportunity to snoop. "It must have been lying under one of her shoes. I guess when I vacuumed I moved everything around." When he was vacuuming Jonathan sucked up quite a few of the smaller rocks in the living room. He is hoping Hilary won't notice. "Why was it in her room?"

Hilary shrugs. "She never did puzzles in her room."

"She's a strange-looking one, isn't she?" Jonathan says when they go down to the dining room to put the piece in the puzzle.

"What do you mean?"

"Her face is all flat, there's no dimension to it."

"You'd look strange too if —"

"If what?"

"If you were just told you were having God's baby."

"Yes," Jonathan says. "I guess you're right." He laughs.

Hilary and Jonathan sit back down in the living room. They found nothing of interest in Becka's room and being in there makes Hilary feel shaky and tense.

Thomas comes into the living room. He has been upstairs in his bedroom going through boxes of his things that he dragged down from the attic.

"What did you find up there?" Jonathan asks.

"So many things. She kept every piece of artwork I think I ever did. My trophies, my yearbooks, my photo albums. She kept everything."

Hilary goes into the dining room. She smoothes the puzzle down, touching the trees and the angel and the angel's wings. Everything is coming together, she thinks. Everything is finding its own place. She moves back into the living room and looks out the window.

"Mother packed boxes like that for each of us. You should take it home with you."

"When is everyone coming?" Jonathan asks.

"Soon," Thomas says.

"It's snowing out," Hilary says. "It's coming down hard." She thinks of her mother, in a matter of hours, lying deep under the cold ground. Hilary has missed her terribly, has ached at the emptiness the house holds. Even though Thomas and Jonathan are here it still seems as if something is missing, as if her mother's presence is needed to make this house a home.

Thomas walks back upstairs. He enters his room again and sits on the bed with his boxes of life. He wanted Jonathan to follow him upstairs, he wanted to share this with Jonathan, but for some reason he didn't know how to ask him. Thomas takes a stuffed teddy bear out of a box. He carried that bear around for years. It is full of holes and musty smelling. He takes out several model airplanes, pieces missing, a toy car his father gave him, a compass, a thermos with Batman on it, and a troll doll with purple hair. These small things mean nothing to him really. But the fact that his mother put them there, placed them together in these boxes, knew which items were his, that means all the world to Thomas. Again, for the hundredth time since he walked off the airplane, he wishes that he had come home to say goodbye to her before she died. And for the millionth time he wonders why he didn't come home. What was it that made him stay away? Is he really that selfish?

Jonathan is standing in the doorway. "How are you doing?"

"Do you think," Thomas asks him, "that I didn't come home because I'm gay? Do you think that I avoided her because of my sexuality? She probably would have accepted me, don't you think? Why didn't I come home?"

"I always thought," Jonathan says, "it was because you are afraid to fly." He walks over to the bed and pulls Thomas's head to his chest. This is the second time this week that someone has hugged Thomas this way.

"Maybe," Thomas says, muffled in Jonathan's shirt, "maybe I'm more afraid to land."

"What do you mean?"

"Maybe getting here is not the problem. It's being stuck here, like I was as a child. It's landing. Landing the plane. You wouldn't believe all the responsibility that comes crashing down on me when I walk into this house, Jonathan. I always had to take care of everything. I feel overwhelmed here."

"Even with everyone grown up? Even with your mother dead? You still feel that way?"

"Yes, even with all that. I still feel the burden."

"I think," Jonathan says carefully, "that if you really look at the big picture, Hilary should feel the burden. She's the one who has spent a lifetime in this house."

14

Burying Becka

Jonathan leaves Thomas in his bedroom and convinces Hilary to decorate the house for the funeral.

"I've been to enough funerals," Jonathan says "They are always lacking in decorations."

They blow up balloons and leave them floating throughout the house. Hilary then gets ready for the funeral. She wears her mother's red dress again. There is a dirt stain on the knee area from when she crouched in the bushes outside of the funeral home, but she thinks no one will notice.

Thomas waits upstairs. He is lying on his bed looking at his collection of old comic books and wondering if they could be worth anything now.

Jonathan stands in the dining room, awkwardly shifting his weight from one foot to the other. He was sitting in the living room but he was gradually becoming afraid to move, suddenly afraid he would break his ankles on the rocks. He stares at Hilary's puzzle. Without the lips and chin, the Madonna looks silly. Or sad.

Jonathan can't decide which.

In the dining room and bedrooms they all wait for Billy and Tess and Sue and they wait for Dick Mortimer in the hearse which will carry the body of Rebecca Hilary Mount through the snow, through suburbia, to the house.

At the funeral home Dick pushes and heaves and rolls Rebecca Mount's closed casket out the back doors of the building and into a waiting hearse. His hands and shoulders ache. Everyone at the funeral home has gone home and, besides, he has to do this alone. Top secret. Dick feels stealthy, he feels invincible. He feels like a teenager again. He wonders what his assistant will say tomorrow, he wonders if Darren will notice that a body is missing and if he will dare question Dick about it. Dick locks the back of the hearse and then walks up the stairs to his apartment, his stomach sucked in, his shoulders high. He strips naked, takes a warm shower, shaves, puts on his mourning suit, all dressed in black, white, and grey, a new man. Dick whistles. He climbs into the front seat of the hearse, starts the engine, and turns on the headlights.

"Lucky," he says out loud, to Rebecca Mount lying shut up in the back, as he drives slowly through the snow.

At Billy's house they are getting ready. They put on their best clothes. Tess is amazed at how loose her dresses have become, amazed that in such a short time she could lose over ten pounds, that the weight must be just dripping off of her. Mostly amazed that ten pounds can make such a difference. Sue says she's losing water from the intravenous, not fat, but what does Sue know. Tess is encouraged with the weight loss, it seems easy so far. She wants to start on a new path in life, regain the years she has lost to overeating, to Billy. She isn't even hungry. A large part of Tess would like to leave Billy, lose weight, be pencil-thin like Sue, and get a job. She imagines herself in a business suit behind a desk somewhere. Tess has never had a job. She moved straight from her mother's house into Billy's life, pregnant with Sue. It's time she got out, saw more of the world.

Billy tries to wake himself up in the shower. He uses more cold water than hot. He lets the water stream down over his face. He tries to think clearly.

Sue wears a black dress and red cowboy boots. She isn't wearing makeup and she isn't wearing jewellery. For just a minute, as Billy carries the empty Scotch bottle to the car, he thinks that Sue looks almost like the little girl he loves so dearly. He feels a knot in his throat. He wants a drink but he pretends that he doesn't need one. Everyone is silent in the car. There is no fighting. Nothing is said about the empty Scotch bottle rolling beside Sue on the back seat, or the smell in the car, or the near miscarriage, or the blood, or Tess's heart attack, or Billy's drinking, or the death of a mother and a grandmother.

The snow falls thickly.

Softly.

And in that snow everyone converges upon Becka Mount's house in the heart of the suburbs.

"Watch the road," Tess says as Billy pulls into his mother's driveway directly behind Dick Mortimer's hearse which is clicking as the heat from the engine dies off. "It's a slippery slope almost, it's a death trap. Drive careful."

Billy comes straight into the kitchen without taking off his shoes, tracking snow through the house. He puts down the empty bottle of Scotch and searches the cupboards for a full one which he finds and opens and pours himself a glass. One hour in the car in traffic with his daughter and his wife, in searing silence, deserves a drink. Or two. Or three. Really quick ones to calm the nerves. He will quit after the funeral. He promises himself this.

Hilary looks at him.

"Don't look at me like that," Billy says. "I can do whatever I want. It's my mother's funeral."

Tess follows behind Billy, stopping to wipe her feet on the mat, and sits quietly in a chair in the kitchen. She sighs.

"How are you feeling, Tess?" Hilary asks.

Dick Mortimer comes in from the backyard where he was standing in the snow looking down into the hole and hoping that it was big enough. He claps his hands together, startling everyone, and shivers. "It's cold out there. We're all going to freeze."

Dick is introduced to Sue and Jonathan and he smiles politely at everyone. He looks at Hilary and is pleased to see her in the same red dress she wore when they went out. He thinks that must mean something about their relationship, it must mean they have a relationship.

"Your neighbour," Dick says, "does he know what's going on?"

"No," Thomas says. "He thinks we are doing renovations."

"He's watching from his upstairs window," Dick says. "He'll see everything."

Hilary goes to the back door. She looks out at the hole in the ground. She comes back in.

"We could put a tarp up so he can't see from his upstairs windows. The fence blocks the downstairs windows. We could pretend we're just having a barbecue."

"I'll barbecue throughout the service," Jonathan says. "You bought hot dogs and hamburgers, right, Thomas? You can hang a tarp from the fence to the tree to cover the hole and everyone standing under. Besides, that will keep the snow off everyone's head."

"What does this black person have to do with planning our mother's funeral?" Billy asks.

"Billy," Tess hisses.

"Jonathan is my friend," Thomas says. "He's trying to help."

"Fuck," Billy says, gulping down the Scotch.

"Billy, watch your mouth," Tess says.

Billy stares at Jonathan.

"You might as well tell him, Thomas," Hilary says.

"No, I don't think now is the time —"

"Billy, Jonathan is Thomas's gay lover," Hilary says.

"What?"

"His boyfriend? Isn't that right, Thomas?"

Thomas's face turns pink. Jonathan takes a step closer to Thomas. Everyone is silent.

"Boyfriend?" Billy says. "Boyfriend?" Billy pulls out a chair and sits down. "I knew something fucked up was happening."

"Cool," Sue says. She puts her hand on the knot in her stomach and starts to laugh.

Tess laughs too. She claps her hands. She looks at Hilary in her red dress, her hair pulled back from her face, and for a minute Tess feels that Hilary is actually attractive. Tess feels that she should try to get to know Hilary a little better, try to see who she really is behind that skinny exterior. She watches the funeral director stare at Hilary. Tess thinks it's funny that Thomas is a homosexual. And in love with a black man. She thinks that this kind of news is good for Billy. She thinks that he deserves to be knocked over every once in a while. It feels good to laugh with her daughter.

"You're a fag?" Billy says. "My mother dies and my brother is a fag? What next?"

"Billy," Hilary says, "be quiet. Grow up." She walks into the living room, across the rocks, and looks out the front window. The street is empty except for a car passing quickly in the snow. The sky is dark.

"Fucking shit," Billy says in the kitchen.

"Where is she?" Tess says, when she has stopped laughing.

Sue goes into the living room and turns on the TV. She sits back on the couch, her feet on the rocks, and holds her belly close.

"How are you feeling?" Hilary asks her.

"I've been better," Sue says.

In the kitchen Tess says again, "Where's Becka?" She looks around. The dolls stare back at her.

"In the hearse," Dick says. "I'll need help rolling the casket around to the backyard."

"This is insane, you know," Tess says. "You could lose your licence. We could all be arrested. You can't bury a body in the backyard."

"It's what Mother would have wanted," Hilary says, coming back into the kitchen. "No one will know about it. We'll be quiet. We'll hide ourselves and be quick about it."

"How long have you been a fag?" Billy asks Thomas.

"When are you going to grow up? There's nothing wrong with a person being gay."

"There is when he's my brother. Jesus, I shared a room with you."

Billy and Thomas look each other up and down. Billy is standing up at the counter. He is playing with the empty bottle of Scotch and he's drinking straight out of the bottle he found in the cupboard. He chooses to forget about his glass.

"It's my life, Billy," Thomas says.

"Have you always been a fag?"

"I'm gay, Billy, not a fag. And yes, I've always been gay."

"Christ. I've showered with you in the gym."

"Which hurts you more, Billy? That your mother is dead or that I'm gay?"

"Fucking Christ," Billy says. He swigs from the bottle. He feels sick to his stomach. He swallows more Scotch and it burns his throat. "I should kick your ass in," he says. "I should beat the hell out of you. You goddamn buggering —"

"Billy," Tess says, "smarten up."

Billy slams the bottle down on the counter and raises his hand to hit someone. "No one tells me I'm stupid," he shouts. He turns around to all the people in the kitchen, his hand high, not really knowing who he wants to strike. He isn't sure if he really wants to hit someone or if he just wants to curl in a corner and cry like a baby.

"Calm down," Dick says. "Let's all remain calm. This is a funeral. Let's respect that."

Billy turns quickly and hits Jonathan. Jonathan falls back, the blow knocks him into the stove, but he remains standing. He turns his face away from Billy.

"Jesus," Thomas shouts, pushing his brother aside.

"You're the one I should have hit," Billy hisses at his brother. "I should kill you."

"What's your problem, Billy?" Tess shouts. "At least Thomas is in love. What's wrong with being in love?"

Thomas checks Jonathan's face for cuts, sees a large bruise forming on Jonathan's dark cheek.

Billy stands back, shaking his fist out. He lost both his jobs. His mother is dead. A black man. His brother fucks a black man.

Hilary wonders if her mother would ever have thought this possible. Her children, gathered around in the same room at her funeral, come together one last time to say goodbye.

Tess's face is drained of colour. She is tired. She is standing now and holding her hand up in front of Billy's face. Billy shakes his hand out. It hurts.

"You," Tess shouts. "You make me sick. I'm sick of this."

"What's going on?" Dick whispers to Hilary.

"Family," Hilary says.

Billy drinks again from the bottle. "Here's to family reunions," he says. He raises the bottle in a toast.

"Family reunions," Hilary echoes.

"Billy's drunk," Tess says to Jonathan. "I would apologize for him but —"

"But what?" Billy shouts.

Thomas says, "You shouldn't have to apologize, Tess. He's not your responsibility."

"Yes," Tess says. "You're right. He's not my responsibility any more, is he?"

"We should get on with the service," Dick says. He doesn't want to release Hilary's hand but he has a job to do. "Is there a tarp around here? We should put your mother to rest before the snow gets too thick, before more of the neighbours are looking out their windows."

Jonathan rubs his cheek carefully. "This is a funeral," he says, "not a gay bashing."

"Wouldn't know that," Billy says. "Look at the balloons." He kicks one that floats past him in the breeze from the forced air of the furnace.

Thomas feels something itchy lodged in his throat. He coughs. His brother hit his lover. This doesn't seem possible. He is mad at both of them, at Billy and Jonathan. He told Jonathan not to come.

"A long time ago Mother would have liked a party," Hilary says. "When Daddy was here, they liked to have parties."

Dick squeezes her hand. "I like it," he says. "It reminds me of an Irish wake."

Sue shouts from the living room. "Can't you guys please keep it down? I'm trying to watch something." The volume goes up on the TV and the people in the kitchen can hear the loud roar of a laugh track.

They are gathered around the hole in the ground, looking down into the whiteness, into the snow that stuck to the earth before the tarp was hung from the tree and the fence. There is no sound but the muffled stillness of falling snow. The air is crisp and cold. The wind is quiet. Dick shuffles his feet.

"Christ, it's cold," Sue says. She stamps her red cowboy boots on the ground.

Behind them the house is lit up. Every room glows. The air from the furnace has pushed the balloons up against the patio doors. Hilary thinks it looks as if ten little heads are staring out at them.

Dick turns towards the gathering and places his hands together in prayer. Everyone follows his lead. But he doesn't pray. He merely holds his hands, palms together, fingers stretched high, and he closes his eyes.

Thomas coughs gently.

The casket sits alone on the front driveway of the house, in the back of the black hearse. MORTIMER'S FUNERAL HOME is written in fancy script on the side doors of the car.

"I'll need some bearers," Dick whispers. He looks up at the gathering huddled under the tarp and then over at the neighbours' houses. He watches Jonathan, wearing an apron, barbecue hot dogs and hamburgers in the falling snow. Jonathan's cheek is swollen and discoloured. His shoulders are slumped as if he's given up the fight. As each drop of snow falls on the coals there is a small hiss and a puff of smoke. Dick feels that something is going to go wrong tonight. Not just the battle in the kitchen but something else horribly dangerous. The air is thick with trouble. The neighbours on one side have the lights in the back of their house off. The neighbours directly behind them seem to be out for the night. Their house is also black. That's a good sign. The fence is high around the property. The nosy neighbour is sitting in his window reading a book, but Dick hopes that with his light on he might not be able to see that much. The tarp covers most of what is going on. Dick thinks that with a little luck and good timing. . . .

"We'll cover the casket," Dick says. "We'll move quickly."

Billy and Thomas stand forward.

"We'll need you too, Jonathan," Dick says.

"He's not carrying my mother's coffin."

"Casket," Dick mumbles.

"I've lived with him for fifteen years," Thomas shouts. "Fifteen goddamn years, Billy. That's almost as long as you've been married to Tess."

Billy looks at Tess.

"Shhh," Dick says. "Do you want someone to call the police?"

"And they're still in love, Billy," Tess whispers. "Some people stay in love after that many years."

"Jesus, Tess," Billy says.

Billy is still limping from twisting his ankle on Hilary's rocks. He follows Dick around the house. Jonathan follows Thomas. On the count of three they pull Becka's casket out of the hearse, place it on a frame with wheels, pull a tarp over it, and roll it awkwardly to the backyard while the women wait. Thomas holds his breath. His lungs feel like bursting. He can't get over how heavy the casket is to push. Billy stumbles in the snow. The neighbour in the window stares down at his book.

Around the back of the house, Hilary gasps when Dick takes the tarp off the casket. "Oh God."

"The burgers," Jonathan says, seeing smoke rise from the barbecue.

"It's lovely, it's beautiful," Hilary says.

"It's a gift," Dick whispers, clearing his throat. "For you, Hilary."

Hilary sucks in her breath and holds it. She wants to touch the casket, run her hands up and down its polished blue finish. "Blue something," she says, with a rush of air. "Wasn't it called Blue Light or something?"

Dick says, "Blue Diamond."

"That's funny," Billy says. "A blue coffin. Do you make pink ones too? You know, one for a boy, one for a girl? Or do some boys like pink?" He looks at Thomas. Billy's stomach is warm, on fire. "A coffin for a present," he laughs. "What would you think of that, Tessy? Want me to buy you a coffin? Or would you prefer perfume? Candies? Chocolate? A blue coffin — Jesus."

"Shut up, Billy," Tess says. "This is a funeral."

"Do you think I don't know that?"

Sue says, "Hurry up, please. It's cold out here." She stamps her feet on the ground and looks down at her footprints.

Dick clears his throat. The casket is raised from the ground. It is high up on the frame with wheels that they used to roll it from the hearse. It is closed. Reflections of lights from the houses around glow on it. White shine. Soft, night-sky blue. Hilary runs her fingers over the surface. No matter what Billy says, the present is wonderful.

"Shall we open it?" Dick asks. He looks out from the tarp and up at the man next door. He isn't in his window any more. Dick holds his breath.

"Open it?" Tess opens her mouth. She feels too close to death. She doesn't want to see it, stare it in the face.

"Yes," Hilary whispers.

"Let's just get this over with," Sue says. "It's freezing out here."

"You can go inside," Tess says. "You don't have to stay for this."

"She was my grandmother."

"And how often did you visit, Sue?" Billy says.

"Open it."

"Oh, honey," Tess says to Hilary, "you're just grieving. Let your mother be. Let her rest."

"We are not opening that coffin," Thomas says.

"Casket."

"Why not?"

"She'll get wet," Billy says. He laughs.

"She's under the cover."

"She'll get cold."

Dick clears his throat again. "It's common," he says, "for the family to have a last viewing. It reassures family to know that it really is their loved one that they are burying."

"Reassures us?" Thomas asks. "To know that her body is going under ground? That's ridiculous."

"I want to put something in there with her," Hilary says. "I want to bury her with something."

"She'll catch a cold," Billy says. "She'll get wet and get sick." He chuckles. He wants another drink.

Jonathan raises a spatula in the air. "Thomas, your sister wants —"

"You shut up," Billy shouts. "I've heard enough from you."

"Quiet," Dick says.

"Let's just bury her," Thomas says, "so we can all go home. Billy needs to sober up." He doesn't want to see her face again, her bald head. "Someone say something and let's just get it over with. The neighbours might call the police."

"I don't need to sober up," Billy says.

"I want to see her," Hilary says. "I want to say goodbye. You have to let me say goodbye. I want to see my mother."

Dick looks over the fences at the houses surrounding them. He feels shivery and worried. The man in the window next door is still missing from the chair he was sitting in. The light is on.

"Lighten up, Thomas," Billy says. "Just open it or we'll be here all night. Most people have a viewing."

Sue agrees. "I wouldn't mind seeing her," she says.

"Go," Tess whispers. "Just go. Just go on."

Dick moves to open the casket. "Those of you who do not wish to view her, please turn around or go into the house."

Thomas turns around.

Tess turns around. "Sue," she says, "avert your eyes." But Sue stays facing forward.

Dick opens the latch and pushes back the top half of the lid. He hovers over Rebecca Mount for a minute, adjusting, straightening her wig, and then he stands tall and looks proudly down at his work.

"A scarf?" Hilary says. "I didn't give you a scarf."

"It's silk," Dick says.

Thomas turns back and sees his mother's face, her wig, her neck covered with silk, her tiny body almost swimming in her purple dress, and he starts to cry. He can't help himself. Jonathan moves to comfort him.

"Jesus Christ," Thomas says. "She looks fine." He is half glad that he is looking at her, that he will now remember her like this instead of the way he saw her in the funeral home, yellow and bald.

"But she doesn't even look like Becka. Is that Becka? Are you sure?" Billy says.

Dick clears his throat. "When the soul disappears there is only the shell left. And the shell is only that — a shell, some skin, some bones."

"What the hell are you talking about?" Billy looks at Dick.

"Something I read once," Dick says.

Hilary looks at her mother, at the transformation that has taken place, and then she looks up at Dick. "She looks wonderful."

"Thank you."

Hilary bends over her mother. Up close she can see the makeup lines. She looks carefully, taking it all in, her eyes filled with tears. She wants to remember every pore on her face. She touches the silk scarf. She whispers something. Dick watches her closely. And then Hilary moves back and fetches something she has hidden on the porch. Her father's old running shoes. She places them in the casket next to her mother, the dirt from the soles spotting the purple dress.

"What are you doing?" Billy asks.

"Burying a piece of Daddy with her," Hilary says. "These are his shoes. They're the last thing she heard of him. His shoes on the linoleum floor. Walking out."

"But he must have been wearing the shoes that he left with. Not those," Billy says.

"I know that," Hilary says. "Don't you think I know that?" Her voice rises.

"It's symbolic," Thomas says. "Let her be."

"This is crazy," Tess says. "This is just crazy." Tess has turned and is looking at her dead mother-in-law's face. She thinks that maybe they had more in common than she ever knew.

Billy limps up to the casket. He looks into his mother's resting face. He picks up the empty Scotch bottle from where it was resting beside the hole, carried out of the house with the tarp, and he puts it into the casket, beside the shoes. "As long as we're giving her things."

"What are you doing?" Thomas asks.

"Burying my bottle," Billy says.

"Don't worry," Tess says. "It's empty."

"What's that supposed to mean?"

"She didn't drink," Thomas says. "What are you doing?"

"I know how it got empty," Sue says.

Billy looks at his daughter, at his wife. "I'm trying to better myself," Billy says. "And none of you care. You don't care what I do."

"Better yourself?" Tess asks. "What's that supposed to mean?"

"I'm burying my Scotch bottle," Billy shouts.

"Shhh," Dick says.

"I'm burying it. Don't you get it? You almost died, Tess. "

Becka is lying there, still. The snow falls down around them. It covers the tarp.

"Nothing is going to change," Tess says.

"Shall I close it now?" Dick asks.

"Wait," Thomas says. "Just wait a minute." He stands there, thinking. He thinks that he should add something to the collection she is amassing, something meaningful. Thomas goes into the house and roots around a while in the kitchen and dining room. He goes up into his bedroom, Hilary's bedroom, his mother's bedroom. He stays inside for quite a long time. Dick is getting impatient. Hilary jumps a bit from one foot back to the other. Dick leans over and wraps his arms around her shoulders and holds on tight. Hilary stops shaking and stands paralysed.

"People change," Billy is saying. "Every day people change."

Tess looks away, out into the night. She holds her hands tight around her large body.

Thomas finally comes out again. He is holding something small in his hand. He found it under his mother's pillow. He places it into the casket. It is easily hidden and Thomas pushes it down towards Becka's lap, under the lid. He shudders when he touches her. She is so cold.

"What was it?" Billy asks.

"Nothing."

Hilary says, "I have something else I want to put in. Wait a minute." She goes inside and gets her doll, the one with the emerald dress that her father gave her, and takes it outside.

"What is this? Is she a garbage can?" Tess asks.

One eye closes on the doll. It's winking at Hilary. She holds the doll for a minute and then she walks over and places it inside the casket, just beside her mother. When she puts the doll in she feels down and touches what Thomas put in their mother's lap. She runs her fingers quickly over the surface. She breathes deeply.

Billy's stomach tightens. His bowels feel loose. "She looks like she's holding a baby," he says. He feels suddenly as if he has the beginnings of a flu. He shakes his head.

The feeling passes quickly. He looks at the doll and at Becka and at his daughter and then he rubs at his eyes. Hard.

Dick closes the casket. "Would anyone like to say a few words?"

Silence.

"Someone say something," Billy says.

"I'm sorry," Hilary says.

"What are you sorry for?" Billy asks. "Stop picking at your face. You're bleeding again."

Dick touches Hilary's hands on her face. He squeezes them. "Shhh," he whispers. "It's all right. Don't say anything. You don't have to say anything. Hold my hand."

"Let's just bury her," Billy says. "Let's get this over with." He looks over at the barbecue, at Jonathan standing there minding the burgers. Billy wants a drink so badly that his hands are shaking. He wants a drink so badly that his mouth is watering. "It's harder to change than you think, Tess," Billy whispers.

Dick stands tall. "I'll need some help lowering her."

"I just want to know one thing," Tess says. Her voice cracks. She's been quiet for so long. "I just want to know if you slept with someone, Billy." She can't hold it in. She is watching the lid close on Becka Mount and she is thinking that she could just as easily be where Becka is now.

"Christ, Mom," Sue says. "Bad timing."

Billy looks at his wife. "Not now," he says. "We'll talk later."

"I just want to know."

"Not now."

"Did you?" Tess stands as tall as she can and she glares at Billy.

"No, for Christ's sake, I didn't sleep with her. I just —" Billy puts his hands over his eyes.

Tess turns and walks quietly into the house. She turns her back and walks away, opening the glass patio doors, releasing the bobbing balloons which float up into the snowy sky. She settles down in the living room, takes her coat and boots off, feels her feet solid upon the rocks, and she stares at the blank TV set. She turns it on. Tess puts her hand on her heart and settles in to watching TV.

An uncomfortable silence falls over the people under the tarp. Jonathan watches the balloons float higher and higher. And then he thinks that he can't wait to go home and feels the side of his face, feels the ache, wonders how long the bruise will take to heal.

"Hey," a voice says suddenly. "What are you guys doing?"

Hilary looks up. "It's the neighbour."

"Oh no," Dick says.

Hilary walks out from under the tarp and sees the neighbour standing on his ladder looking down at the plastic blue covering.

"We're having a party," she says.

"In the snow, in the cold?" he asks.

"Don't you have anything better to do than spy on your neighbours?"

The man looks at her. "I —"

Hilary suddenly shouts, "When I need something, no one ever comes. And then, suddenly, everyone is here. Why don't you just leave me alone? Leave me in peace. I didn't mean to hurt anyone."

The man looks up at his well-lit window and then down at Hilary. He clears his throat and climbs down the ladder and goes back into his house. Hilary feels a blush spread across her face. She is shaking, she is dizzy. She stumbles back under the tarp.

"Good for you, Hilary," Dick says. He reaches to steady her. "Now he won't bother us any more."

"He'll call the police, I bet," Sue says.

Billy is standing still with his hands over his eyes.

"Billy?" Thomas says. "Hey, Billy."

"What?" Billy shouts. "What?"

"We have to put her in the ground. You have to help."

No one says anything. Hilary starts to cry. She leans on Dick's shoulder and cries. Then she straightens up, wipes the tears from her face, and moves away from Dick. She stands next to the closed casket, looks at it, sees her reflection in the blue shine.

"Hilary," Thomas says, "it's okay, really." He moves to comfort her.

"I have this doll," Hilary says. "Daddy gave her to me. He

brought her home in a large box with a plastic bag around it. She was so pretty, all dressed in green. Her eyes winked at me and her smile was perfect. I have this doll and that's all I have of him."

"Isn't that the doll you just put in there?" Billy points towards Becka's casket.

"Shut up, Dad," Sue says.

"Why couldn't Daddy have helped me? Why couldn't he have stayed with us, helped us?"

"Hilary," Dick says. "It's all right now."

And then there is no sound. The snow muffles the traffic on the road out front. A dog's bark several houses over comes at them, ghostly and thin.

"Help us, Jonathan," Thomas says after a minute. "Help us lower the casket. We have a funeral to finish."

"Be careful," Dick says. "Be steady."

The men slowly lower Becka's casket into the ground, using ropes and straps. A light flashes on in the house just behind. Dick lowers quickly. His hands are shaking. The casket is off-centre. The men work at it. Righting it. Resting it properly. They sweat.

"She was calling for help," Hilary whispers as the casket makes a final move and then stops. Her whisper stops abruptly in the padded stillness of the snow. "There was no one there to help me. None of you helped me. I'm sorry, Mother." She steps outside of the tarp and she looks up at the sky. The drops of snow hit her face and the weight seems unbearable.

"Just be quiet for a minute, will you?" Thomas says fiercely. "I don't want to hear it."

"All this talking," Billy says. "You're giving me a headache."

"I knocked the glass of water on the floor," Hilary says. "I knocked the pills off the table. It was an accident."

"Accidents happen, Hilary," Thomas says. "I'm cold. I want this to be over."

"Her breath hushed over my face." Hilary touches her cheeks. "It stained me, can't you see? The stain is all over my face."

"Jesus Christ. There's nothing there. It's all in your mind. There is nothing on your face. You didn't do anything, Hilary. Just be quiet. Just stay quiet. Everyone be quiet." Thomas is shouting. A door slams in the neighbourhood. The dog several streets over begins to bark again and its high-pitched yapping takes over, grows stronger, drowns out all else.

The family in the backyard stands still. No one moves a muscle.

"I don't know why everyone can't just be quiet once in a while. Stop talking," Thomas whispers. "Just stop."

15

The End

"I need a goddamn drink." Billy is the first to speak.

Dick reaches over to Hilary. He pulls her towards him and hugs her tight. She is shaking.

Thomas whispers, "There's nothing there, Hilary. I'm sorry. There is nothing on your face."

"Haven't you ever heard of dry skin?" Billy says.

"Let's bury your mother," Dick says. "There's nothing else left to do."

Thomas looks at his hands. He feels helpless. He reaches for one of the shovels Dick has thought to bring and he begins to load the first bit of snow and dirt on Becka's casket. Billy picks up a shovel too.

The light in the neighbour's window goes out. A door bangs shut like the blast from a gun and the dog suddenly stops barking.

Billy and Thomas and Dick stand before the hole, shovelling in the snow. Hilary joins them. They form a semicircle. They bow their heads to the work.

Jonathan stays by the barbecue, afraid to move close and help when Billy has a shovel in his hand.

There is little sound in the air except the static of snow falling, the heavy thud of the dirt on the casket. The shovels toss the dirt which thumps lightly on the closed lid of the Blue Diamond casket.

Slowly they finish and, one by one, move into the home.

Quietly.

Jonathan unties the tarp from the fence and tree and then carries the burgers and hot dogs into the house. He puts the plate on the table. The kitchen is light and warm. Hilary stands in front of the stove and her mind spins; she touches the stove and thoughts about having a bun in the oven, about her mother, about the Madonna, about her own reason for being tumble around her head. Billy tries to find another glass for his Scotch but he can't find one because Jonathan moved everything. He continues to drink straight from the bottle. No one says anything to him about burying his habit. Dick watches Hilary, inspects her every movement. Thomas stands by the sliding-glass doors, looking out at the backyard. He begins to cry silently. He wipes his eyes and watches the snow as it sticks on the mound of dirt now that the tarp is gone. Sue joins Tess on the couch, and the noise from the TV fills up the house. Tess puts her arm around her child and holds on tight.

Hilary takes one step forward, towards the centre of the kitchen. She opens her mouth as if to say something and then, thinking better of it, she closes her mouth and takes one step back. She leans against the stove again, feeling the warmth, hearing the clicking sounds as it heats up to keep the food warm.

Rebecca Mount's body lies resting under a mound of fresh dirt and a sprinkling of snow, six feet under, in cold, damp ground. And in the Blue

Diamond casket, right beside the dead woman, is Billy's empty bottle of Scotch, her husband's pair of dirty, old running shoes, the emerald green doll with both eyes shut, and Thomas's contribution, the missing piece of Hilary's puzzle — the Madonna's mouth, lips pink and painted thin, closed tight and speechless.

MICHELLE BERRY is the author of two short story collections, *How to Get There From Here* and *Margaret Lives in the Basement*. She publishes short fiction in magazines and journals throughout Canada and is a reviewer for the *Globe and Mail*. Berry teaches at Ryerson University and has served on the board of PEN. She lives in Toronto.